A Whispering Pines

SHORT MYSTERY COLLECTION #2

SHAWN MCGUIRE

Secret of the Winter Woodsman

Chapter One

I hurried down the stairs, taking care not to trip on my long skirt, and rushed across the cottage. Someone was knocking on the front door. I opened it to find Blind Willie Haggerty and Lucy O'Shea standing there with overflowing baskets in hand.

"Blessed be, Morgan. We come bearing gifts." Lucy's smile was big and bright, although a bit of the usual sparkle was missing from her eyes.

I opened the door wider and let them in. "What are you two doing here?"

"Just told you," Willie replied in his charmingly gruff manner, "we're bearing gifts." He stomped the snow off his big boots, then kissed my cheek as he entered.

"We wanted to make sure you had enough to eat." Lucy set her boots on the shoe tray by the door, then strode straight to the kitchen with her package. "It's been almost a week since our last delivery."

"And we wanted to check on your patient. How's she doing today?" Willie kicked off his boots and placed them next to Lucy's then followed her path.

I pulled my shawl tighter around my shoulders and

glanced up at the second floor where our bedrooms were. My heart was heavy but growing a little lighter each day.

"She's sleeping now but has been taking fewer, shorter naps this week. She had a pine needle bath a little while ago so is quite content." At Willie's confused expression, I laughed. A hearty, endorphin-releasing guffaw. When was the last time I'd laughed like that? "I toss a cheesecloth sachet of pine needles, Epsom salts, oatmeal, and a few drops of cypress essential oil into the tub and let it steep while she soaks."

"What's all that do?" He stoked the fire in the kitchen hearth.

"It performs a bit of nature magic. The Epsom salts help with achy muscles. Oatmeal soothes itchy skin."

"And we all know the benefits of pine," Lucy added while pulling a container from the basket.

We did know. Our village was surrounded by a pine forest, after all.

"The scent of pine," I explained, "clears sinuses and bronchial passages. It helps with circulation. And especially beneficial for Mama, it aids in mental clarity."

A little more than a month ago, Mama had a stroke. Thank the Goddess it was a minor one.

"It's unlikely she'll return to one hundred percent," her doctor cautioned after a few days of observations. "Her speech will get better, but it could be slower and a bit garbled from now on. Other than that, if things continue as they have, I expect her to have a full, satisfying life. Her strength should return to near normal, although she may need a nap now and then."

"Don't we all?" I joked, scared to death.

While Lucy prepared a plate and mug of tea for me, she asked, "When did you last eat? As in a meal. Not just a handful of something as you flit about." She was always worried about people having enough food.

I let Willie usher me to our small round dining table by the fireplace. When I dropped onto a chair, my body was instantly grateful for the rest. "Mama wanted butternut squash soup, so I made some for dinner last night."

It took nearly an hour for her to finish the bowl, but she had been able to take small sips and declared it delicious.

"Did you remember to add an apple for a bit more depth?" Lucy set the plate in front of me.

"Of course." I picked up my fork, and my mouth watered as I gazed down at roasted winter vegetables and something that looked like meatloaf. "Is this what I think it is?"

"Nut roast," Willie declared. "Lentils, mushrooms, cheddar cheese, a bunch of different veggies, and seasonings . . ."

I smiled at him. "You sound familiar with this recipe."

He puffed out his chest. "Thinking it'll be my contribution to the Yule gathering next week. I brought you a whole loaf, so you'll have a few meals covered. You can also tell me if you think it's good enough."

"You've got a nice variety here from the villagers." Taking items out of the baskets, Lucy detailed what else I had to look forward to. "Scones and granola from Sugar. Gingerbread cookies from Honey. Mince pie, hard-boiled eggs, and chia pudding from Wesley. Assorted nuts, a couple big hunks of cheese, dried fruit, fresh fruit, and cut up veggies from Peyton and the gang at Sundry. I made buttermilk bread and lentil salad. There's also a small jug of Willie's cider and another of Maeve's Wassail. Go easy on those last two. They pack a punch, and you've got a patient to keep an eye on."

"Good goddess," I said through a laugh. "That's enough to feed us for a month."

"It sounds like a lot, but it's just a bit of this and a bit of that."

"Remember," Willie reminded me, "you're supposed to call us when you need a break."

"I know and I will."

"I haven't received a phone call yet." He crossed his arms and pouted.

I had the best friends and neighbors. Starting the day of the stroke, they made sure I had plenty to eat even though I didn't have much of an appetite at first. Someone stopped by every day so I could take a bath or lie down for a few minutes without worrying Mama would need something. And then there was Willow.

"Don't even think about the shop," our irreplaceable attendant, and my dear friend, had said. "Your only concern right now is nursing Briar back to health. I've got everything under control there."

She started working with me and Mama at Shoppe Mystique a couple years after we graduated high school. Her aunt had passed on to Summerland, and Willow needed both money and something to keep her busy. She started with a few shifts but by the end of her first summer season she'd become the perfect full-time shop assistant. Not only was she great with the customers, she knew almost as much as Mama and I did about herbs, crystals, spells, and so on.

I placed a forkful of nut roast in my mouth, and my body relaxed even more. Savory, stick-to-your-ribs goodness. And so satisfying. Like getting a hug from someone you dearly loved.

"Surprisingly fantastic, Willie." I winked at him. "You really are a good cook."

His eyes misted over for a moment, then he gave a little smile.

I added, "I'm so glad I was wrong about you all those years ago."

"Wrong about him?" Lucy set three mugs of tea on the table. "What happened years ago? I'm missing something."

I gazed longingly from my forkful to her and back.

"It'll be a story," Lucy concluded from my reaction. She picked up one of the mugs again. "Tell you what, I'm going to run upstairs and take a peek at my girl. You eat."

My girl. Mama and my grandmother were the first two people to join the O'Shea family here in Whispering Pines. Nana and Lucy had been the closest of friends, and since Mama was the same age as Lucy's Dillon, Mama had always been like a daughter to her.

I was almost done with my meal when Lucy came back downstairs ten minutes later, wiping her eyes. She looked sad but brighter than she had the last time she'd seen my mother.

"She was sleeping soundly," Lucy reported, "so I didn't wake her. Just watched her sleep."

I did the same thing. Completely content to sit there and watch her chest rise and fall.

"You absolutely need to bring this to the gathering," I told Willie when I'd eaten the last bite of nut roast. "And I'd like the recipe, please."

After refilling our mugs, Lucy asked, "Are you ready to tell me what you were wrong about?"

"Can I tell the whole thing?" I asked Willie.

"She already knows the big reveal at the end. Go ahead."

"It was three days before Yule, and I was fifteen years old . . ."

Chapter Two

F ifteen Years Earlier

The card hanging on the small container read: *Sugilite (soo-ja-lite) helps increase positive energy, decrease negative emotions, and soothe loneliness. It enhances meditation practices and spiritual connections.*

It went on and on, listing things like psychic awareness, forgiveness, getting in tune with one's higher self, banishing nightmares . . . Two things on the list stood out to me. *Helps in connecting with spirit* and *aids in making life decisions.* I dumped the contents of the small white bowl into my left palm and placed my right hand over it. Out of the dozen or so stones, one made itself known by practically vibrating against my skin. I plucked that one from my palm and put the rest back.

"Are you what's been calling to me lately?" I asked the small purple stone with magenta speckles and darker purple lines. It seemed every time I entered Shoppe Mystique lately, I felt pulled to the crystals and stones corner. Curious to learn more about this stone, I went to the reading room.

Except while I could get to the bookshelves that lined one wall, the room was anything but the peaceful, cozy reading spot it usually was. Small pine crates of handmade Yule ornaments, wood splint baskets filled with pinecones, and a pile of formerly fresh pine boughs that had dried out two weeks ago sat stacked in front of the windows and fireplace. Right where Mama had placed them three or four weeks earlier. There was a nearly identical scene in our living room at home.

Yule was three days away, so there was no point decorating now. I should just put them away. We'd try again next year. Plus, there were hardly any tourists in the village. (Not that we got many this time of year. Whispering Pines was more of a summer place.) There weren't many villagers either. Once school let out for the holidays, everyone scattered. It was like someone cast a spell to scare everyone away. Why did Mama even bother to open the shop this week? Worse, why did I *have* to be here with her?

"Traffic has been very light this week," she said this morning while making our tea. "It's the perfect opportunity to prepare for the new moon ritual."

"I can do that here."

She fixed her blue eyes on me. "But *will* you?"

Probably not. Being a green witch was a huge badge of honor for her. Something passed down through the bloodline from one Barlow woman to the next. Whoopee. Maybe it was time for that tradition to end. It's not that I knew what I wanted to do or be, but I'd sure like it if the decision was mine. Not something forced on me. Maybe this was why the sugilite called to me so loudly. So it could help me with decision making.

What I wanted to do this morning was go back to bed and sob my eyes out. Seemed Mama couldn't understand that my heart was broken into a billion pieces. After all, if anyone in this village *should* understand how I felt, it was her. And it's not like I didn't try to talk to her. I told her about the actual physical pain I got in the center of my chest every time I thought about my grandmother. The person I adored more than anyone in the world. Mama's reply was, "It's grief, sweetheart. You're okay. Try to focus on something else."

I was far from okay.

Mama poked her head into the reading room, startling me. I shoved the sugilite stone into my jeans pocket.

"How about that new moon ritual?"

"Why can't you just leave me alone?" I stormed past her into the main shop . . . and cursed myself. Why did I say that? It's not what I wanted. Not at all. I *wanted* her to tell me I wasn't the only one shattered by Nana's passing. That she understood how I felt. But of the many, *many* things she had said to me over the past weeks, I hadn't heard any words of understanding.

I felt like I was stranded in the middle of an ocean or desert and had no idea which way to go or what to do. Was there anyone in Whispering Pines who understood me?

Just then, Blind Willie walked in. With his white beard, big belly, forest-green coat, and tan leather leggings, he looked like the Holly King himself. Or Santa Claus. (But we've never really done that holiday here.)

Mama beamed when she saw him. I mean, she lit up like a Yule log. I had to admit, the tension decreased dramatically when his big personality took over the shop.

"Good late morning, Briar. Morgan." He put his hand to the furry hat on his head and gave us each a salute.

"Good morning, Willie," Mama greeted, suddenly all happy. "Are you here about our dinner plans?"

Dinner? Were they going out? Like on a date? He was at least thirty years older than her. Eww!

"Yep. Figured we should discuss the menu."

"Oh good, a happy topic." She shot a glare my way. "With someone who won't yell at me."

"I didn't yell."

Willie looked at my mother then me. "Am I interrupting something? I can come back later."

"No big deal, Willie," I promised.

I welcomed the interruption. This would have turned into the same discussion (aka argument with *possible* yelling) we always had.

You need to study more, Morgan. Your skills won't improve if you don't practice, Morgan. You know you're a full year behind because the sabbat and esbat rituals can only be done at specific times. You missed the last two.

Behind based on whose schedule? I wasn't in a rush.

I wandered back to the tea cart by the reading room. Far enough away that I couldn't be dragged into whatever they were going to talk about, but close enough that I could still hear what they were saying. While I messed around with adding different herbs to my mug, taking note of the amounts in case I liked the blend, they started talking about having Yule dinner together. *At our cottage!*

Five minutes later, while I was sipping my tasty tea, Willie said, "Good menu. I know you have every herb possible, so that's covered. I got plenty of veggies from my garden this year. I'll bring a variety."

"I'll bake gingerbread and mince pie."

I loved Mama's gingerbread. The mince pie was okay too.

"And I'll make a pork roast." Willie pointed southeast. "My next stop is Sundry, so I'll pick up that and the ingredients we're not sure we have."

"This is wonderful, Willie." Mama's voice shook as she spoke. "There hasn't been a lot of joy around here lately. It's good to have something to look forward to."

"I agree. I'll drop everything off at your place tomorrow, and we can do a final ingredient check."

I waited until he'd left Shoppe Mystique and stomped over

to her at the checkout table near the front door. "What's going on? Is he actually coming over for Yule?"

Mama sighed. "For years after the village was founded, the Original families would get together to celebrate special occasions. Not just religious holidays. If it was something worth celebrating, we did it together."

Was she avoiding my question?

"At some point," Mama continued, "we stopped gathering for everything and saved group events for the eight sabbats. I was about your age when we—Nana, Lucy, Dillon, Willie, and me—started getting together for meals. Sometimes it was for special occasions like birthdays. Other times it was simply because we hadn't seen each other in a while." She paused. "Nana obviously isn't here this year. Neither is Lucy. She and Keven decided to spend the holidays overseas. And you know they cancelled the Yule gathering this year."

That's why all of my friends left. No gathering meant no one stuck around. "Right. Because Mr. and Mrs. O'Shea aren't here, the rest of us can't celebrate either. Is that how it goes?"

Seemed to me we'd want to be together even more at a time like this. The first sabbat without Nana.

"Everyone is mourning, Morgan," Mama said using her soothing voice. "The villagers loved her so much." She closed her eyes and let her head drop back. Was that actual emotion? "It just doesn't feel right to have a big celebration without her."

And the Whispering Pines Yule gathering was a *big* celebration. The folks at The Inn went all out and put pine boughs, candles, bells, and mistletoe everywhere. Everyone dressed in either green, red, white, gold, or silver. A huge pine tree was the center of attention in the dining room. Gifts were piled beneath it and spilled out across the floor. They set up tables for cookie decorating and beeswax candle-making. And of course, at all our gatherings, there was always more food than we ever thought we could eat. By the end of the night, though, there would hardly be anything left.

The highlight for me was that Nana, Mama, and I (the village's official maiden-mother-crone trio) got to light the Yule log. We saved a piece of the log from the year before and used it to light the new log. An ancient tradition Mama said they adopted the first Yule in Whispering Pines. That act, she said, connected us to the villagers of the past.

"Who's going to light the Yule log?" I demanded. "What's the matter with these people? Don't any of them care about tradition?"

"Morgan, honey, we'll take care of it. The villagers voted, and it was a unanimous decision for everyone to celebrate privately this year."

"I didn't get to vote." Tears filled my eyes. "I look forward to the gathering and the three of us lighting that log."

Yes, the tradition connected us to villagers from the past, but what about my connection to my grandmother? There wouldn't be anything special about this Yule for me.

"Willie doesn't have anywhere to go," Mama continued. "I invited him over, so he won't have to be alone. And he's going to cook for us. Willie's a great cook. Wait until you taste his pork roast."

This was a complete disaster on all levels. "Something else I don't get to vote on? If I hadn't been standing here listening to you two, would you even have told me, or would I have found out when he walked in with the groceries?"

"Morgan, no, that's not—"

"In case you care, I hate everything about this." I grabbed my down jacket and backpack and left the shop before she could say another word.

Chapter Three

S tanding outside Shoppe Mystique, I tilted my head back and took a deep breath. One that went clear down to my belly. And then one more. Yes, I was feeling sorry for myself, but I didn't know how to pull out of this. I missed Nana so much I thought my chest might split open.

A puff of frigid air sent a chill through me, so I slipped on my jacket, pulled the zipper all the way up, and took my thick woolen mittens from the pockets. Despite the temperature, I felt better outside. A little time away from Mama would help, too, because lately we were either fighting or not talking at all.

A walk through the woods would surely lift my mood. I loved the trees and the quiet and the peace of being alone. I'd head east along the Fairy Path, cut south to the lake, follow the shoreline west, and then turn north to home. But my plan fell apart three steps away from Shoppe Mystique when the villagers I was sure had left for cheerier places were suddenly everywhere. Okay, not everywhere. There were only ten or twelve of them on the red brick pathway surrounding the Pentacle Garden, but they were all looking at me.

"Hey, Morgan. How are you doing?" Schmitty's dad asked, his voice full of sympathy.

People always asked that question, but they didn't want to hear the whole answer, so I replied, "I'm all right."

"Good. Good." He nodded, then scurried off without waiting for me to say more.

Two villagers, Mrs. Jardine and her son, Basil, who was five years below me in school, came out of Treat Me Sweetly. Basil carried a pie box with such care it was like it might explode if he let it tilt off level even the slightest bit. Mrs. Jardine had a bulging tote bag over her shoulder. Loaves of bread poked out of the top and made me think of the brown squirrel that lived in that maple tree near our cottage. She (the squirrel, not Mrs. Jardine) scurried into a cavity twenty feet up the trunk whenever I went out there and then peeked out at me. Pitch, my pure black rooster, loved to taunt her. Pitch loved to taunt anything that entered our garden. He was a great security guard.

I smiled at the memory of them chasing each other, and Mrs. Jardine assumed the smile was for them.

"Good morning, honey," she greeted. "Or is it afternoon?"

I wiggled my hand. "Right on the threshold."

"Say hi to Morgan, Basil."

The poor kid turned holly-berry red and murmured something that sounded like hello. He had a crush on me, but I never teased him about it. His sister, Violet, took care of that torture.

I passed another woman who gave me a tight-lipped smile and looked like she might burst into tears at the sight of me before she finally said, "You look so much like Dulcie."

Like that was my fault.

When two more villagers turned and went the opposite way when they saw me coming, I decided walking through the commons to the Fairy Path felt a little like running a gauntlet today. To make everyone more comfortable (myself included), I changed my route by slipping between Shoppe Mystique and Treat Me Sweetly. Doing so took me directly into the woods, and while this path didn't have a boardwalk, we hadn't gotten any snow yet, so I wouldn't have to trudge through knee-deep drifts or risk my ankles on icy patches.

As I walked, I thought about Pitch. He showed up in our garden not quite a year ago. Nana, Mama, and I were doing our daily tending, and he seemed to appear out of nowhere. He ran right over to me and then followed me around the garden all morning.

"Looks like you've got yourself a familiar," Nana declared.

Pitch was so unusual I went to our tiny library to see if they had any information on chickens. Or roosters in this case. They did. Turned out he was an Ayam Cemani from Java. Then I needed to look up where Java was. Indonesia, clear over near Australia. Colonists in the 1920s brought the chickens and roosters to Europe. They arrived here in The States fifteen or so years ago. (Right around the time I was born.) The people of Java believed the birds had mystical qualities. I liked that.

The big question was, how did tiny Pitch end up in the Northwoods of Wisconsin?

My next questions were, what was it like in Java? And, would I ever get there? Would I ever travel anywhere further than central Wisconsin with Mama on day trips? There was so much to see and experience (like a country filled with black chickens) and I only got to know about them through books and the internet.

"Don't you want to see more of the world?" I asked Nana once. "Don't you get bored here?"

"Not at all," she replied immediately. "Everything I need in my life is right here. If there's ever something I can't buy at one of our shops, the gang at Sundry can order it for me, or someone will pick it up when they're out and about. Before

Shoppe Mystique became so busy, your mama and I would make two or three trips a year to sell at the markets. That was enough for me. Now I'm content to stay right here." She grew quiet for a moment. "I think Briar would have liked to see more. Maybe I should have encouraged her to explore."

I wanted more. *I* wanted to explore. Nana got to see and do so much before she moved them here. It wasn't fair that we had to stay trapped inside the Whispering Pines dome. If that's really how Mama felt, why did she stay? Why didn't she travel? Even around Wisconsin?

All my friends were leaving. Two years from now, I'd be the only one my age left here.

Don't exaggerate, child, Nana scolded in my head.

Okay, I'd be one of four. Everyone else already knew what was coming next. Aster was going to marry Alder Flowers. (He didn't know that yet.) Schmitty planned to work for Mr. Powell in village services as soon as he turned sixteen next month. (Mr. Powell knew this.) And Willow would disappear into the forest with her aunt and become a wood sprite or something. The other three were going to college, to a tech school, and off to the Rocky Mountains to learn how to snowboard. All of them had big plans and then there was me. The lost one.

What would I do after graduation? This was what I thought about while I walked. It's what I thought about every day. Maybe I'd run away to Java and start an Ayam Cemani chicken farm.

"That's ridiculous." I put my hand over the little bulge in my jeans pocket, the sugilite stone, and sent out a plea that it would help me start making reasonable decisions soon because lately they'd been way off the charts. Chicken farmer, tea maker, join a band (even though I couldn't sing or play an instrument) . . .

"I'll be back for the food tomorrow. I can't carry everything."

I blinked and realized I'd somehow ended up over by Sundry. I hadn't even been heading this direction. Through the trees, I saw Blind Willie leaving the store, his big voice carrying easily across the two-lane highway.

"No problem," a softer voice from inside the store responded. "We'll have it ready for you."

Willie had a package strapped to his back, making him look even more like Santa. A closer look showed that it was a cardboard box, approximately two feet square. From the way he bent at the waist, it must have been heavy. Hauling groceries would be a challenge with that box on his back. Groceries for my Yule dinner. *Our* dinner.

Suddenly I felt bad that I'd complained about him. He seemed nice enough. Mama sure was happy about him coming over. My irritation was with her, not him. I didn't really know anything about Willie. Other than he believed weird conspiracy theories about the government and big business. He probably believed in Big Foot and aliens from Mars too. That's where his nickname came from. People said he was blind to reality.

I was about to run over to the parking lot and offer to help him by carrying the groceries when a ringing sound came from . . . him.

He pulled a satellite phone out of his coat. We all knew he had the thing because it was kind of a big deal. No one else here even had a cell phone. No need since the village was in a pocket that couldn't get service, so we dealt with regular old landlines. Satellites were all over the sky, though, so his phone worked anywhere. I guess it kept him in contact with the company he owned somewhere out west.

"I got it," Willie said into the phone, stopping to check both ways before crossing the highway.

He was coming this direction, so I hid behind a pine tree.

"You didn't need to send this stuff to me," he continued. "You could've just—"

He stopped talking. Even stopped walking in the middle of the road for a second. Worried he'd get hit by a car coming around that blind corner, I almost called out to him to keep moving. He did so on his own before I could say a word.

"You put *what* in the box?" He paused to listen. "You're serious? After all this time, they found evidence?"

Chapter Four

W ho found evidence of what? I let him pass by me and then crept along silently behind him. He spoke softly, looking around every few seconds. Making sure no one was listening? Well, I was. Mama told me to focus on something other than Nana's death, and I couldn't ignore this. He lowered his voice, so I had to strain my ears to hear what he was saying. Either that or get closer, and doing so didn't seem like a good idea.

"I was sure the death would remain a mystery forever." He nodded while he listened and didn't seem happy about this *evidence*. "Yeah, makes me glad I'm tucked away in the Northwoods. They can't find me here. Right? You swore you'd keep my location secret. No one knows where I am?" He grew quiet, listening. "Good. And yes, I had to ask. Anything else going on that I need to know about?" Another pause. "That's fine. Let's talk about it later. I gotta haul this box you sent me through the woods. Should probably pay attention to my footing. We'll talk in a few days . . . Yeah, Merry Christmas."

We all knew how reclusive Willie was. He built a log cabin somewhere in the northwest corner of Whispering Pines, which was pretty far from here. We rarely saw him during the tourist season and pretty much only for village gatherings during the rest of the year. He stayed put until he needed supplies. Or, apparently, if someone invited him to dinner.

I had so many questions: Who was Blind Willie Haggerty? How did he end up here? Why did he run his company via a satellite phone? Was that one of his employees he was talking to? Didn't sound like a business call to me. And what was in that box? What evidence was he talking about? Whose death? Was Willie a murderer? Had he been hiding out in Whispering Pines for nearly forty years because he'd killed someone?

I kept following him, doing my best to not step on sticks and give myself away. But keeping my eyes on the ground meant I got jabbed by branches. More than once, a low-hanging pine bough brushed through my hair. How many needles were stuck in there? I'd have to clean up before going home. Mama would have plenty of her own questions if I walked in wearing half the forest.

Willie groaned beneath the weight of that box, stopping now and then to readjust it on his back. I couldn't say how far or how long we walked, but eventually we ended up at a log cabin. It couldn't possibly be his place, though. Everyone said he'd built his home himself with little more than an axe. I pictured a rustic one-room hunting cabin. This place was really nice.

It was about the size of our cottage but without the second floor. It had a big covered porch and a cool fieldstone chimney. From where I stood a good fifty yards away, it looked like the creek wound past his property too. Nana chose the location for our cottage because the creek was so close. We had a constant supply of water for our garden. That's probably how the owner of this place chose the spot.

My mouth dropped open in surprise when Willie walked straight inside. He didn't knock. Didn't open the door, stick his head in, and announce himself. Just strode on in like he owned the place. I waited a couple minutes to see if he'd come out again. When he didn't, I sneaked around to the side with the chimney and peeked in the closest window. Willie was sitting at a desk along the far wall typing on a keyboard. Along with the computer he was using, there was a bunch of high-tech looking equipment all over that desk. Guess this was his place.

When he moved, like he'd either heard me creeping around or was simply ready to get up from the desk, I ran. Knowing the creek would take me home, I followed it east.

I'd been walking for nearly fifteen minutes, and nothing looked familiar. I lived my entire life in Whispering Pines, a good deal of it in the woods. Sometimes I foraged for edible plants with Mama. Sometimes I explored on my own. I never got lost. If I followed the creek, I'd be fine.

"Morgan? What are you doing up here?"

I turned, looked, and looked some more. When I said that Willow would disappear into the woods and become a wood sprite, I was only partially joking. She dressed in shades of brown, gray, and green, and the only thing that gave her away was her long red hair.

My face flushed hot with embarrassment. "I might be lost." Some green witch I was. Thought being one with nature was in my blood.

"Have you ever been up here before?"

I shook my head. "Well, to the circus but never in this area."

"Then you being lost is understandable. When I go down to your end of the village, I go to school and come back home. Sometimes I have to stop at Sundry or one of the shops in the commons, but those are obvious routes. If I wandered around your woods, I'd get lost too."

She was being gracious about my missing sense of direction today, which was nice of her, but I knew how to navigate the woods. "I was following the creek."

"This creek?" She pointed at the one we were standing next to.

"Yes," I answered slowly.

"You know there are two, right?"

"I've never heard that, no." How could I not know that?

"They start as one coming out of Lake Superior, I believe, then it splits. This one runs past the carnival, that weird church thing that woman is building, Blind Willie's place, and then heads west away from us."

"The one I thought I was following," I explained, "enters the village from the east. It cuts past the rental cottages and makes a swoop north past our place. Then it goes by the Meditation Circle, the campground, the Fortune Tellers' Triangle, and the O'Sheas' property before emptying into the lake. I always wondered where you folks up here got your water."

"You'll never get home if you follow this creek." She made a *follow me* swoop with her hand. "Come on. I'll walk with you."

Willow practically glided through the woods. She was so at ease. It was more like she was part of the forest rather than passing through it. Sometimes I felt that way in our garden. I guess if I spent more time in the woods, I wouldn't be tripping and stumbling and getting pine needles in my hair. They told me I was a green witch. Willow appeared to actually be one.

"Where exactly do you live?" I'd never seen it (not sure many villagers had), but I'd heard that her aunt's garden was so perfectly natural, folks were sure woodland creatures tended it for her.

Willow pointed over her shoulder behind us. "Along the creek. If you go back to the spot where I found you, and follow the creek northeast for about five minutes, you'll find it."

I approached my next question cautiously because Willow

didn't like to talk about her home life. "And you live with your aunt?"

She nodded. "Since I was ten. My parents died in a car crash, and my grandparents were too old to take on a kid. Aunt Zyl was the only other family I had, so she took me in. Now, she's my only family. Grammy and Grampy passed on a couple of years ago."

"Zyl," I repeated. "I don't think I've ever heard her name."

"It's short for Zylina, which is Greek for *wood-dweller*. Super appropriate, don't you think?"

"Are you Greek? Is she?"

"No and no. She heard the name while traveling a couple decades ago, loved it, and adopted it."

I sighed.

Willow shot me a questioning look. "What's the sigh for?"

"With graduation only a year away, I've been thinking a lot about traveling. Do you ever wonder what's outside Whispering Pines?"

"It's been a while, but I came here from the outside."

That was true, she had. "What's it like? Do you remember?"

She gazed up into the treetops, thinking, her feet sliding past ruts and over dips like they weren't there. "We lived in a big city. I'm talking tens of thousands of people. Buildings everywhere. Stores and factories and homes. Cars, trucks, motorcycles . . . *So* many automobiles." She paused to think again. "It was stifling."

"What do you mean?"

"There were so many rules. Although maybe it only felt that way because I was little. And my parents were a lot stricter than my aunt."

Even more cautiously, I asked, "Do you remember your parents?"

"I do, and I miss them a lot. I love my aunt, but I wonder

all the time what my life would be like if my mom and dad hadn't died."

"Understandable. I wonder what my life would be like if my father was in it." We both grew quiet for a moment, then I said, "I always thought you didn't like to share things about yourself."

"Oh, I'm fine sharing. No one ever asks." She glanced at me. "So you want to travel?"

I sighed again. "More than anything. Mama wants me to stay right here, like she did, and take over Shoppe Mystique. What about what I want? I mean, don't I get a say?"

"Sure you do. It's not like there's a bubble around the village keeping us here. If you want to go see what else is out there, go."

"How? Walk? Ride a bike? How do I pay for food and stuff?"

Willow grinned at me. "Good that you're thinking about that now before you grab your knapsack and stick out your thumb."

I frowned at her. "Why would I stick out my . . . Oh. You mean I could hitchhike." My face flushed hot again. Sometimes I felt like the dumbest, most sheltered person in the world. "You seem like you've got it all figured out."

She laughed hard at that. As in, she bent over and clutched her belly she laughed so hard. "You couldn't be more wrong." She held her hands out to the trees. "I'm standing in the middle of the place I know best, so it *seems* like I know what I'm doing. You plunk me down in that big city again with those thousands of people, and I'd feel exactly like you do."

Except I didn't feel like I had a place I knew best. Not even the garden felt right anymore. Not without Nana there.

"You're thinking about your grandmother, aren't you?"

I nodded.

"Sorry about her passing. I know how that feels."

She did. And just that fast, I didn't feel quite so alone.

"You never answered my question before. What are you doing up here? Not that you're not allowed or anything like that."

"I was following Blind Willie."

She waited for more, then asked, "Why?"

"Because I think he might be a murderer."

She stopped walking and turned to face me. "I'm going to need more than that."

I told her about the mysterious box, the phone call, and what he said about being happy to be *tucked away in the Northwoods*. "Have you ever seen his cabin?"

"Many times."

"I only got a peek through the window, but I saw the computer stuff. It's like some high-tech secret hideout."

"Or the office of a man who owns a really successful business."

I deflated. "Now you think I'm strange."

"We're all strange in our own ways, aren't we?" She stared up into the trees again, almost like there was something up there feeding her information. "I can see why you might suspect him of something. He kind of has that vibe about him. Like he's holding on to some huge secret. But if you're right, and he is a murderer, is it a good idea to be following him through the woods by yourself?"

Now she thought I was stupid too. "Probably not." I flashed her a big smile. "Does that mean you'll go to his cabin with me?"

She stiffened. "To Willie's cabin? What are you going to do there?"

"Try and find some proof. From what I heard of that phone call, there's evidence in that box connected to the murder."

"So you'll break in?"

"I don't have to break in. He leaves the front door

unlocked." I gave her a minute to absorb all that. "Will you go with me?"

"When are you planning to do this?"

"In the morning. He's supposed to go to Sundry and pick up groceries for the Yule dinner he's making us." I shrugged. "Figured I'd go up early and hide in the woods until he leaves, then look around."

She frowned, not liking my plan. "I'll think about it overnight and meet you back here if I decide to go."

"How am I supposed to find this spot again?"

Willow pointed out a fairly wide path on our right that intersected with the one we were on. I hadn't even noticed it. "Follow that path. It will lead you straight to the Meditation Circle. You can probably find your way from there."

And now she was picking on me. The Meditation Circle was like a quarter mile from my cottage. "Pretty sure I can. Is this the only intersection?" She nodded. "Then I can for sure find it. If you're not here, I take a left and follow the creek west to Willie's place."

"See? The woods aren't so hard."

Instead of leaving, I stood there, still feeling a bit lost even though I knew where I was now. "We've known each other for five years. How come we've never hung out or even talked like this before?"

She shrugged. "I don't know. Why do people ever do something they've never done before?"

A new feeling formed in my chest. Had I just made a friend? One I could talk to and have fun with?

"It's almost Yule," I declared.

"Two more days."

After a rare split-second decision, I said, "I want to give you a gift, and I *really* hope you'll accept it."

Her auburn-brown eyes bore into mine. Almost like she was trying to read my thoughts. "The gift of friendship?" She enclosed me in a gentle hug. "I accept and give you the same."

Chapter Five

Full dark descended as I walked the final stretch between the Meditation Circle and our cottage. I took my time going home, letting the events of this strange day play through my mind. (Although, pretty much every day since Nana died had been strange.) I thought of Willow but mostly about Blind Willie. What was in that box? Who had he been talking to on the phone? *Was* he a killer? And that cabin of his!

"You seem to be in a better mood," Mama stated when we sat down to dinner. She'd made vegetable stew with fresh everything from our garden including herbs, big chunks of potatoes, sweet potatoes, carrots, celery . . . A bowl of stew and a hunk of bread was one of my favorite winter dinners. "Being out in the woods always agrees with you."

My first reaction was to snap at her. How did she know what agreed with me and what didn't? I didn't feel like fighting again, though. Between the energy drain of our earlier arguments, a jolt of fear over inviting a possible murderer into our home (to *cook* for us!), and all that traipsing around in the woods, I was wiped out.

"I ran into Willow."

"What was she doing down here? A trip to Sundry probably. Her aunt really doesn't like leaving her property. I think Zylina has a social phobia."

"Willow wasn't down here." I placed a spoonful of stew into my mouth and let her complete that circle.

"You walked all the way to the north side?"

"Yeah." I paused, debating if I should say anything about Willie being involved with a murder. Maybe he wasn't a killer. Maybe the person on the phone was and Willie was their accomplice. No, best to not say anything until I had proof. "I admit, I got a little lost. Willow got me back on track. We talked about where she had lived with her parents and traveling."

Mama continued stirring her stew. Was she even listening to me?

"Have you ever left Whispering Pines?"

"Sure I have. Nana and I used to go—"

"I don't mean shopping trips or to markets to sell herbs and crystals. I mean a vacation. Exploring. Seeing what else is out there."

She shook her head and loaded her spoon. "No. I never went exploring."

"Didn't you want to?"

Her eyes took on a faraway gaze. "When I was in my late-twenties, I thought about getting out there and seeing more of the world."

Was there a wistfulness in her voice? "Why didn't you?"

"It's a very strange phenomenon, but the older you get, the faster time passes." She laughed softly. "Like I said, I thought about it, then life got busy, and before I knew it, almost twenty years had passed."

"You're blaming me?" Despite my intent to not get angry, I was heading there. "It's my fault you were trapped here?"

"Not at all. I love Whispering Pines. Like my mother, I feel like this is where I'm meant to be."

"But how can you *know* that if you've never seen anything else?"

She took her time tearing off a bite of bread. "I know because I had the opportunity for something else and didn't take it."

It was like the stew warming my belly had turned into a rock. "You're talking about my father. Are you saying we could have been a family? That he could have been a part of my life? We could be living somewhere else?"

She shook her head and wouldn't look at me. "No, I'm not talking about your father. Another opportunity arose when you were a baby—"

"What opportunity? A job? Another man?"

"I simply never felt the desire to leave Whispering Pines. This is my home, and I love it here."

"And what about me? You're so much like Nana. You make the decision, and I have no choice but to go along with it."

"Morgan, I never said you have to stay."

"You said you want me to run Shoppe Mystique."

"Meaning, I'd love it if you did. Not that I expect you to." She tapped her chest. "I believe to the very depth of my soul that you have tremendous potential. If you focus on your craft and let me teach you, you'll be unstoppable. I know you're wondering what comes next, every teenager does, but that's your decision to make. I never said you must do as I say." She tilted her head side to side. "Well, for now you do. You're only fifteen, but after graduation . . ."

We sat in silence for a few minutes, finishing our dinner, and as Mama wiped her mouth with her napkin, signaling she was about to get up from the table, I asked, "Did Nana say the same thing to you?"

"About what?"

"That you had potential and should focus. Did she say you should run Shoppe Mystique?"

"Nana taught me a great deal about Wicca and green witchery. She was a hands-off sort of mother, though."

"But? I can hear it in your voice."

She set down her napkin and, after a minute, said, "There were so many things I had to learn on my own. She was right there whenever I wanted help with plants or to learn a new spell. But in day-to-day life situations, my mother was too much of a hippie. I could have used a little more of her at times. Believe it or not, too much freedom isn't always a good thing."

I seriously doubted that but thought about it while I cleaned up the kitchen after dinner. (That was our agreement. Whoever cooked the meal didn't have to do the dishes.) Too much freedom, to me, meant running wild. Mama never left Whispering Pines, so that definition didn't fit. Was Nana too hands-off, or had Mama simply been a needy teenager?

Hoping to get more guidance from my grandmother, I went to the room where I felt closer to her. Not *closest*, that would be her bedroom, and I wasn't ready to go in there yet. I was pretty sure Mama hadn't been in there either. She shut the door the day Nana left us, and we had to walk past it on our way to our bedrooms every day.

The conservatory was a few steps away from the kitchen. The glass ceiling and three glass walls gave us a full view of the garden and let in oodles of sunlight. We kept house plants here and started seedlings in late winter for planting in the spring. Before the first frost, we brought in the tender plants that wouldn't survive northern Wisconsin's harsh winters. We also grew a few tropical plants that wouldn't do well in this climate any time of year.

A few houseplants, for some reason, always acted out when we brought the tender outside dwellers inside. My spider plant, for example (the first I'd learned about since it's one of the easiest plants to grow), had me stumped. The tips of all the leaves had turned brown. New leaves curled, turned brown, and died almost immediately after sprouting. Nothing I did helped. More water, less water, more sunlight, a new pot, more shade, differing amounts of fertilizer . . . Always the same result.

"You have to share this space," I told it. "Everyone is welcome here, you know. The sooner you accept that, the sooner you'll thrive again."

I heard a soft chuckle and looked up to find Mama standing in the doorway smiling at me. She always puffed up proudly when she caught me talking to the plants. I rolled my eyes and shook my head at her in return. She only smiled bigger and walked away.

An idea regarding the spider plant struck me. Something I hadn't tried yet. "How about I leave you alone for a while? It's not that I'm giving up on you, but sometimes, especially during the full moon and new moon phases, Mama gets a little demanding with me. *You need to practice. You're falling behind.*" I tucked the pot into a spot where it would get bright light but not too much of it. "What she doesn't realize is if she'd leave me alone, I might do exactly what she wanted."

After a quick lap around the room, calling out greetings so no one felt ignored, I went to our altar. The nine-foot-long oak table with a Triple Moon Goddess symbol etched into its surface was my favorite spot in the room. Along with being the place where Nana, Mama, and I prayed and did our spellwork, it doubled as our gardening work table. Tucked behind the altar/table was a bookcase filled to bursting with books about gardening and nature.

I knelt in front of the case and scanned the selection, hoping to find something to help Spidey, and found a new book on the bottom shelf. Or rather, one I'd never seen here before. I had *seen* Nana's grimoire plenty of times. She either read something in it or wrote something in it every day. She recorded notes and observations about the garden. Her thoughts and feelings regarding Wicca. Any spell she ever tried and whether it was successful or not. Mama had one as well. The two of them gave me a beautiful, huge, leather-bound grimoire for my last birthday.

"We share a lot in this house," Nana said in that free hippie way she had, "but a witch's grimoire is for her eyes only. Use this somehow every day. Keep it in your bedroom where only you will see it."

That's where they kept theirs too. We didn't enter each other's bedrooms without permission. And *never* looked at each other's grimoires.

I'd opened the front cover of mine to find they'd left a simple inscription on the inside cover: *Given to Morgan Barlow on her fifteenth birthday. With all our love, Mama and Nana*

From somewhere nearby, Pitch let out a crow. His coop, attached to the side of the conservatory, allowed him to come inside or stay outside as he chose.

"Inside voice, please." I'd taught him to make a sort of throat-clearing growl sound, like he was about to give a full crow but stopped before letting loose. His regular cry was loud outside and ear-shattering inside.

He strutted straight up to Nana's grimoire and pecked it.

"Really?"

He pecked it again.

"Okay, okay. Don't scuff it."

He laughed at me using his growl. His point being, the leather was scratched, stained, and velvety soft after decades of daily use. A little peck from his beak would only add to its character.

"All right." I took the grimoire to the overstuffed lounge chair in the corner. After settling in with my legs in crisscross, I grabbed the throw draped across the back, tucked it around me, and looked down at the rooster. "What am I supposed to read? Is there something about spider plants in here?"

This time, Pitch walked away. Guess the rest was up to me.

I opened the front cover and found an inscription: *Given to*

Dulcie Barlow on her fifteenth birthday. With all our love, Mama and Nana

We were nothing if not consistent in this family.

I flipped through a few pages and found myself getting emotional at the sight of her handwriting. I slammed the book shut and slapped my hands over my face. At Nana's memorial service, dozens of villagers all promised the same thing, that the pain of her death would lessen with time.

"That doesn't mean you won't miss her." Mrs. O'Shea wrapped her hands around mine and stared into my eyes. "We *always* miss those we love. I only mean that you'll be able to think of the good, happy times, or even the not-so happy times, without heartache overshadowing those memories."

But no one said how long *with time* meant. It had been seven weeks, and every morning I was still sure I'd find her in the kitchen drinking her tea when I went down for breakfast.

I dried my eyes on my sweatshirt sleeve, propped the book on my knees, and opened it to a random page. *Samhain* was written in her beautiful, swirling script at the top of the page along with notes about the holiday.

Based on the ancient Celtic practice of starting a new day at sundown, Samhain, October 31st, is the start of the witches' new year . . . On this night, the veil is thin and those who have passed walk among us . . .

I knew all this. Nana died on November 2nd, so I was going to have to wait practically a full year before she'd be near me.

At that moment, something on the other side of the conservatory made a noise. Sounded like a pot tipping over.

"Pitch! Be careful."

He crowed in response.

I flipped a chunk of pages, but they fell back to almost the same spot. Must be how it was resting in my lap. *Yule.*

This page was filled with shorter, more random thoughts rather than longer contemplative ones like she wrote about Samhain.

Shortest day. Longest night.

Sunlight is about to grow stronger again. The earth will warm. Spring plants will hear the whisper to start waking soon.

A time to reflect upon on personal intent.

What do I hope to find in the new lighter season?

How do I intend to grow in my practice?

Do I intend to grow, or is this as far as I want to go?

Shall I continue along this same path or follow a different route?

I thought of the creek splitting into two. Why did it do that? Was it simply the lay of the land, or did the water (a living, life-giving thing as far as we were concerned) think there was something better waiting for it in another direction? A better place where it could become all that it was meant to be?

I pushed those thoughts out of my head. They were silly. But these words from my grandmother, when had she written them? Did she leave them for me? How did she know back then (whenever then was) what I would be feeling now?

"We're all more alike than not."

Startled, I looked around for Mama. No one else was in

the cottage with us, so it could only be her voice I'd heard. Unless Pitch learned to talk. But Mama wasn't here.

Holding tight to the grimoire, I threw off the blanket and stomped toward the kitchen. The acoustics in this cottage were such that we could often hear each other from another room. The lights were off in the living room, and only a small, dim lamp on the counter that we left on all night illuminated the kitchen. She had to be upstairs in her bedroom.

I flipped off the lights in the conservatory and then climbed the stairs. In the hallway, I hesitated for half a heartbeat outside Nana's room before continuing to Mama's. I blew out a hard breath, centering myself a bit, and knocked.

"Come on in."

I found her sitting in her bed, pillows propped all around her, a novel resting on top of the pillow on her legs.

"I thought we were going to bury Nana's grimoire with her." I held up the book as evidence of catching her doing . . . something.

"That was the intent, but I—" Her words cut off abruptly as she saw what was in my arms. "Where did you find it?"

"In the bookcase in the conservatory. Bottom shelf. Did you put it there for me to find?"

"Did I what?" She laughed. "Of course not. I looked everywhere in her room for it." Her gaze turned to one of warning. "You didn't read it, did you?"

My face went hot. "Only a few pages, I promise. And it was only about Samhain and Yule stuff that I already knew."

"You know our grimoires are private. We pass knowledge along verbally and via demonstration, not through our writing."

"I swear, I didn't read anything personal. And besides, Pitch told me to. Twice." I explained what I'd read, especially the words on the Yule page. "What was that about? And the question about should I stay on this path or follow another one, it's like she put those words there specifically for me to read. And then right after I wondered how Nana could have known what I've been thinking, you said, *we're all more alike than not.*"

Mama paled. "I didn't say that. I've been right here for half an hour." She licked her lips as though they'd gone dry. "Is that exactly what you heard? Those exact words?"

"Yes," I snapped, getting irritated again. "Those exact words."

She dropped her head back and started laughing.

I stiffened. "What's the matter with you?"

"Oh, Morgan. I swear, it wasn't me. That's what Nana used to say all the time, and it drove me nutty. I'd tell her that the saying was *we're more alike than we are different.* We argued about that every time even though neither of us really cared which version was right."

I clutched Nana's grimoire tight to my chest. "What are you saying?"

"That maybe your grandmother doesn't need the veil to be thin to visit you."

Chapter Six

I was so hopeful that Mama's explanation for what had happened in the conservatory last night was right, I laid awake for hours waiting for Nana to show up again. She never did. I drifted off at some point and woke again to a pale-gray early-morning sky. Then I lay there thinking about Blind Willie. And Willow. I told her I'd meet her at the intersection of the two paths. Would she be there?

As quietly as I could, because our cottage was creaky on winter mornings, I rolled out of bed and got dressed in jeans and the heavy black alpaca sweater I got from Effie the fortune teller a couple years ago. ("Better for hiking around the woods than a too-warm jacket," she'd said. She was right. I always ended up overheating in my jacket.) The air held a bit of dampness this morning. Maybe snow was finally coming. Before I even left my room, a shiver raced through me, so I added a long-sleeved insulated T-shirt under the sweater. My usual black lace-up boots were perfect for wandering the woods, but I'd need my thick woolen socks and mittens today too. As I grabbed my scarf, I realized it was the same magenta-purple color as the sugilite stone sitting on my nightstand. I tucked the stone back into my pocket and crept downstairs.

Mama's tea mug was sitting in the kitchen sink. Again. She must have had a hard time sleeping last night. Again. Chamomile helped, but she said it wasn't working as well lately. She didn't know, but I'd been studying some of our books on herbs (keeping notes in my grimoire) and was pretty sure I had the right recipe for a blend that would work better for her—chamomile, peppermint, lavender, rose, and a bit of valerian root, although it was a work in progress. I'd mix up the blend tonight and give it to her for Yule tomorrow.

For now, I turned on the kettle and reached for our breakfast tea, then thought of all that I'd learned about herbs. Why not give something new a try? As I took bottles from the cupboard, I stated my intention for each herb aloud.

"Peppermint to enhance psychic clarity, spearmint for mental clarity, sage for wisdom, and lavender to make wishes come true." I added pinches of each to my infuser and then stated my intention for the blend overall. "I ask for psychic and mental clarity and the wisdom to see that which I need to see. My intent is to uncover the truth about Blind Willie Haggerty." I said this three times, turning the infuser to mix the herbs each time. When a huge yawn sneak-attacked me, I added a good pinch of black tea for energy.

While my experiment steeped in my insulated mug, I tossed an apple and a small bag of nuts into my knapsack, as Willow called it. Then I spotted the scones Sugar had given me as I passed Treat Me Sweetly two days ago. She had paused when she saw me, a look of sorrow crossing her face. It's like people were fine until they saw me and then remembered their beloved Dulcie was gone. Instead of trying to console me, which I appreciated, Sugar held up the brown paper bag in her hands.

"I tweaked my Yule scone recipe." She stared at the bag,

then reached in, grabbed one of the scones, and broke off a bite for me. "What do you think?"

We all looked forward to her cranberry-orange scones every Yule. As far as we were concerned, they were perfect as they were. What more could they need? I closed my eyes as the pastry melted in my mouth. "Oh my Goddess, Sugar. What did you do to them?"

"I added vanilla. People think it's bland or boring, but vanilla is perfect on its own or as an enhancer. These are for Mr. Jardine at Ye Olde Bean Grinder." She seemed to be debating something, then shoved the bag at me. "I've got plenty more inside. Merry Yule to you and Briar."

Now, I grabbed one of the scones from the covered platter Mama had put them on, took another for Willow, wrapped them in a tea towel, and headed out. Then I turned back and left a note. Mama wasn't used to me waking up before her, let alone leaving the cottage first.

I'm off on a hike. Meet you at the shop later.

I turned right onto the path outside our front door and followed it and *our* creek (as I now thought of it) west until I got to the Meditation Circle. Then I took another right and sipped my tea as I strode, repeating my intention in my mind with every sip. As far as I knew, Willie hadn't caused any problems here, but if he killed someone, no matter how long ago, he needed to be held responsible for that.

As I closed in on the intersection, my spirits dimmed. Willow wasn't there. Although, I hadn't given her an exact time. I could wait a few minutes. I pulled the apple out of my knapsack. If she didn't show up by the time I finished eating it, I'd go without her.

She never came, but Martin Reed did. He was another village kid who spent tons of time roaming the woods.

"Hi, Morgan."

He didn't make any noise when he walked, so it was a good thing I'd seen him coming up the path, otherwise he would've scared me half to death.

"Are you following me?" I teased. Sort of.

"I saw you walk past our cottage. I was in the backyard."

"So early in the morning?"

"That's what I thought about you. Just going for a walk?"

I'd already told Willow about my suspicions regarding Willie. Martin was a quiet kid, but who knows what an eleven-year-old would do or say to impress his friends.

"Yeah, I've got to help my mom at Shoppe Mystique later, and it gets dark so early. Figured I'd try an early-morning hike."

Now that I thought of it, there were a lot of us kids who wandered the woods unsupervised. I couldn't recall any of us getting lost or hurt, and most of us went by ourselves.

"Okay." He turned and started back down the path. "See you later."

Martin was another odd one.

Willow's words, *we're all strange in our own ways,* came back to me.

I rephrased my thought. He was a nice enough kid, just quiet. Really quiet. We were pretty sure that was because of his mother. She was super strict. His dad was a good guy, though.

Following the creek west took me right to Willie's cabin. I saw the smoke rising from his chimney before the cabin itself came into view. Standing behind a huge pine tree allowed me to hide from Willie's sight while still being close enough to see him inside. Then I realized I had no idea when he'd leave. If he didn't go to Sundry until lunchtime, I'd be standing behind that tree for hours.

I hadn't planned this stakeout very well. I should've shoved a blanket and more food into my pack. A stocking cap would be nice too. I draped my scarf over my head and then around my neck to keep away more of the chill, which was seeping in fast now that I'd stopped walking. Brilliant.

With nothing to do but wait, I glanced around the property. Like us, Willie had a garden. It wasn't anywhere near as big as ours, but we grew herbs and plants to sell in the shop as well as to use for cooking, cosmetics, and our spells. His wood stack, however, was three times the size of ours, but only some of the logs were cut to fireplace size. The rest were full tree trunks. He must use those big ones for his woodworking projects. We all knew Willie was a talented woodsman. Not only did he build this cabin, he made all of the signs throughout the village, and I'd heard people talk about furniture he made for them.

I turned my attention back to the cabin to find Willie in the window. I slid further behind the tree so all except one eyeball and the top of my head was hidden. The window in question was next to the chimney, so I guessed he was doing something with his fire. Banking it so he could leave rather than adding to it, I hoped. He glanced outside, so I ducked completely behind the tree until I heard the front door open and his heavy boots clomp down the stairs. Then I peeked again.

He took the same route as he did yesterday. The less defined one I followed him along while he carried that box. He whistled as he strode away. Only once I couldn't see him or hear his whistling anymore did I dare to make my move.

I only saw a bit of the cabin through the window yesterday, but now, standing inside on his doormat, I was even more in awe of his abilities. The cabin was a single large room. Knowing he made furniture for others, I assumed the heavy pine log pieces were his creations. A loveseat, chair, coffee table, and side table were grouped near the fireplace to my right. A small dining table with two chairs sat near the kitchen at the back, which was a modern dream. We talked about updating ours. Mama loved our sage-green cabinets so would never change those, but a stove and refrigerator like Willie's would be nice.

His bed was tucked into the front corner on my left with his desk at the foot. His computer setup was like nothing I'd ever seen before. Along with a desktop computer, it was covered with multiple monitors, keyboards, mice, and other equipment I couldn't even identify. I'd been so happy when Nana and Mama agreed to bring a laptop into the shop. Keeping track of inventory (my job) became a snap. We could email our handful of distributors and easily take orders from tourists who wanted more of whatever they'd purchased during their summer visit. Willie's high-tech system put our simple one to shame.

An adrenaline rush hit me when I spotted the box beneath his desk. I set my backpack on the floor by the door and went to the box. My excitement plummeted as fast as it had spiked. The box was still taped shut. I couldn't open it. He'd know someone had been in here. And that might send him on a murderous rampage.

Hoping to find something else that would prove my suspicions, I searched through stacks of papers and peeked inside kitchen cabinets. (I drew the line at looking in his dresser drawers, though. The last thing I wanted to see was Willie's underwear.) I didn't find anything. Of course, if I'd been living in the Northwoods for forty years, hiding from the authorities who wanted to take me into custody for murder, I wouldn't leave evidence lying around either.

I glanced at the box again. No. I could not open that box.

A framed picture on a small table next to his bed caught my eye. It was a wedding picture, and it took me a minute to realize Willie was the groom. The man in the photo was thinner, had a neatly trimmed medium-brown beard, and none of the wrinkles covering the face of the Willie I knew.

The pretty, earthy redhead with freckles across her nose

was his wife? Willie was married? Where was she? Why wasn't she here?

Then, as loud as Pitch's crow, someone called out, "Hi, Willie."

I sneaked to one of the windows by the front door and spotted Martin Reed outside talking to him.

Chapter Seven

There was no way Willie had hiked all the way to Sundry and back already. He must have forgotten something. And why was Martin out there?

Through the window, I watched as Martin led Willie around to the back of the cabin, loudly saying, "I was thinking I'd clean up the wood pile in our backyard as a Yule gift for my dad this year. Figured you'd be able to tell me the best way to do that."

Willie stared down at him. "You came all the way up here to ask me how to stack wood?"

Martin shrugged. "It's not like I made a special trip. I'm up here all the time."

I ducked down beneath the sill when Willie looked directly at the cabin. "All right. I'll show you how I do it, but then I need to get going. I was on my way to pick up groceries at Sundry, but I forgot my wallet."

Another suspicious statement from my suspect. I knew for a fact Sundry let villagers put things on credit. All the businesses did that. He didn't *forget his wallet*. What was he up to now?

Once they'd disappeared around the corner, I snagged my

backpack by one of its straps as I darted out the front door, took a second to make sure the door was shut tight, and then ran full speed into the woods. I hid behind the biggest pine tree I could find and waited for Martin and Willie to reappear. They did a few minutes later.

"Thanks, Willie. There's wood all over our backyard. My mother hates it." He paused for a second. "Guess that means this will be a Yule gift for her too."

"Double duty is always the way to go." Willie clapped him on the shoulder. "Anything else you need my guidance on?"

Martin shook his head, the puffball on top of his stocking cap wobbling like it might fall off.

"See you around, then," Willie told him and headed up his deck stairs.

As I cut through the trees to intercept Martin, I crossed all my fingers that I hadn't left anything else behind that would give me away. "Did you do that for me?" I ask him.

"Distract Willie? Yeah, I didn't want you to get in trouble."

"That means you followed me here."

He stared at the ground. "I've seen you hiking around other areas of the village but never up here. I had a feeling you were up to something. You were waiting for someone before, weren't you?"

This kid was really observant. "Willow said she might meet me. Guess something came up. And how do you know I never hike up here?"

"Because I explore these woods all the time. As in, pretty much every day." He kicked at a pine cone. "It's not like I have anything else to do."

"Why not?"

"My mother . . ." He threw his hands up in exasperation. "I can't go to my friends' cottages, and they can't come to ours."

"She doesn't want you to hang out with other people but doesn't care if you wander around the woods by yourself?"

An almost wicked little grin turned his mouth. "She thinks I'm in the backyard. She has no idea what I do all day. I'm totally serious. As long as I'm inside by the time Dad gets home for dinner, she never even wonders. Never asks. Never looks out the window to see if I fell out of a tree or something."

"Did you ever fall out of a tree?"

"Once. Didn't hurt myself, though. Just twisted my ankle a little."

Poor kid. "Doesn't sound like it's very fun at your house."

He shook his head. "Or your house right now either. Sorry your granny died."

These were probably the most genuine words of sympathy anyone had given me. I opened my mouth to thank him, but nothing came out, so I smiled and nodded instead.

"She's got a real pretty headstone."

I cleared my throat. "How do you know?"

He looked at me like I was dense. "Just told you, I'm up here all the time. Plus, my grandma's and grandpa's graves are in the same graveyard."

I debated for maybe two seconds. "Will you take me there?"

It took him another two seconds to understand. "You haven't been to your granny's grave?"

I shook my head. "Couldn't do it. Hurt too much."

"Okay." He seemed happy to have a job to do. "Follow me."

I took the scones out of my backpack and gave one to Martin. We'd been walking and talking and eating for maybe ten minutes when we came to a fieldstone wall, about four feet tall, that surrounded what looked like a park in the middle of the forest. Five brownstone obelisks, taller than me, so maybe six feet, stood at equal distances from each other inside the wall. Five smaller pillars had been placed in between and a few feet in from the obelisks.

"Connect the dots and it's a pentacle," I murmured.

"*That's* what it is," Martin blurted. "I wondered why they put them there like that."

"Where's my nana?"

He led me to a grave by the pentacle's spirit point. There, a beautiful, gleaming black-granite headstone stood as though waiting for us. There wasn't a birthdate or death date. Other than my fifteenth birthday, Nana never made a big deal about age. Maybe Mama honored that by not including her life dates. Instead, it simply read:

Dulcie Barlow
Making the gardens in Summerland more beautiful.

"I'm gonna go say hi to my grandma and grandpa." Martin pointed across the graveyard. Almost like he understood I wanted to have a private talk with my grandmother. Or maybe he just wanted to visit his grandparents.

I took off my mittens and placed them on the frozen ground so I could kneel next to her and pulled my sweater sleeves over my hands. For the longest time, words wouldn't come. When they finally did, they were accompanied by tears.

"I miss you so much it hurts, Nana. As in, I get a literal pain in the center of my chest. The first time it happened, I thought I was having a heart attack or something. I didn't know *the pain of losing someone* was physical." I inhaled and sopped up my tears with my sleeve. "Did you visit me last night? In the conservatory, was that you speaking to me?"

At that moment, a gust of wind blew through the trees, making them sway. And I swear on my life it sounded like they were saying *Yes*.

Of all the Originals, Nana was the first to really connect

with the land. Even more deeply than Mrs. O'Shea. So it wouldn't surprise me at all to learn that she could communicate through the trees or plants now.

I smiled, and my heart swelled. "I'm going to take that as you saying yes. Partly because I need something good in my life right now. And partly because I really hope you're still around."

I told her about my possible new friendship with Willow. (I wasn't positive about it since she didn't show this morning.) Then about Mama inviting Willie over for dinner. "She says he misses you and doesn't want him to eat Yule dinner alone. Turns out, you were a pretty big deal around here. They cancelled the Yule gathering this year even though I know you'd say we should come together not pull apart. Even the O'Sheas left the village. So it'll be just the three of us."

The trees whispered again. This time it sounded like *Nice*.

Inching closer to her headstone, I whispered, "Something's going on with Willie." I told her about the phone call and the mysterious box. "I think he was involved with a murder. You knew him better than most people here. Did Willie kill someone?"

No whisper this time. In fact, the trees stood absolutely still.

"I'm going to find out what he did. I mean, if he's dangerous, I don't want him hanging around us." I swallowed the lump that suddenly formed in my throat. "We're all kind of emotional about you right now, and people do stupid things when they're emotional." (Like yelling at their mother to leave them alone when what they really want is for her to tell them about her sore feelings.) "I don't want him blowing up at us tomorrow because he wishes he was with you and Lucy."

I waited for another message, but nothing came.

"Now you're angry at me, aren't you? I'm sorry, but I'm trying to protect Mama. We're fighting with each other a lot lately."

A single, angry gust blew through.

"I know. We should be consoling each other or whatever, but she's making me crazy with this. She keeps pushing me to learn a moon spell or study about a sabbat or learn about plants and never asks if I even want to learn these things." I rubbed my cold hands over my equally cold face and blew through my sleeves to try and warm my fingers a little. "I know about the maiden-mother-crone thing and how every Barlow woman learns from her mother and grandmother and then becomes this powerful green witch. But what if I want to choose a different path? I was excited about the whole triple goddess green witch thing when I was little. Then it became more fun to play with my friends after school than go home and experiment with the many things I could do with lavender or whatever. After you two gave me my grimoire, I sort of became interested again, but now—"

I stopped talking. My words stuck in my throat.

After a long moment, there was a little puff of wind. Like a nudge.

Tears made my vision blur. "All I have is the mother now. I don't have the crone to teach me anymore, so why bother? I mean, if I'm going to do this, and I'm not sure I even want to, I'm supposed to learn from both of you. Aren't I?"

The trees stood still. Then another puff.

"She's all I've got left, Nana. You were my only other family member. It was always the three of us. What if something happens to her? Is this why she's so desperate to teach me this stuff? Because she's going to leave me too? How am I supposed to carry on the maiden-mother-crone tradition by myself?"

Still.

Tears stung my eyes again. "Please, one more sign."

But the pines had stopped whispering, so I sat there and even though I couldn't hear her, it felt like she might be there with me. Just hanging out.

"Morgan?"

I turned to see Martin standing a few feet away.

"Are you ready to go?" he asked. "We can stay if you want. I don't need to leave. You said something about helping your mother, though."

I inhaled a lungful of cold air. The shock of it felt good. "Yeah, I should probably get going."

To prove I was at least trying to become this oh-so powerful witch, I told Martin I was going to lead him back to the spot where I was supposed to meet Willow this morning. "No hints. I can do this on my own."

"Sure you can," he said. "It's not that hard if you let the trees guide you."

Like it was that simple. How would he know? There was no green witchery in his bloodline. His aunt was a really strong kitchen witch. His mother, well, none of us could tell exactly what kind of skills she had, if any. His dad was our constable and not a witch at all as far as I knew.

Now that I'd made my claim, that I could lead us, I doubted my abilities.

But the wind blew, and I thought the trees whispered *Trust*.

Okay. If this connection to all things plants really was in me, then Martin was right. This shouldn't be that hard.

"We're going that way." I pointed toward *their* creek. I hoped.

"All right," Martin said, stone-faced. When I waited for more, he added, "You said no hints."

Years ago, Nana had told me to always be sure of my intentions whenever I set out to do something. Once I knew what I wanted, I should state it clearly either out loud or in my head. "People walking past don't need to know, for example, that you're trying to find the closest bathroom."

I looked into the trees and declared, "We're going to the creek that cuts west through the village."

Despite the intention thing, I still felt moments of

hesitation as we walked. But instead of not trusting myself, I decided it was my instinct or some sort of internal compass guiding me and adjusted slightly. After five minutes, I started wondering if I was foolish to believe I was a human compass and was instead getting us completely lost. (I kept that thought to myself. Martin and the trees didn't need to know about my doubts.) After ten minutes, my doubts had eased. I was *almost* positive we were going the right way. After fifteen, I knew for certain.

"Great job, Morgan," Martin said like the little forest guide he was. "The creek is twenty yards ahead."

When we came to the path that ran along the creek, I took a right without hesitation.

"Can I give you one tip?" he asked.

I smiled. He'd stuck by me for fifteen minutes without correcting me even once. "Sure."

"People think a tree is a tree, but that's not true. If you look closely, you'll see every tree is different from the one next to it."

I studied those closest to us. Trunks bent at different spots and leaned in different directions. Branches did their own thing. The bark patterns were unique to each tree too.

"You're right," I praised. "Trees are kind of like people."

He laughed good and hard at that. "Do you think when there's a group of people walking through the woods the trees think we all look alike?"

"No," I decided after a bit of thought. "I think trees are more evolved than people."

"Hi, Morgan. Martin." Wood sprite Willow appeared before us. She had to be the best hide-and-seeker ever. "Sorry I wasn't here this morning. My aunt was having another one of her episodes."

I didn't know what that meant but figured she'd tell me if she wanted to. "That's okay. This way, you can't get charged with helping a trespasser. Fortunately, Martin followed me and saved me from disaster. Willie came home when I was inside his cabin."

Willow gasped. "No."

"Yes," Martin confirmed. "And you know how private Willie is. Can you make it home from here, Morgan?"

I pushed my shoulders back. "Yes, I can, because I am one with the forest." I pointed at the path that headed south. "And I know that one will lead me straight to the Meditation Circle."

"See you later, then." And he disappeared into the trees to explore, I assumed. Or maybe to go home and stack wood.

"Did you find anything?" Willow asked.

"That big box he hauled up there yesterday is in there, but he hasn't opened it yet, and I wasn't about to rip off the tape."

"Maybe it's a Yule gift."

"No, it sounds like he knows what's inside it. He told whoever he was talking to on the phone that they didn't need to 'send that stuff' to him."

"So you didn't find anything."

"A wedding picture on the table by his bed. Is Willie married?

"He was. I heard she died."

"When?"

She thought for a moment and then paled, which was concerning considering *pale* was her normal shade. "Just before he moved here."

Chapter Eight

Tomorrow was Yule. Mama talked about it so much while we ate dinner, I let my mind wander to other topics.

"Did you hear me?" she asked.

Like a squeegee clearing a window, I blinked, sweeping away thoughts of Willie's deceased wife. "Willie's coming to cook. I know that."

"Bright and early in the morning."

I'd missed that part. "If he's doing the cooking, why don't we eat at his cabin?"

That way, while he was busy with his roast and vegetables and whatever else he planned to make, maybe I could get a look inside that box.

"Because he doesn't have enough cookware. And before you say it, it's silly to haul our stuff there. Besides, we've got more room."

That was true. He only had two chairs at that tiny dining table. I paused, my fork suspended partway between my plate and mouth. I hadn't said that out loud, had I? I waited for Mama to ask how I knew what kind of furniture Willie had, but she didn't react.

Once I'd done the dinner dishes and checked on my plants in the conservatory, I sat in the chair in the corner, waiting for Nana to come back with more to tell me. When an hour had passed and I'd heard nothing but silence, I moved up to my bedroom. I curled up in my window seat and tried to read, hoping that, like with my spider plant, if I didn't try so hard, I'd get better results. But after reading the same page six times and still not knowing what it said, I gave up on that too. There were too many distractions. Such as the sight of the first snow of the season falling outside the glass (just enough to leave a dusting on everything). Remembering how the trees seemed to deliver messages to me today. Thoughts of Nana. And Willie. And Willie's poor dead wife.

I needed to try again. I had to find out if Willie was involved in his wife's death. If that meant ripping the tape off that box, I'd do it. And if he was responsible, I'd go straight to Constable Reed with the evidence. We couldn't have a killer wandering around Whispering Pines. I'd leave the cottage before Mama woke in the morning and sneak into Willie's cabin again.

With a plan in mind, I figured I'd fall asleep in minutes. Instead, I tossed and turned all night. Finally, I gave up and threw back my covers. I'd be exhausted for Yule, but with all my questions answered, and satisfied that I'd done something to protect the villagers here, I'd surely sleep soundly tonight.

Quiet as I could, I made some tea, grabbed the last scone from the covered platter, and added more nuts to my bag. By that time, it was light enough that I'd be able to see in the woods, so I headed out. As I reached the path in front of our cottage, I realized I forgot to leave a note for Mama. If I went back inside, the sound of the door opening again might wake her up. Hopefully she'd guess I was out for another early hike.

Even though I walked quickly, it felt like it took forever to get to Willie's place this time. Once I got there, I hid behind the same pine tree, the one that gave me a good view through the window next to his fireplace. The clouds that brought that tiny bit of snow last night had drifted away, so with nothing above us to trap in the heat, it was a cold morning. The sun would rise fully soon and start warming the air, but I'd worked up a sweat during my hike, and now I was shivering.

"You don't need to be in such a hurry," Nana had told me one September morning a few years ago. We were on our way to the Mabon baking competition in the commons area, and I was anxious to see what the contestants had made. "We'll still get where we're going, and we can take the time to enjoy our surroundings."

"This is the same route we take every day," I objected, itching to get my hands on some free samples. "I've seen all this hundreds of times."

The words had barely left my mouth when two young bucks appeared on the path a few dozen yards ahead of us. They butted their heads together, small antlers clicking and clacking.

"They're hurting each other," I insisted and was about to yell and hopefully scare them out of their fight.

Nana put her hand on my shoulder. "Slow down, child. Take a moment and watch."

I did and, after a few seconds, realized they weren't fighting. "They're playing."

"They're practicing," Nana amended. "In a year or so, they'll use these skills to prove dominance and attract a mate."

"How do they know what to do?"

"The same way human children learn. By mimicking their adults."

I thought of the tearful plea I'd made to Nana yesterday. *I don't have the crone to teach me anymore, so why bother?* Maybe she'd already taught me more than I realized. Like, if I hadn't been in such a rush to get here, I wouldn't have gotten so sweaty and wouldn't be shivering now.

Thank the goddess Willie left after only a few minutes.

With a sack thrown over his shoulder, he reminded me again of Santa Claus. I waited until I couldn't see him walking through the forest anymore and darted over to the cabin and straight inside. Taking a second, I wiped my boots on the mat and then went to the fireplace to warm my hands over the still hot coals. As I stood there, I looked over my shoulder at his desk. The box was still there.

Before I could think about it too hard, I strode over to the box and slid it out from beneath the desk. It was heavy, so I had to give it a good tug. Then I froze. He'd opened it. The clear tape still held the flaps closed, but tiny bits of torn cardboard stuck to it made it obvious that it had been ripped loose since I was here yesterday. I took hold of the loose edge, pulled about an inch of it up, and stopped. Something inside the box would prove he either was or wasn't a murderer.

Was it worth it?

As far as I knew, he hadn't done anything to anyone in the almost forty years he'd lived in Whispering Pines. He was a recluse who built a cabin in the woods, made useful items for the other villagers, and kept to himself. Most importantly, he had cared a lot about my grandmother.

"I can't do it," I said, releasing my grip on the tape. "I can't invade his privacy."

"You already have."

I screamed and slapped a hand over my mouth while spinning toward the door.

Willie stood there looking very disappointed. "What are you after, Morgan? This makes two days in a row. What's so interesting that you would enter my cabin without my permission?"

"I wasn't here—"

"You smell like an herb garden. You left your aroma behind."

I looked down, embarrassed. I'd been experimenting with body lotion and bath soap. My latest was rosemary, lavender, and honey and was my favorite so far. Mama liked it so much she said she'd sell it in Shoppe Mystique.

"Real pretty, but I noticed it the second I walked in yesterday. Course I already knew you'd been here. Or that someone had. Didn't know for sure it was you 'til now."

"How *did* you know?"

"Couple ways." He set his sack down on the floor mat. "Martin stops by to see me every few days. I showed him how to stack wood this summer. Their backyard has never looked so good. I noticed when I walked by the other day, so I knew he was up to something the second he asked. Turned out to be a little white lie to protect a friend."

Gutsy kid. "What's the other way?" I needed to know where I'd messed up.

"You ever notice how certain people blend in with the woods?"

Willow the wood sprite immediately popped into mind. "Willow blends so well she's practically invisible."

"Indeed, she is. That girl has scared the wahoobies out of me a number of times. What's the similarity between her and, say, a deer hunter?"

I thought for a minute. "What they wear, I guess. They're camouflaged."

"Right. What color is your scarf?"

My face flushed. "Magenta."

"Nothing that color in the woods. Not this time of year, at least. Try a nice olive green or chocolate brown next time."

Now he was picking on me.

"I hate using locks," he continued. "Tend to lose the keys. Sure hope this is the last time you'll do this."

I nodded. "It will be."

"Good. Now why don't you tell me what's piqued your interest so much."

I willed my voice to stay even and said, "I heard you on your phone the other day. You were leaving Sundry with this box and were talking about evidence of a murder. Then you said that evidence was inside the box. *Then* I learned your wife died." I wanted to be closer to the front door, but he was still standing in front of it. Just that fast, my mouth had dried out, so my next question came out sounding like dead leaves blowing about. "Did you kill your wife, Willie?"

He took off his jacket, hung it on a peg next to the door, and then took off his big boots. "This is what comes from drawing conclusions after hearing only one side of a conversation. I don't recall saying evidence of a *murder*. I do recall talking about a death. And no, I most certainly did not kill my wife." He pointed at the chair by the fireplace. "Sit."

While I unwound the offending scarf from my neck (no more bright colors for me), Willie retrieved the box from beneath his desk. He carried it over and set it on the coffee table, stared at it for a long while, but didn't open it.

"I'm going to tell you how I ended up in Whispering Pines. It's a time in my life that isn't easy for me to talk about, so don't say anything until I'm done. If you do, I probably won't finish the story."

"Okay." Different emotions swirled inside me. Curiosity and excitement because few people knew Willie's story. Fear. What if he told me something awful? Could I get away from him? Much as he probably wanted me to, I was not taking off my boots.

He paced around the cabin for a bit, psyching himself up, I guessed, got us each a glass of water, and then sat in the middle of the loveseat. After another few seconds, he blew out a breath.

"Joanna and I got married on April 3rd, 1965. It was a picture-perfect day. Blue sky with no clouds, not too cold, not too hot. Small gathering of our families and closest friends." He blew out another breath, not quite as forcefully as the first. "My best friend, Oscar, was also my business partner. We'd been talking about a business idea for a long time. Our wives encouraged it and were also very involved in getting it going. That meant a lot of sixty- and seventy-hour workweeks for Oscar and me. We figured that would ease a little once we opened for business, but the weeks stayed that long or even longer. Joanna supported me a hundred percent, though, and gave me pep talks when it got to be too much.

"About a year after we opened the doors, we were doing well. Sales were good and getting better each month. Honestly, the money was flowing in like someone had left the faucet running. Around that time—" His voice caught, and I was afraid he'd stop there. "Around that time, Joanna told me she was pregnant. No idea if it was a boy or girl. They didn't have that ability yet. Didn't matter. We'd be thrilled either way."

He took his glass of water from the coffee table and wrapped his big hands around it.

"She was about seven months along when she was run off a mountain road. They found her car but never found her body. The police searched for weeks but eventually had to quit, so I paid a private eye to keep looking. He never found her. Or my baby."

Willie took a long drink of water.

"Having nothing else in my life, I threw myself into the business even more. Our six-figure quarters quickly became seven figures. Oscar said I was working myself to death. I said I didn't care. Finally, he insisted I take some time off. The only person in the world I trusted more than him was Joanna, so I agreed to leave him in charge and went on a sort of walkabout."

Having made it through the worst part of the tale, his dark expression brightened a little.

"I started in the Pacific Northwest, the Oregon border near Idaho specifically, and headed east. Didn't have satellite phones then, so I called Oscar collect from a payphone every day and told him where I was and where I planned to head the next day." Willie chuckled at a memory. "He told me every time that if he didn't hear from me in the next forty-eight hours, he'd send out the search and rescue folks to look for me. After a few weeks of walking ten or fifteen miles a day, sometimes twenty if daylight, terrain, and the weather cooperated, a few things happened. With no one else around, I had to face my demons on my own. Only thing harder was losing Joanna and my child, but I did it. I also lost weight and became fitter than I'd ever been. More importantly, I found I liked solitude. It got to the point that even a quick stop in a grocery store or restaurant where there were more than ten people was too much for me.

"Eventually, I ended up here in Whispering Pines. To this day, I don't know how. My intended route was northeast from Oregon into Montana, head southeast to the Black Hills and the Badlands in South Dakota then continue east to Minneapolis. I was going to catch a flight home there. Except I ended up way off course. I had no idea where I was, not even which state I was in, but when I got here, it was like I was meant to find this village. Lucy let me stay at her house for a while. I called Oscar from there, and he was spitting tacks mad at me for not calling for so long. He didn't believe me when I said I hadn't seen a single person, let alone anyplace with a telephone, for two weeks. I assured him I was fine and gave him Lucy's phone number. Eventually, she offered me this little piece of land. I agreed as long as she let me pay her monthly rent. Every year around this time, I give her an extra big check to show my appreciation."

Mama had told me Willie was the reason the village had basic necessities, like electricity, water, and sewer. Among other things.

"I hiked around Lucy's woods, found this spot, and decided to try building a cabin so asked Oscar send all my tools here. Sure, I could've bought new ones, but nothing new would stand up to the set my grandfather left me. When I was ten years old, give or take, he started teaching me about woodworking. The hobby quickly became a passion." He paused and cleared his throat again. "Built a cradle for the baby I never got to meet. Gave it and everything we bought for him or her to one of our employees. Anyway, there's a little log shed tucked into the trees on the west side of this cabin. That's where I slept while I built this place. It was just meant to be a vacation home, and I was beyond thrilled to have it.

"Once the main structure was complete, I went back west to get back into the business, but Oscar could tell my heart was here now. We spent a long weekend discussing options and ultimately decided that with the right equipment and regular communication, I could help him run the business from here. And we've made that work very well for almost forty years.

"Now, turns out, it's time for Oscar and me to retire. We're not ready to step away completely, but we found someone to take over the day-to-day operations. That meant it was time to clear out everything I left behind, which means the contents of this box."

"What's in there?" I asked, figuring it was safe to interrupt him now.

"Bunch of legal paperwork I should probably have." A shadow crossed his face. "The police report from Joanna's accident is in there. I don't need to look at that. The pictures from the scene will only upset me. They also sent a copy of a signed deathbed confession from the hit-and-run driver who killed her and the baby. He died a few weeks ago. They said his version of events lines up with what they found at the scene. Oscar read the confession and said I should too. Maybe I will someday, but it's not like it'll change anything." He patted the box. "Her purse was still in the car. That along with whatever else of hers was in the car is in here."

My heart hurt for him. "A purse is full of treasures. Did you look inside?"

He nodded. "A dozen grocery lists and twice that many receipts. Three pairs of sunglasses in case she lost a pair, which she did every couple of months. Her little datebook scribbled full of appointments. Baby's due date circled about twenty times. Pack of gum she never opened." He blinked and the shadow turned into a smile. He reached inside the box and pulled out a picture of them in a frame identical to the one next to his bed. "This was always on my desk. It was taken when we were on our honeymoon in Vancouver." Next, he pulled out a thick stack of envelopes rubber banded together. "Every peptalk came with either a card or a little note. I kept every one of them in one of my desk drawers."

"You left all those things behind when you moved here permanently?"

"I couldn't look at them then. For years, seeing her face in a picture or handwriting on anything ripped me wide open again."

I thought of seeing Nana's handwriting in her grimoire and understood how he felt. "Did you look at them now? Does it make you feel closer to her?"

Willie stared at me for a long moment. "Not such a little girl anymore, are you?"

"No, sir."

"I looked at her grocery lists first. That only ripped me a little then I sealed back up again. Think I'll read those cards before I go to bed tonight."

A perfect Yule gift from the past. Guess the villagers were right. Time does lessen the pain of loss. "Can I ask, did you ever have another woman in your life?"

He sighed. "If you mean a girlfriend, no. Joanna still holds my heart. I can't see ever giving it to anyone that way again. But this is where Lucy and your grandmother come into my story. The three of us became close pretty quickly after I got here. The others accused us of having something going on, if you know what I mean."

I did, and my traitorous habit of blushing told him so.

"Turn down your cheeks, missy. There was nothing going on between us but friendship. We told each other our deepest secrets. Other than the two of them and Oscar, you're the only other person I've ever told this story to. It's important to have someone you can talk to that way, and Dulcie took a piece of me with her when she left. I've still got Lucy, though, so I'm not alone yet."

I wanted to cry for him. "Hopefully Mrs. O'Shea will be with us for a good long time yet. While I don't know your other secrets, I do know the big one now, which means you trust me, I guess."

He smiled like I'd just wrangled him into something. "Guess it does."

"I know I'm young enough to be your granddaughter, but we can be friends, can't we? Like you, Nana, and Mrs. O'Shea?"

His eyes glistened with tears. "Far as I know, there's no age requirement for friendship." He glanced at the clock on his mantle and jumped to his feet. "Your mother is going to have words for me. I should be cooking already."

"She'll have a few for me too. I didn't leave her a note when I left this morning."

He wiped his eyes. "I actually came back here for a reason other than to catch you. I forgot the cider I was going to bring for us to enjoy today." He grabbed a jug from his kitchen pantry. "Let's get going."

He took the jug and told me to carry the sack because it was lighter, and we stepped outside.

"Why are you grinning at me?" he asked with a scowl.

I shrugged and grinned even bigger. "I'm so glad I was wrong about you."

Chapter Nine

Willie and I kept a steady pace on the way to our cottage but one that also allowed us time to talk. I told him about what I had been feeling lately. Not just about Nana's death but also being trapped in Whispering Pines.

"This is just my opinion," he began, "but if a person had to be stuck somewhere, I can think of far worse places."

I looked around the forest and smiled. He was right about that. "Didn't you ever feel like that, though? Like you had a massive decision to make and everyone else had ideas about what you should do?"

"Multiple times throughout my life regarding multiple things. People like to help, and the more they know and love you, the more they want to help. If it's folks that know you, let them talk, gather all their suggestions and opinions, and then make your own decision. If it's people who don't know you, smile and nod and forget what they said the moment they walk away."

I laughed at that. "It's the make my own decision part that I'm having a hard time with. How am I supposed to know what to do when I don't know what all my options are?"

Willie nodded his approval. "A very good question. One way is to get out and explore."

"As in, go see what's beyond the border of Whispering Pines. Like how you went on your walkabout."

He held up a hand. "Hang on now. I never said you should go walkabout. At the risk of sounding like a chauvinist—"

"You were able to defend yourself, and I'm just a scrawny girl."

"Can you physically defend yourself?" He arched an eyebrow in challenge. "Have you ever had to?"

"Not sure and no," I answered.

"I think this is a conversation you need to have with your mother. I know you're being the angry teenager right now and think no one understands you, but we all feel pretty much the same thing at fifteen."

"We're all more alike than not."

He chuckled. "That's what Dulcie used to say. It's true, even if she said it wrong."

We were coming up on the Meditation Circle, which meant we'd take a left soon and then only had another quarter mile to go. Suddenly I was glad he'd be spending Yule with us. I liked talking with him. I didn't necessarily like *everything* he told me, but he was honest, and I appreciated that.

We were almost to the cottage when he said, "Something I forgot to mention earlier."

"What?" I prepared myself for something big and wise.

"Remember how we talked about your magenta scarf?"

I scowled at him. "Something I'll never forget."

"Do you know what happens when someone walks through the snow? Even a small amount of it?"

Oh, dear goddess, I was such an idiot. "They leave footprints."

"That's the other way I knew someone was in my cabin. You may have more potential than anyone else in this village when it comes to plants and crystals and the like, but stealthy, you are not. You need to get more in touch with nature if you're going to follow in Dulcie's and Briar's green witch footsteps. No pun intended."

I was momentarily stunned by what he'd said. He thought I had more potential than *any* other villager? That was saying something because there were a lot of green witches in this village. And he said *if* I was going to become a green witch. He had no expectations of me doing so.

"There you are," Mama snapped at both of us when we walked in. "I was about to start that roast myself." To me, she added, "And I don't care that today is Yule, Pitch needs tending to."

Her words were sharp, but there was a twinkle in her eye. Happy to see us safe? Happy to see us together?

I took the kitchen door out to the garden and followed the first pea-gravel pathway on my right all the way to Pitch's coop. He was fairly easy to care for. Every few weeks, I gave him fresh straw and added the old stuff to our compost bin. Every day he got clean water and more food. He always supervised this process.

"Did I do it right?" I asked when he gave me a gentle peck on the leg.

He growl-crowed at me.

I picked him up and held him close. "Happy Yule, little one. I've got a gift for you."

He gave a squawk and wiggled for me to put him down when he saw the small pumpkin I'd hidden in his supply bin. I set it on the ground next to his coop, and he immediately started pecking at it. That would keep him busy all night.

Back inside, Willie had taken over the kitchen. There were pots, pans, bowls, cutting boards, and utensils all over the place. How long had I been outside?

"Are you always a sloppy cook?" I asked.

He laughed. "Can't be too sloppy at my cabin because I don't have anywhere near as much stuff as you two do."

"My mother had a weakness for yard sales," Mama explained. "She loved wooden spoons. Said they were not only handy in the kitchen, they were great for digging small holes in the garden." Her voice grew shakier with each word. "She would also use them as markers by writing the name of the plant on the bowl and sticking the handle in the ground."

She covered her face with her hands and burst into tears. Willie and I went to her and wrapped her in a hug until she stopped crying. Then Willie said, "Morgan, take your mama someplace where you two can talk. Dinner won't be ready for a good while yet, so you've got all the time you need."

We went to the conservatory. She, Nana, and I spent countless hours together there. I dragged a second chair through the jungle of plants, and we settled into the corner where I read Nana's grimoire.

"That's the first time I've seen you cry," I told her once her tears had stopped.

"I promise you, it's not the first time that I have."

"Why were you hiding them from me?"

She sniffed. "Because a mother is supposed to protect her daughter. You had enough going on in your own head. You didn't need to worry about what was going on in mine."

"You know I hate it when you—"

"It's what I thought was best, Morgan. I figured when you were ready, you'd come to me and we'd talk. And here you are."

"Only after Willie told us to." I immediately regretted the snippy tone in my words. "Sorry."

"At some point, maybe even later today, we'll talk for hours about your grandmother. There will be more tears but some laughter too. Eventually, the reverse will be true, and there will be more laughter than tears. For now, I want to know what's going on with you."

"And what about you?" I objected. "It might be hard to believe, but I care about what's going on with you too."

She hesitated, then said, "My part is simple, so I'll go first. I miss my mama." Tears threatened to spill again. Hers *and* mine. "She had a life before I came along, but she's been part of every day of mine. Every day for forty-four years." She blinked, stanching her tears this time. "That's it for me. Promise. What about you? I know you're thinking about what comes after high school and wondering what else is out there."

My mouth dropped open with surprise. "You were listening?"

She gave me the tiny smile that meant she wasn't as clueless as I thought. "One of my Super Mama abilities is that I can listen to every word you say while appearing to be doing something else. Because when it looks like I'm paying attention, you clam up."

"That's not true."

"It's completely true. Now, tell me what's on your mind." She pointed at the wall. "I'll stare into the corner, so you think I'm ignoring you."

"Stop it," I said through a laugh while softly slapping her knee.

I started by telling her that I felt like I had no choices regarding my life. "You and Nana just expected me to learn how to be a green witch and take over Shoppe Mystique."

"The choice is one hundred percent yours," Mama insisted. "We thought, because of our bloodline, you'd have natural skill, which you do. If you want to follow a different Wiccan path, or none at all, that's completely your decision, but I'd like you to consider two things. First, sometimes we're given a gift. Accepting, following, and using that gift can make life easier."

"Or harder. A gift isn't always a blessing."

She didn't object. She didn't agree with me either. "Second, you know how those who came here to live all say they felt called to Whispering Pines. Some of the tourists say the same thing."

I'd heard the others talk about that. They didn't even know the village was here but felt the need to come to this unknown place in the Northwoods. Willie had said something similar this morning. *I had no idea where I was, not even which state I was in, but when I got here, it was like I was meant to find this village.*

I disagreed again. "The *adults* felt called here. The kids had no choice but to tag along."

She locked her blue eyes onto mine, but there wasn't the flash of anger I'd expected. "I know exactly what you mean."

Chastened, I lowered my proud chin. Mama had no say when Nana brought her here either. I guess that's true for any kid anywhere. They had to be with someone who would take care of them.

"Even though we didn't choose Whispering Pines," she continued, "I feel like you and I are meant to be here too. Nothing can make you stay if you don't want to, but I ask that you factor in those two things. Your gift and your calling. If you think finding out what else is out there will help you make that decision, then you should do that. I won't stand in your way."

My heart raced with excitement. "Really?"

"Really."

Ask and she says yes. It couldn't be that easy, could it? "Willow told me about where she lived before coming here. She said there were thousands and thousands of people, buildings, and automobiles everywhere. And there were all these rules she had to follow." We really only had one here: harm none. That was pretty easy to follow. "I don't know if I'd like a big city. Are smaller towns like that too?"

Mama smiled. "That's a question I can't answer. I've never been to the heart of a small town, only to the outskirts where we set up our tent to sell herbs. And I've never been to a big city."

I approached the next topic cautiously, knowing it could end with her throwing up her wall again. "There's one other thing that's been bothering me." I swallowed. "I want to know who my father is. It's not fair that you never tell me."

She nodded. "I understand how you feel. I never knew who my father was either."

That was her standard response, and that was as far as this discussion ever went. Mama didn't know anything about my father. Nana didn't know about Mama's. That's just how we Barlow women were. Stupid automatic response.

I threw my hands in the air in frustration. "Didn't that bother you? Didn't you ever demand Nana tell you?"

The wall didn't go up this time. "I did, many times, but she couldn't tell me. *Couldn't*. Not that she didn't want to. She only knew his first name but not where he lived or how to get in touch with him."

An awful thought occurred to me. One I'd never considered before. "He didn't . . ."

"No. Your grandfather did not force himself on her. Your father didn't force himself on me. I've told you that Nana was very free and loose regarding things like that."

"She was a hippie." And a Wiccan. (Talk about your countercultures.)

"Right. The freer and looser her lifestyle could be, the happier she was. That's why this village suited her so perfectly."

"And you followed her lead. Down to not knowing anything about the man who fathered your child."

She paused, debating something. "Do you want the blunt answer?"

My pulse quickened a bit. "I just want *the* answer."

"It was time. I was approaching my thirtieth birthday, and it was time to bring my maiden into the world. Not that the clock was ticking or anything like that." She tapped her chest. "I felt like it was time."

I made a face. "So you just picked someone?"

"It wasn't quite that random. He came to the village for a weekend, and we kept running into each other. After the fourth occasion of us ending up in the same place at the same time, I watched him with his friends. He was good looking, laughed a lot, and seemed very kind. My gut told me he was the right one, so we spent some time together and, well . . ."

I made explosion hands next to my face. "Surprise!"

"For the record, you were planned, wanted, and loved all along."

My cheeks heated up, but this time the blush was from happy feelings, not embarrassment regarding my mother's sex life. "Was Nana's story the same?"

"It was similar, yes. Some would say we didn't follow the proper path. To that I would say, they're right. We followed *our* path. Even though I often felt like I was brought here rather than called here, I'm happy. There were times when I was younger when I questioned everything. Just like you're doing now. That's what we do when we approach adulthood or any big change in life."

"Are you questioning everything now? With Nana being gone, I mean."

She paused, then took a breath. "I'm questioning a lot. Such as, did I miss something? Should I have seen that this was coming and tried to prevent it?" She shook her head. "Some things are simply beyond us. We don't get to choose everything in life. Death is one of them." She circled a finger randomly around the conservatory. "You heard your grandmother in here, so you know that the death of the body is not the end."

After a moment's consideration, I nodded in agreement. My heart clenched as I said, "I miss her hugs, though."

"Oh, my dear, so do I."

Nana gave the greatest hugs. She'd open her arms wide when she saw me coming, wrap them tight but not too tight around me, and hold on until she was sure I'd received whatever message she was delivering at that moment. Love, empathy, compassion, joy. My grandmother had the full spectrum of emotions to hand out and did so freely whenever they were needed.

"I assume," Mama prompted, "that you feel like your life has somehow been lacking because your father wasn't part of it."

I frowned. "You assume correctly. There must be some way to find him."

"Sure there is. If you really want to, we could hire someone to try and track him down. That will be expensive and likely take a good deal of time. And there's no guarantee we'd find him. If it's that important to you, that's your option. While you think about that, consider your life to this point. What *exactly* is lacking for you? If it's a father figure, some of the men here, Willie being one of them, filled that role for me. Nana never once made me feel like I was missing anything by not having a male parent in it. Like you, I didn't fully agree with that and thought now and then about trying to find my father. Eventually the question faded from my mind, and now I can truly say that I don't feel like I've missed out on anything."

I stared at Mama for a moment. "You've never told me any of that before. Why are you suddenly willing to tell me so much?"

She placed a hand on my cheek. "Because you are suddenly willing to hear my answer."

Chapter Ten

N ot ready to leave our little nest among the plants, Mama and I stayed right where we were in the conservatory and talked a little longer about random things. What it was like here before the tourists started coming. (Peaceful and free, but almost a little too much so. The tourists provided structure and purpose.) What might be wrong with my spider plant. (She didn't know either but agreed that sometimes giving a problem some space helped the solution surface.) My possible friendship with Willow. (Mama was one hundred percent in favor.)

After a while, the wonderful aromas of whatever Willie was making for us floated into our corner of the conservatory. "Smells like it's almost ready," Mama said as both of our stomachs growled.

"We should probably go see if we can help," I suggested.

Before she let us leave the room, she gave me a hug. It was practically a Nana hug. I couldn't imagine a better Yule gift. The whole scene, from sitting down together to revealing truths to respecting each other's decisions, was so nice. Like a breath of the chilly, pine-scented forest air. I felt a little older (in a good way) and definitely closer to my mother.

We found Willie elbow deep in soapy dish water. A mountain of clean dishes sat to his left, dirty ones on his right. While Mama helped him by drying and putting the clean ones away, I set the table. Willie said I should warm up the cider and we could have a "little tipple" while the roast reached perfection.

"What's a tipple?" I asked.

"He means it's got alcohol in it." Mama narrowed her eyes at me. "You're not planning to run off into the woods again, are you?"

"Not tonight," I promised.

"Then you may have some."

We gathered around the living room fireplace (the best we could, at least, with the crates of decorations in the way) and Mama unwrapped the bit of Yule log left from last year. Together, she and I lit that sliver of log in the flame of a candle and then used it like a match to light this year's Yule log. Once this one had burned down to little more than a stick, we'd smother the flame, pull it out, and wrap it up to continue the tradition next year.

The three of us talked about many things while setting out a few select decorations and putting the rest away. Nana, of course, came up, and we toasted her through tears and laughter. Willie decided to tell Mama his big secret too.

"It isn't fair for Morgan to carry all that around with her while living under the same roof as you." He started telling his story the same way he had for me. "Joanna and I got married on April 3rd, 1965."

He added a few details he hadn't told me, like how he sold his house in Oregon once the exterior of his cabin was done. That he made a trip to the spot where they'd found his wife's car every year on the anniversary of her presumed death date. As for his comment about being tucked into the Northwoods, he was hiding from the reporters that kept trying to get an interview with him about his wife and the accident, not the police.

"I have answers," he said, his voice gruff. "I think I can finally put the incident to rest."

"Thank you for sharing that with us." Mama had tears in her eyes again. "We won't tell a soul."

By then, dinner was ready. Willie carved the roast, Mama put all the side dishes on the table, and I, in a flash of inspiration, whipped up a new tea blend—pine needles, spearmint, rosemary, and chamomile.

"Oh, Morgan," Mama declared, "this is delightful."

"Needs to be a permanent addition to our Yule festivities," Willie agreed. The emphasis on *our* made it clear we'd be having many more meals with the woodsman.

Once we'd eaten our fill, I couldn't wait to give Mama her gift. I handed her a glass jar with a hinged lid, decorated using a length of twine and pine bough sprig. "I made a special tea blend for you. I'm calling it Chill Out and hope it will help you sleep tonight. I know you've been having problems with that."

Her hands went to her heart. "How thoughtful. I've been waking up at midnight and it takes hours for me to fall back to sleep. I can't wait to taste it."

I looked at Willie. "I made plenty and can bottle some up for you too."

He nodded his head. "I'll take some. And if you have more of that Yule blend left, I'll take that too."

"Now you," Mama told me, "should go to Nana's room. It's only been a few weeks, but it's time we start taking care of her things. I took what I wanted while you were gone this morning, so you can choose from what's left."

Willie gave a firm nod and looked me in the eye. "Remember, things are not your loved one. A keepsake or two, like cards or pictures, are great. The rest only weighs on your heart."

Mama's request for the door to stay closed was one I didn't mind honoring. I'd been afraid to even peek inside, afraid I'd be overwhelmed by Nana's scent and the sight of her things. I was ready now. With my hand on the knob, I blew out a breath and twisted. The smell of sandalwood and patchouli hit me first. I'd been prepared for it, though.

The room was a riot of color. Mama said Nana had redecorated it a few years before I was born. Changing it from vibrant, psychedelic orange, yellow, and hot pink to the more subdued amethyst purples and sapphire blues that now covered everything from the walls to the patchwork quilt on her bed, to the velvet sitting chair . . . that was no longer there. Mama must have taken it. Even though the colors were darker, the room was anything but depressing or heavy. It was cozy and comforting, like Nana's hugs. A perfect place to end a day with a book and mug of tea.

My first thought was that I wanted everything. The quilt, the scarves covering the lamps, and all of her jewelry. Willie's caution sounded in my ears, though. Too much would only weigh on me and become a blur. Maybe it was better to select only a few things that would make me smile and think of her when I saw them.

First, I went to the lamp in the corner where her chair used to be. How many bedtime stories had she read to me in that chair? How many invitations to sit in her lap, even when I was almost as big as she was, and tell her what was bothering me? She must have done the same with Mama. No wonder she wanted that chair. I had always loved the midnight-purple shawl draped over the lamp, softening the light that came from it. The shawl was embroidered with flowers, birds, and butterflies. Black fringe hung from the edges. I wrapped it around my shoulders and crossed the room to look in the full-length mirror standing in the corner. I gasped. I saw myself looking back but also a bit of Nana. A closer look showed me

Mama too. They were both a part of me, and I'd carry them with me for the rest of my life.

"Midnight-purple," I murmured to myself. "Don't know if it will camouflage me in the woods, but I think I've found my new favorite color."

Knowing that Nana and Mama and maybe my other great-grandmothers had viewed themselves in this mirror, I decided I wanted it too. If I stared into it without focusing on anything in particular, I saw them gathered around me. I swear one of them placed a hand on my shoulder.

Next, I went to her dressing table and loaded my fingers with Nana's silver rings and draped a few of her necklaces around my neck. I painted my nails with her black polish, and while it dried, I stood in front of the mirror again. I looked different but somehow even more myself than I had a few minutes ago.

Next, I went to her closet. My blue jeans weren't right. I wore them because that's what kids wore, but I was never comfortable in them. Dresses, skirts, tunics, and flowy pants weighed down the closet's hanging rod to the bowing point. The shawl and jewelry were a good start, and I'd find my own style with time, but I didn't want to wear jeans anymore. I flapped my hands to finish drying my nails and then carefully touched one to make sure they wouldn't smudge. I wiggled out of my jeans and took Nana's long, black wool skirt from its hanger. I'd always loved this skirt and loved it even more when I saw it paired with my other treasures from Nana's room.

"Almost forgot." I took the sugilite from my jeans pocket and tucked it into the pocket of my new skirt. The stone had done a great job aiding me with spirit connection. I hoped it would help with life decisions and healing abilities too.

"Look at you." Willie let out a long, slow whistle when I appeared back downstairs.

Mama's hand went to her mouth. "Oh, Morgan. You look . . . perfect. And so much like your grandmother."

"I feel perfect. I'd also like her mirror, but it's heavy."

"I'll move it for you before I leave," Willie promised.

Looking down at myself, I said, "This was the perfect Yule gift. Thank you."

"That was from Nana," Mama said. "My gift to you—"

Willie cleared his throat.

She smiled. "Our gift to you is outside."

I couldn't imagine what it might be. Something in the garden? A mate for Pitch so we could have a whole garden of little black chickens? How fun would that be?

"Front door," Mama corrected when I started for the back one.

There, sitting in the spot where people parked if they ever drove here, was the cutest little black car I'd ever seen. I pointed at it. "That's for me?"

"For months you've been saying that you want to do some traveling," Mama recalled. "I decided that you should."

"Your mother knows nothing about cars," Willie added, "so I helped her buy it."

Mama placed her palms together and bowed to him in thanks. "You can't drive by yourself until you're sixteen, which gives us a couple of months to recruit some folks to give you lessons. I don't know how, and Willie hasn't been behind a wheel in decades."

She handed me the keys, and I rushed over for a closer inspection. It wasn't big, but it had enough room for me and a couple bags. Maybe a passenger. Mama came to mind first. Much as I loved her, I wasn't planning a mother-daughter adventure. Not right away, at least. Maybe Willow.

"I love it. Thank you both so much." As I covered them with hugs and kisses, I started mentioning all the places I wanted to go. Which was basically everywhere.

"First you'll learn," Mama announced, "and then you'll start with short trips. To Ashland or Rhinelander. Then Eau

Claire or Green Bay. Once you're comfortable with that, you can try the southern border."

"Of the country?" I asked hopefully.

"I was thinking of Wisconsin. Don't be in such a rush, my dear."

You'll still get where you're going, Nana whispered in my ear.

We each had some more of my Yule tea (after I'd bottled some for Willie), gingerbread, and the moon cookies Nana always made. Now Mama would carry on that little tradition. By then, we were all exhausted from our long, emotional, beautiful day. Willie gave us each a kiss on the cheek and said goodnight. I banked the fire in the living room while Mama took care of the kitchen fireplace. Then we headed upstairs for bed. Willie had left Nana's bedroom door open after moving the mirror for me. We decided that was okay.

"That will make it easier for her to roam the cottage at night," Mama decided.

While she washed her face and brushed her teeth, I got into my pajamas.

"Mama?" I asked a few minutes later as she arranged the covers around her legs, mug of Chill Out waiting on her nightstand. "There's one more thing I'd like."

"What's that?"

"There's a new moon next week. Will you teach me the ritual?"

She did a fabulous job of tempering her excitement. "Not only is it a new moon, it's on New Years' Eve. A perfect night to declare new intentions. I think we'll both have plenty of those."

Chapter Eleven

P resent Day

Lucy popped the last bite of her pumpkin-maple scone into her mouth. I was so grateful Sugar had brought a box over for us. They were absolutely delectable. Better still, when these hit the shelves, we all knew the cranberry-orange-vanilla were coming next. That last tweak she made fifteen years earlier, adding vanilla, had skyrocketed them to the top of the most popular list.

"I can see why you'd think he was a murderer," Lucy teased. "He was such a curmudgeon then. Nowhere near the marshmallow of a man he is now."

Willie simply shook his head and laughed softly.

"We should get going." Lucy pushed away from the table, then cleared our plates and took them to the sink. "Would you like me to wash these?"

"No need," I assured. "I actually enjoy washing dishes.

Doing so allows me to stand still for a while and stare out into the garden."

"And warm up your hands," Willie added.

I nodded. "Another checkmark in the positive column."

"Can we see the patient before we leave?" he asked, almost sheepishly.

"She'd love to see you. Let me get a tray ready for her, and we'll go up together."

While they waited, I made a mug of green tea and placed three bites of pumpkin scone on a napkin. Mama loved the scones, but she was supposed to limit the amount of pastries she ate. Three bites, she insisted, was just enough to satisfy her.

Willie held the tray while I opened the door. "Mama? Are you awake?"

She was sitting up in bed, a book in her lap. "I've been awake for a while. I heard you three talking and thought about coming down. But then I'd steal the show, and I didn't want to interrupt your conversation."

We chuckled at that. She really did hate being the center of attention.

"Do you remember the Yule right after Nana died?" I asked.

All these years later, there was still a touch of sadness in her smile when she thought about Nana. "How could I forget?"

"Remember how your girl," Willie added and pointed at me, "thought I murdered Joanna?"

"And had been hiding out in Whispering Pines for forty years." Mama laughed so hard at that, the three of us laughed along with her. "Such a dramatic teenager you were, Morgan."

I took the tray from Willie and set it on her bedside table. Then I sat in the purple chair in the corner while the three of them chatted about plans for this year's Yule gathering.

"Morgan and I will be there," Mama insisted.

"Course you will," Lucy said. "You two have to light the Yule log. It's tradition."

They talked for another few minutes and then Willie said it was time for them to go.

I moved the tray to the bed so Mama could have her tea and scone bites. "I'm going to see them out, then I'll be back with more tea."

At the front door, I thanked them again for the food. "I never realized how long it takes to put together even the simplest of meals. Those ready-to-eat donations are a real blessing for me. And as you heard, Mama is determined to make it to the Yule gathering this year."

Lucy shook her finger at me. "Even half an hour is enough. No one expects her to party all night."

"I thought we'd do a trial run by going out to dinner at Grapes, Grains, and Grub a few days before. And I need to ask the village council for permission to use a golf cart to get her there."

"As head of the council," Lucy stated importantly, "I grant permission."

"I second the motion," Willie agreed. "You'll call me if you need anything. Anything at all."

It was an order, not a request.

"You're at the top of my call list, Willie. Always."

He stared down at me with misty eyes, and I let him pull me into a hug. "You need to take care of yourself, too, you know. What you've done for Briar is admirable, but we're not about to let anything happen to you in the process. Not even a head cold."

I laughed, pulled away, and stood on tiptoes to give him a kiss on the cheek. Then I gave Lucy one too. "You two be careful going home. We've been sitting here talking for far too long. It's dark already. You're staying at Lucy's tonight?"

"I am," Willie answered. "We've got some of that nut loaf

in the fridge ready to heat up. Then we'll watch a movie or play cribbage or whatever."

"Sounds like a great night between great friends. I'll see you two soon."

As I watched them walk away, I thought again about that Yule all those years ago when Blind Willie Haggerty worked his way into my heart. While I had received numerous blessings over the years, the gift of my woodsman would forever be one of the best.

Secret of the Season's Fortune

Chapter One

I turned the corner onto the gravel driveway feeling tired and hungry, but accomplished after finishing the Christmas shopping and weekly errands so quickly. My best friend, Cybil, usually went with me, but this week she refused. At least the kids stayed with her. That's probably why I got done in record time. Having the kids in tow always slowed progress.

As soon as I approached our building, I understood why she didn't want to come. Well, not the reason behind why, but what she had been doing while I'd been gone was immediately obvious. She, Rae, Gabe, and Vanda all stood in the cold next to our craft trailer, our meager belongings in a disorganized pile next to it. The kids were shivering and seemed a little shell-shocked over whatever had happened.

"What on earth is going on?" I asked. "It's freezing today. Why are you all out here?"

All Cybil would say was, "We have to leave. Now."

"Leave? Why?"

She shook her head, opened the back door of our station wagon that I'd just filled with gasoline, and started loading the boxes and bags.

"Cybil, please, tell me what's—"

"Effie! *Divinò!*"

I'd been so surprised to hear our codeword, I didn't question her further. Just helped her load our things. An hour later, when the shock had mostly worn off, memories from ten years ago tried to push their way to the front of my mind. Cybil had been only sixteen, me seventeen, and—

No. I couldn't think about that. What mattered was Cybil stood by my side then, so I had to now. *Divinò* was her grandmother's Creole word for seer, fortune teller, or mind reader. To us, the word also signaled the agreement we made that day in 1958 when we fled Jamaica. It meant, *please just do as I ask without insisting I tell my secret.* I had used it first and promised Cybil I would do the same for her if the time ever came. Today, it was my turn to repay the debt.

After three hours on the road, I decided while it would be nice to know why we left, I wasn't too upset about it. That place hadn't been right for us. It didn't accurately reflect who we were.

Although, Cybil seemed to be doing fine there. I, on the other hand, had been slowly dying for months.

Now, another couple of hours had passed. The kids had fallen asleep forty miles back. Out of the corner of my eye, I saw Cybil's head bob forward and then snap back. Maybe now, when she was half asleep, was a good time to try again.

"We've been driving for more than six hours," I began, cracking open the topic. "Where are we going?"

"Why ask me?" She flung a hand across the car's bench seat. "You're driving. You can stop any time you want to."

She always made it sound like I insisted on doing the driving. It's not like I had a choice; she refused to get a license. As for stopping for the night, I feared this pine forest might never end. And who knew how safe we'd be out here. It was 1968, after all. The world was a bit chaotic.

Staring straight ahead, hands at ten and two on the steering wheel, my eyes itchy and vision blurring, I continued down the two-lane highway. After another five minutes of silence from her and soft snoring sounds from the backseat, I said, "The sun is setting."

"I see that."

"And we're nearly out of gas."

This set her off. "How could you let that happen? Why didn't you stop before? Do you even know where we are?"

"Have *you* seen anyplace to turn off in the last hour?" I shot back. "We're in northern Wisconsin. That's all I know. And it's late December, so we're lucky there isn't snow and ice on the ground or that there's a raging blizzard blowing."

Cybil crossed her arms. "You chose the direction."

Except I didn't. Not consciously at least. She was adamant to *go, go, go*, so I just started driving. I headed north out of Kenosha toward Milwaukee in a sort of trance. Not that I wasn't paying attention, I'm a very good driver, but I had no destination in mind. It was almost like some strange force had taken over and my job was to keep the car and trailer between the lines on the road. Before I knew it, we were passing Wisconsin Dells, then Black River Falls, then Chippewa Falls. The last sign I saw was for Hayward, but that was at least an hour ago.

I blew out a breath, steeling myself for the blowback, and cautiously said, "I have no idea where we are."

Thankfully, she didn't yell. Maybe she could tell how stressed and scared I was. The lives of my best friend, her son, my daughter, and the teenager who had basically adopted us were in my hands. We hadn't seen a single car in nearly an hour. If we ran out of gas, we'd have to sit alongside the road until someone came by, because walking anywhere in the dark and cold was a fool's errand. At least we had blankets. If I pulled over with a couple of gallons left in the tank, I'd be able to run the heater for a few minutes at a time throughout the night to keep us warm. We didn't have any food or water, though, and hadn't eaten since lunch. I'd be fine, but my daughter, Rae, would complain that she was hungry soon. She'd barely eaten her burger. I knew we should have picked up some snacks the last time we stopped for gas.

"Effie." Cybil's voice was soft. "You're doing a great job. I'm sorry I didn't at least help you figure out which way to go. It's cold but not subzero. We'll be okay."

I nodded. "Let's give it ten more minutes. Then we should find someplace to pull over for the night." I told her my thoughts about leaving enough gas for the heater. She agreed.

We both stared ahead into the waning light, looking for a turnoff or house. Anything. The constant blur of trees along the sides of the road was really getting to me, and I'd need to stop soon regardless of sunlight or our remaining fuel level.

With our self-imposed deadline ticking down, Cybil pointed ahead. "Up there on the right. It looks like a road or maybe a driveway."

Praying it was a driveway, I slowed and switched on the right-turn indicator. Not that there was anyone around to see it.

The dirt road looked like it got used often, which made my dying hope gasp another breath. After about half a mile, according to the odometer, my hope dimmed again. We were off the main highway now, so I'd need to turn around. Somehow. That would be a challenge. Not only was the station wagon long and the dirt road narrow, we were towing our craft trailer. I'd never be able to back up all the way to the highway without running into a tree.

"What is that?" Cybil pointed ahead. "Cars? Is that a lake? Or a river? Can't tell from here."

I saw it too. Vehicles and a body of water of some kind lay about a hundred yards dead ahead.

"Where are we?" Gabe asked from the back, waking Rae and Vanda.

"We're not exactly sure," his mother answered. "Hopefully someplace where we can stay for the night. Or get directions to where we can."

The forest ended abruptly, and I entered a clearing that looked a bit like a small parking lot. There were four vehicles parked in a neat row next to a garage big enough for two more. A wide strip of lawn browned from the cold butted up against a beautiful tree-lined lake. Maybe we were on the outskirts of a town. One that had a restaurant and gas station. Maybe a hotel.

Looking to our right, I gaped at the house standing there, a simple rectangular structure with windows everywhere—to take in the view, I imagined. It was painted gray, the color of the sky when it was planning to storm, with bright white trim. And it was big. Three stories tall and very long.

"That can't possibly be a family's home," I murmured. "Unless it's a really big family."

"Maybe it's an inn," Cybil said, "or a bed-and-breakfast."

"With this many cars, you might be right." I shifted the station wagon into park. "Let's go see if they have a room for the night. Or directions to the nearest town."

"Can we get out?" Rae asked as Vanda slipped out of the back driver's side door.

"Yes," I replied, "but don't go wandering off. Stay nearby and away from the lake."

As Cybil and I approached the front door, we noticed carefully tended shrubs along the house and sidewalk. The ground was currently covered with a thick layer of pine branches, protecting whatever grew there in the spring and summer.

I rang the bell, then took a couple of steps back to stand next to Cybil. After maybe ten seconds, the door opened, revealing a woman about our age—late twenties—with short, dark-brown hair cut in a bob, bangs hanging just past her eyebrows.

Her brilliant smile faded as her head tilted with confusion. "Sorry, only two people ever ring our bell, and you are neither of them." She opened the door wider and leaned against the jamb. "I'm Lucy O'Shea. How can I help you?"

Chapter Two

I held out my hand. "Hello, Mrs.—"

"Goodness, no. Just Lucy, please."

I began again. "Hello, Lucy. I'm Effie Crain, and this is Cybil Grace."

Cybil stepped forward. "You have a beautiful home."

"We don't get many folks through here." She looked between us, a slight smile returning to her mouth. "It must have brought you here for a reason."

"*What* brought us here?" I asked.

"This place." She gestured at the cars in the driveway. "A few of the others unexpectedly found themselves here as well. Or do you know where you're going and simply need a rest?"

"We don't really know where we're going or where we are," I explained with a laugh. "Guess we can't be lost if we don't have a destination in mind."

"That is a very true statement." Lucy's smile deepened. "So, you're looking for a place to rest. We can help with that."

"Could you tell us how to get to the nearest town?" Cybil asked. "We've been driving all day and are almost out of gas."

"How much is *almost*?" Lucy asked.

"We've got two gallons at most," I guessed.

"Oh, dear," Lucy said with a sigh. "The nearest town is forty miles away."

"Forty miles?" I blurted. "I thought for sure there would be one just up the road. You live forty miles from the closest town?"

"Isn't it glorious?" She gazed past us, presumably at the trees surrounding every bit of her property except for where the lake met the yard. Then she realized we were still standing in her open doorway. "I'm being rude. You should come in. It's cold tonight."

I pointed toward our car. "We've got kids with us."

"How many?" Lucy wanted to know, unfazed. "And what are their ages?"

"Rae is eight," I began, "Gabe is seven, and Vanda thirteen."

"Perfect. We've got five ranging from six to eight. Go get your kids and come inside. Door's open, no need to ring again. And bring in your bags. You'll be pushing your luck if you try to find gas now. You can stay here tonight, and we'll figure out the rest tomorrow."

We walked back to the kids and the station wagon, both of us a little stunned by Lucy O'Shea.

"Do you suppose it's safe?" Cybil wondered.

"To stay here? You'd rather sleep in the car along the highway tonight?"

She poked my shoulder with her long, pointy fingernail. "You are too trusting."

I blinked at her. "You're right. I'm sure this is all a setup. Probably a cult of some kind. I need to sleep before driving any further and would prefer a bed over a car seat. Since I drove all day, you sit up all night and make sure we're not killed in our sleep. Then in the morning—"

"Effie?"

"Yes?"

"Shush."

I chuckled softly, pleased with my performance. "I got no bad vibes off Lucy. And her home is very welcoming. We'll be fine."

Cybil grumbled to herself but didn't object further. Like me, she was tired, hungry, and cold. I knew she wanted a bed as badly as I did.

Then, as I pulled my suitcase out of the back of the station wagon, a cloak of happiness surrounded me. I felt warmth, contentment, and friendship. It wasn't a vision exactly. I hadn't had an unbidden vision in months. This was more a reassurance that we'd be okay here. What brought that on?

The kids, being kids, didn't hesitate when we told them we were staying here for the night. Saying it as though this had been the plan all along helped. A minute later, looking like complete vagabonds, we stood in Lucy's entryway with our suitcases and waited for her to tell us what to do next.

To our left was a dining room with two simple, unmatched dining tables surrounded by seven chairs each. That was it, no other furniture. To our right, a sitting room was more completely furnished with a modern orange sofa and two blue chairs. Wood side tables with lamps and trinkets flanked the sofa, and a coffee table sat on a yellow shag rug in front of it.

From the front door, we could see all the way to the back wall of the house. It was floor-to-ceiling windows that must look out at the lake. The view had to be amazing. There was also a huge, perfectly shaped Christmas tree.

Lucy appeared from the right at the end of the entryway/hallway, a man and little boy following her. She smiled warmly at the kids. "This is my husband, Keven, and our son, Dillon."

Dillon offered a quiet smile as Keven greeted, "Welcome. Lucy says you're in a bit of a bind."

"You could say that," Cybil agreed with a tone. Did she blame me for this?

"Come on in," Lucy beckoned, "and meet everyone else. Leave your bags, we'll take care of them later."

We entered a large living room to find eight adults lounging on two mismatched couches and a collection of chairs, also mismatched. Now that we were closer, I could see that along with simple white lights, the tree was decorated with orange slices, pinecones, strings of cranberries, and feathers. Not a normal ornament in sight. What an unusual way to decorate. Pine boughs with even more pinecones, orange slices, and cranberry strings decorated the fireplace mantel. Smaller sprigs of pine were tucked all around the room. Near the tree, a group of three children sat playing games while two others read books.

"Everyone," Lucy began, "this is Effie and Cybil and their kids."

The adults greeted us with hands raised and calls of "Hello" or "Welcome."

One of the little girls, with long black hair and brilliant-blue eyes, leapt to her feet and grabbed Rae with one hand and Gabe with her other. "I'm Briar. We're almost done playing Trouble, and then you can play either Operation or Kerplunk with us."

"Hang on." A woman with shoulder-length blond hair held back with a headband and flipped up at the ends stood from her seat on the sofa. She propped her hands on her hips and scanned the suddenly guilty-looking kids. "Where did you get the Kerplunk game?"

All the kids turned to look at one girl. She had the same color hair as the woman and a sour expression.

"That was a Christmas present," the woman scolded.

The girl shrugged. "It had my name on it."

The man the woman had been sitting next to said, in a German accent, "It's okay, Oksana. Since Flavia doesn't care about Christmas traditions, we'll just take the rest of her presents back. Or distribute them among the other kids."

The girl, Flavia, glared at him and then turned bright red when the kids snickered at the threat.

"They're the Long family," Lucy said with an amused grin. "Flavia and Reeva, the other blondie over there, go with Jurgen and Oksana. On the other couch are Rupert and Gregor Reed. Horace is their son."

A dark-blond boy stood, waved, and dropped back to the floor.

"Don't worry about remembering all our names right away," Lucy told us. "You'll figure us out with time."

Seconds later, a woman wearing a frilly yellow gingham apron appeared from a room to the right. Presumably the kitchen since she waved with a wooden spoon in hand. "Hi, I'm Fern. Your timing is perfect. I'm just about done with dinner. Lucy says you've been driving for hours. You must be starving. I hope you like chicken and squash."

That's what was making my stomach rumble. Between a chicken dinner and the pine boughs, this house smelled fantastic.

Fern gestured at the other little girl sitting next to Reeva. "Laurel, say hi, honey."

"Hi." She waved with both hands.

Finally, a woman with long, wavy black-brown hair, flared jeans, and a purple striped sweater crossed the room in a few long strides. She greeted each of us by touching our shoulders with the tips of her fingers. "Blessed be. I'm Dulcie Barlow. Briar is my daughter. We're so happy you found us." She inspected Vanda's long checkerboard prairie skirt made out of a dozen different fabrics. "This is groovy. I absolutely love it."

"Thank you," Vanda replied in her heavy Romanian accent. "I made it myself."

"And now I love it even more," Dulcie praised. "Why don't you all have a seat in the dining room and relax? We'll have food for you in a few minutes."

Cybil, Vanda, and I took seats at one of the two tables. As

soon as I settled, exhaustion spread through my body. If I wasn't so hungry, I'd go find a corner to curl up in and sleep.

"They are nice," Vanda noted, smoothing her beloved skirt. I'd taught her how to sew, and she made most of her clothes by cutting up and reusing her mother's things. The girl definitely had her own style.

"They do seem nice," I agreed. "Cybil?"

She swatted a hand in the air. "Yes, yes."

Before any of us could say more, Lucy appeared carrying a tray with glasses. She disappeared and came back seconds later with pitchers of water and milk. "We've got Ovaltine and Tang if you'd prefer that." She looked at me and slumped a bit, mimicking my posture. "You couldn't care less right now, could you, Effie?"

"I appreciate your hospitality so much," I began, "but as soon as I'm done eating, I'd be very grateful if you would show me where I can sleep tonight."

"You bet. The others will get dinner out shortly. I'll go figure out sleeping arrangements for you five. Hope you'll be okay in the same room."

"We'll be just fine," I promised.

While we sat and waited, me barely able to keep my bleary eyes open, Jurgen and Gregor brought leaves to extend the tables and five extra chairs.

"Will you sit with the adults or the kids?" Jurgen asked Vanda.

She debated for a long moment. "With the kids. I will keep them from trouble."

I placed a hand over my heart in thanks and smiled at her. Cybil patted her back. She was such a great girl.

The guys proceeded to make an adult table with ten chairs and a kids' with nine.

Next, Rupert came with plates and utensils and set the tables. Then Oksana brought two platters loaded with squash, and Fern brought roasted chicken. The aromas perked me up and made my mouth water.

"What else?" Fern tapped her chin. "Bread! I nearly forgot Oksana's bread." She left the dining room and called out for everyone to take their seats. The kids all came running in, laughing and squealing. Vanda jumped to her feet, herded them to their table, and like a drill sergeant, explained the rules.

I caught her eye and gave her a wink. She grinned, pleased with the praise and the role she'd found for herself.

The chicken dinner was very good. Those at our table discussed chores that needed to be done tomorrow, and a celebration for something called Yule, which would happen on Friday.

"I was thinking," Gregor began, "that in the spring—"

"Nope, nope, nope," Dulcie cut him off. "Let's not look that far ahead. Many wonderful things will happen here next year, but for now, let's enjoy the moment." She looked at Cybil and me. "And our new friends. Tell us about you."

"Yes," Fern agreed before jumping up to check on the kids, even though Vanda was doing a fine job of maintaining the peace. "Where did you come from? Where were you headed?"

Fern barely stayed in her chair long enough to hear my answer. She took a bite, then rushed to the kitchen for more bread. Was this how she always was?

"We came from Kenosha," I explained. There were certain details about us people didn't always understand. I didn't want to make an otherwise nice meal awkward so left it at that. Instead, I repeated what I'd told Lucy earlier. "We didn't really have a destination in mind."

They all exchanged knowing glances across the table.

"Ready for a fresh start," Dulcie murmured.

"We all understand that," Jurgen said with a nod.

"A fresh start," Cybil echoed. "That's a good way to look at it. How do you all know each other?"

I'm glad she asked because I was about to. Although, I suspected Cybil's question was more an attempt to deflect attention away from us than genuine curiosity about these people who let us into their home.

"Forces we can't explain brought each of us to this spot." Dulcie raised her hands as though to accept a gift that might fall from Heaven. "The Universe works in mysterious ways. The longer you're here, the more you'll feel it."

"Feel what?" I asked. It almost sounded like she was talking about supernatural forces. Did that mean these people would understand Cybil and me? *Could* I tell them more about us?

Dulcie held my gaze for a long moment. As though trying to read my mind? "Don't sweat it, Effie. There's nothing strange going on here. Unless you think us living in a getting-back-to-nature way is strange."

"Not at all." Now I felt foolish. Considering how tired I was, it was best for me to not open what would surely be an involved conversation. I gestured at the property in general. "You've got all the modern conveniences plus plenty of room for gardens. Sounds like the perfect setup to me. I assume the lake has fish, and there is probably plenty to hunt in the woods."

Dulcie smiled but didn't say more. Seemed she was also holding back on details.

"The longer you're here," Keven parroted Dulcie's words, "the more you'll understand what she means."

He seemed a little different from the rest. Less earthy and more . . . mainstream? Practical? Not sure how to define it. Guess I'd understand him more with time too. Of course, we wouldn't infringe on their hospitality for long. In the morning, after a hopefully good night's sleep, we'd figure out how to get enough gas to take us forty miles and move along.

"You look ready to drop, Effie," Fern said.

I laid a hand on my full belly. "Sleep would be welcome."

"We should get you settled in a room." Fern stood as if about to guide me.

"Fern, for heaven's sake," Lucy scolded. "You've taken maybe three bites of your dinner. Sit and eat. I will show our guests to their room."

"The dishes," I objected. "You were so kind to feed us. The least we can do—"

"Go with Lucy," Cybil ordered. "You drove all day. I'll help with the dishes."

Momentarily stunned, I stared at her. Cybil volunteered to wash dishes? Maybe there really were mysterious forces going on here.

Between Lucy, Dulcie, and me, we got all of our luggage up to the second floor. At the top of the stairs, we took a right, went past a small sitting area, and continued to a large bedroom. There were two beds separated by a cozy chair, side table, and a floor lamp, as well as a small pine tree decorated for Christmas, much like the big one downstairs.

"This is someone's room," I noted, taking in the possessions that filled it. Toys and stuffed animals on one side. Stacks of books, a collection of candles, and jars filled with what looked like dried plants on the other. Dozens of houseplants scattered all about and filling the window seat gave the room a greenhouse feel.

"It's mine and Briar's." Dulcie adjusted the star made of sticks atop the tree. "We'll stay in another room for tonight."

"We'd offer you that one," Lucy said, "but it's not big enough for the five of you."

"We can't take your room, Dulcie," I insisted.

"Of course you can. I already changed the bedsheets."

She took the suitcase from my hand and set it with the others near the bathroom. Did every room have its own bathroom? Whoever designed this house was very smart.

"You can figure out who sleeps where. We're out of mattresses, but we could create a cozy nest of pillows and blankets there." Lucy pointed to the open space in front of the reading chair. "I hate making one of you sleep on the floor, though."

"Gabe will be fine there." Then I changed my mind and gestured down the hallway. "Actually, he'd probably rather be in that little nook at the top of the steps, if you wouldn't mind. That would get him away from all the girls for a while. It's tough being the only boy in this group."

Dulcie smiled. "Fortunately, we've got plenty of them here for him to hang out with."

"I've got a standing screen that will give him a bit more privacy." Lucy scooped up an armful of pillows and gestured for Dulcie to take the blankets. "We'll get him set up down the hall. You get some sleep. We'll show the others up when they're ready."

"Feel free to use any of the supplies in the bathroom," Dulcie said as she headed for the door. "I make it all myself and have plenty."

"*Plenty*," Lucy agreed with an eye roll. "Sleep well, Effie."

I got ready for bed and chose a jar of lotion in the bathroom labeled *Sleep*. It was lavender scented and wonderfully rich and creamy. I expected to lie awake, thinking about what tomorrow would bring or wondering if staying here really was okay. These people were friendly and welcoming, but almost too much so. Was there such a thing? Before I could think about that further, my brain quieted and sleep hit me hard.

Chapter Three

I awoke as early morning light started to fill the room and was surprised to find Vanda sleeping next to me. I'd expected my daughter to be there. Cybil wasn't used to sharing, however, and I could imagine her telling the smaller Rae to crawl in with her so she'd have more room in the bed. I smiled at Vanda. Like always, her wild hair was everywhere. Sometimes she tied it back with a bandana or headband, but she really loved the feel of it being free and loose. I leaned close and placed a kiss on the top of her head before getting out of bed and pulling on a sweater and thick socks.

Both Cybil and Rae were still out cold in the other bed as I tiptoed across the room toward the door. Good. I loved starting my day quietly and cherished the early morning minutes before everyone else got up. At the end of the hall, I paused to peek at Gabe, and my heart swelled to see him snug in his little nest. Then I made my way down the stairs.

Last night, I must have been even more tired than I'd realized because now I saw that there was more than pine branches and things from nature decorating the house for the season. It reminded me of the international Christmas market we visited the year we moved to America. Like the different styles of furniture throughout the house, there was a mishmash of holiday decorations. Some were modern and American, whereas others had a more traditional European or Scandinavian look.

I headed for the kitchen, hoping Lucy wouldn't mind if I snooped around for coffee, but as I got closer, the aroma of fresh brew filled my nose. It seemed Lucy felt the same as I did about early mornings. She was standing near the windows, staring out at the lake.

I gasped, startling her. "Sorry. This is my first peek at your lake. It's so beautiful."

Contentedly, as though completely at peace, she replied, "This is how I start every day. A cup of something in hand and my eyes on that view. It hasn't been all that cold yet, so the water is just starting to freeze along the shoreline."

"Well, I'm happy to see it in liquid form." I went closer to the windows to take it all in. It appeared the house was on a sort of peninsula, like a small version of Florida sticking out into the ocean. Other than the expanse of deep-blue water and clear-blue sky, there was pine forest, the trees dusted lightly with snow, for as far as I could see. "You're blessed."

"In many, *many* ways. Help yourself to coffee or tea. I've set everything out."

In the kitchen, I noted the mismatched collection of drinkware—china, ceramic, plastic, glass—and then figured it out. "Everyone contributed their possessions."

Lucy tilted her head in question.

"The unusual mix of furnishings and holiday decorations," I explained.

"Oh, yes. There's a little bit of everyone throughout this house. Good thing they contributed because I don't have enough of anything to accommodate this many people comfortably."

My first sip of coffee from the electric percolator, with plenty of sugar and a bit of milk, was just what I needed to chase away the morning cobwebs. I sighed. "Perfect, thank you."

"You're welcome. How did you sleep?" Her small smile suggested she already knew what my answer would be.

"Better than I have in a long time. Between the dinner, the silence here, and whatever magic Dulcie mixes into her Sleep lotion, I don't think I moved all night."

Her smile deepened. "I'll be honest, it took me a while to get used to the lack of city noise. And I didn't come from a very large town. Now I need to stuff cotton in my ears at night whenever we leave here. Which isn't often." She pulled out a chair at the kitchen table for me as she sat in another. "Please, join me. If you want to."

"I'm happy to." I settled in the chair that afforded me a perfect view of the lake, the morning sun just working its way above the horizon. "You want to know our story, don't you?"

"I'll tell you ours if you tell me yours."

How to begin? It's not that I planned or wanted to hide anything. Everyone in and around Kenosha knew who and what we were. I took a deep breath and blurted, "We're fortune tellers."

Lucy didn't react. There was usually a snort of disbelief, eyebrows raised in judgment, an uncomfortable fidget . . . something. Lucy barely blinked. Had she heard me?

"Go on," she urged. "I'm listening."

Acceptance? Right away? This was different. "Cybil and I have had our abilities since we were young and have used them to earn money in both Jamaica and the States." I paused as dark memories tried to work their way into this conversation and forced them back into the past where they belonged. "About ten years ago, we both had what you could call whirlwind summer romances. We met two military men, fell madly in love, and came to America with them after an intense two weeks of being together constantly. It was like it was meant to be."

"Mm-hmm. That happens sometimes." Lucy's eyes narrowed as she gazed suspiciously at me over her coffee cup. Like she knew I was only giving her part of the story.

"As soon as we got here, to the States," I continued, "we got married. When they started sending men to Vietnam, both of our husbands went." I paused, remembering the days the uniformed men showed up at our door. "Cybil's husband died first. Mine a few months later."

Lucy put a hand on my arm. "I'm so sorry."

I nodded and swallowed. "After my husband passed, we stayed with friends who gave us two rooms in exchange for helping around the house. Vanda wasn't with us yet, so it was plenty of space. We were also able to make some money from our spiritual gifts and the crafts we sell. It was tight sometimes, but we got by. After six months, though, we decided it was time for something new. We came north."

"Why north?" Lucy asked.

"We were already in the south and had never been north so thought we'd find out what it was like."

Lucy cocked a knowing eyebrow. "And?"

"It's cold." I laughed. "Much like we did yesterday, I just started driving. We had car problems on the Illinois side of the border with Wisconsin. Fortunately, we had the money for repairs, but it took a few days because they had to order parts, so we used the time to figure out what to do next. We were at a diner in a little town I can't even remember the name of, and I took out my pendulum to ask for guidance. Should we stay? No. Should we return to Florida? No. Should we go back to Jamaica?" The memory tried to work its way in again. "No. A woman saw what I was doing and slid a chair over to our booth. Didn't even ask if she could join us. She said her name was Bonnie Bristol and she had an idea to set up events where people could have readings done or sit in on séances, that kind of thing."

"Was she legit?"

"We wondered the same thing. Cybil is especially cynical, I'm more trusting, but Bonnie spoke our language. By that, I mean we spoke to her the way we speak to each other regarding our abilities, and she followed us completely. We never once felt like she was conning us. And for the record, she wasn't."

Lucy took our cups to refill them. "This is what Dulcie means when she says the Universe works in mysterious ways. What are the chances you'd run into someone like that in the middle of Nowhere, Illinois?"

"That's what we thought. We told her we'd think about it overnight. Cybil and I discussed it and decided that since we needed to land somewhere, we could give it a try. Bonnie asked for our opinions from the start and let us have a big say regarding our events. Everything was going great."

Lucy set my cup on its saucer, waited a beat, then asked, "Until?"

I stirred a bit of sugar into my coffee. "That's the thing. I don't know what happened. Everything seemed fine, for Cybil at least, until she did a group reading Friday night."

"What's a group reading?"

"It's done for an audience instead of individuals. Normally Cybil limits them to no more than twenty people, but Bonnie wanted her to do a big one. She promoted it like crazy and sold more than a hundred tickets. During these kinds of readings, Cybil walks among the attendees, and when she gets a vibe off someone, she stops in front of them."

"Then she repeats the message she gets?"

"Correct. Not everyone will get a reading. The audience knows this and is cautioned before purchasing a ticket that if Cybil senses something, she will say it out loud for all to hear. No warning, no permission asked, just a public announcement."

"Uh-oh. Did she pick up on someone's deep, dark secret?"

Lucy looked entertained by this, as most people were. Until it was their private life being revealed.

"Probably, but she won't tell me. She says the big secrets are often easier for her to pick up on, because the person is working so hard to prevent the thing from being revealed it's like they're announcing it over a spiritual bullhorn." I warmed my hands around my cup and stared out at the pine trees frosted with a hint of white. "She's done hundreds of these over the years. Not as large as this one, but that shouldn't matter. I can't imagine what could have happened that would make her want to leave town so quickly."

"She won't give you even a hint?"

I shook my head, and out of nowhere, a snippet from a conversation I overheard played in my ears.

"You look like you remembered something." Lucy leaned forward slightly, waiting for details.

"I overheard two women talking about Bonnie when I took Rae out for lunch on Sunday. Our weekly mother-daughter date." I took a sip of coffee, letting more of the memory form. "One of them was really angry. She said, 'it's a complete scam' and used the words *fraud* and *cheat*." I gasped as another thought occurred. "I bet it was Astra."

"Who's Astra?"

"One of the other tellers in the commune. She's horribly vindictive and jealous of Cybil's popularity. She was furious when Bonnie announced Friday night's reading. It was the biggest one yet and attracted a lot of people. I wouldn't be at all surprised to find out Astra has been badmouthing Cybil."

But would that be reason enough to invoke divinò?

"Back up a second." Lucy twirled her finger like turning back the hands on a clock. "Commune?"

"Bonnie's goal is to have weekend-long events where people can choose a teller and get readings on the spot or attend séances. That kind of thing. Word spread, and other mediums and fortune tellers said they wanted to be involved.

Bonnie owns land with outbuildings and lets all the tellers live there."

"Were you happy living that way?"

I gave her a pointed look, then held a hand up, indicating her home. "Isn't that basically what you've got going on here?"

Lucy burst out laughing. "I guess it is. This isn't a permanent situation, though. Dulcie is building a cottage about two miles from here. Fern plans to build on the other side of the bay. I'm sure the others will want their own places too." She brought us back to my story. "You said this Astra woman was, possibly, raising a fuss. How does that lead to you leaving Kenosha?"

"I've been wondering the same thing. Cybil was upset when she got home Friday night, and her mood only darkened with each day. There has to be more to this than Astra being nasty, because when I got back from running errands yesterday morning, Cybil had all our things packed. Even our craft trailer was ready to go."

"The thing attached to your car? I thought it was a tent trailer."

"That's what it used to be. Unlock a few latches, and the sides lift to elevate the roof. That's how we haul and display our crafts when we go to craft markets."

"Ingenious."

I smiled and nodded. "My husband designed it for us."

"You must miss him."

"Every day. I can't believe it's been more than a year already." I blinked away the memories and needed to change the topic. "Tell me about you and this group. How did you end up here with all these people?"

She told me about something called Wicca. "Dulcie introduced me to it after we met at a gardening class. Wicca is a pagan, nature-based religion, not a devil-worshipping cult as many believe. Much like farmers do, we follow the seasons and moon phases, draw energy from the elements, and honor both goddesses and gods. Turned out Dulcie knew more than our instructor that day. The more she taught me about plants, the more it felt like a true connection with nature was what was missing in my life. I was tired of the hustle and bustle of society and yearned to get away."

"And this is what you wanted? Just the three of you all alone in the forest?"

"The two of us. Keven is gone a lot for work, so it was just me and Dillon here most of the time. I learned to be tough, but I admit it was very lonely, and Dillon didn't like that there weren't any other kids. I needed help with landscaping so invited Dulcie to come for a visit." She held up a hand, stopping my next question. "Yes, even out here in the middle of the forest, I wanted a properly landscaped yard."

I leaned back, smiling. "You'll get no judgement from me."

"Dillon and Briar got along immediately, so I talked to Keven, and he liked the idea of there being others here with us. I asked Dulcie if she wanted to stay, and she said yes. Briar did too."

"Just like that?"

"Yes, but it wasn't exactly a spur-of-the-moment decision for her." Lucy paused, gathering her thoughts before explaining, "People have a hard time accepting things that are different from what they're used to. Like Wicca. Dulcie experienced a lot of . . . *hatred* is the only way to say it. People couldn't accept her ways, and she wasn't about to change who she was. So they moved here.

"Dulcie knew Fern and that she was feeling the same way so asked if it was okay to invite her and Laurel to come for a visit. They spent a long weekend here in April and were in love by the time they had to go back. I honestly don't know how the rest heard about us. I swear, like with you five, something summoned or guided them here. Gregor, Rupert, and Horace were camping, ended up taking a wrong turn down our driveway, and after a few days, asked if they could come back permanently. The Longs have a similar story."

"Very mysterious place you've got here, Lucy O'Shea."

She looked at me over her coffee cup. "Can I ask you something?"

"You can ask," I replied without guarantee of an answer.

"You said Cybil was packed and ready to go. Why did you agree to leave?"

Oh, what a big, involved question. "Cybil and I have been best friends since childhood. She's like a sister to me. When I got home and she hysterically insisted we needed to leave, how could I say no? If my husband was still alive, I would not have agreed, but there was nothing tying me to Kenosha."

In fact, it was the excuse I'd been looking for to get out of there.

Lucy studied me for a long while. "You're the fortune teller, but *I'm* sensing there's more to it than that. What's the real reason?"

Could I trust this woman? If I told her my deepest secret, would she tell the others? Would it matter if she did? We were leaving as soon as we had gas for the car, and I'd never see her or any of these people again. Was this my opportunity to finally unburden my soul?

"You can tell me, Effie. I'll keep your secret."

Before I could overthink it, I blurted, "I'm the reason we had to leave Jamaica."

Chapter Four

"**W**hat do you mean," Lucy began with a gentle tone and a suspicious, arched eyebrow, "that you *had* to leave Jamaica? You said you left to get married. Are you in some kind of trouble, Effie?"

I had opened the topic and was about to tell her the truth when the door to a bedroom near the kitchen opened.

"We'll talk more later." Lucy laid a hand on my shoulder, and then a big smile displaced the concern on her face. "Good morning, Fern. Always the first one up."

"First after you," Fern amended. She greeted me with a smile. "And Effie, it seems. Want to know a secret?"

Lucy winked at me. "Always."

"I wake up shortly after you do," Fern whispered. "I'm a light sleeper and hear you moving around out here, trying hard to not make much noise."

"And you don't come join me?"

Fern dismissed the question with a *pfft* sound. "I figure you let us all move into your beautiful home, you're entitled to a quiet start to your day."

"That's kind of you." Lucy's hand went to her heart, but

she didn't object and say that Fern should join her. Now I felt bad for infringing on her alone time.

"An easy, small gift." A heartbeat later, Fern got to work. "Time to start breakfast. Everyone is scattering today, so I figured something easy. Scrambled eggs, fruit, maybe some bacon. I think we still have blueberries, so I could whip up some muffins quick."

"That's an easy breakfast?" I asked with a laugh. "I expected you to take out boxes of cereal."

"I could," she agreed, "but which would you rather have?"

An easy decision. "Eggs, fruit, bacon, and a muffin."

"All of it?" she teased.

My stomach rumbled. "I'm hungrier than usual this morning."

Lucy stood and went to help Fern. "You had a big day yesterday, Effie. Your body needs fuel to process all of that."

She was right, but despite being ravenous, I felt revitalized and ready for whatever this next phase of my life would bring. Guess that's what a good night's sleep could do for a person.

"How can I help?" I pushed away from the table.

"Where do your skills lie?" Lucy asked. "Fern is a great cook. I am not, so my role is to get her what she needs and wash dishes."

"I can cook," I said humbly, "but since Fern has a plan and a helper, how about I set the table?"

"Perfect. We eat breakfast in here instead of the dining room." Lucy pointed out where I'd find everything, and I got to work setting out plates, coffee cups, juice glasses, and utensils.

As the smell of bacon and blueberry muffins spread through the house, everyone slowly made their way to the kitchen. Cybil was the last to arrive and the only one fully dressed and ready for the day.

"Did you sleep as well as I did?" I asked while tightening the belt on my bathrobe.

"How would I know how well you slept?" She was always grumpy in the morning, so I let it go. The dark circles beneath her eyes were less intense this morning, so it looked like getting away from whatever had upset her in Kenosha was the right thing to do.

"Fern made a wonderful breakfast," I told her, ignoring her grumpies, "and Lucy just made a fresh pot of coffee. Come sit. Did you see the view yet?"

I took her arm and led her to the kitchen window, and she relaxed the slightest bit when she gazed out at the lake. And when I brought her a cup of coffee, I noticed she hadn't moved a muscle. Her attention was still on the lake and the trees as though they held her under a spell.

Later, when dishes started piling up near the sink, Rupert took over washing duty so Lucy could eat.

"You were up early this morning," Lucy said to Keven as she sat next to him at the table. "What were you doing?"

"Making a few phone calls," Keven told his wife. "I have to leave. Emergency business trip."

"What?" she objected. "You promised you were done with business until after New Year's."

"It should only take a couple of days." He took her hand in his and held her gaze. "It's important."

"Will you be back for Yule?" she relented but was clearly disappointed.

He kissed the back of her hand. "I will make every effort to be back in time for Yule."

"It's *Christ*yule," Briar said, reminding them of . . . something.

"Did you forget?" Dillon asked.

Looks of confusion crossed other faces. Glad I wasn't the only one who didn't know what they were talking about.

"We decided to celebrate both this year," Dulcie told the kids. "A small celebration of Yule on Friday, and then we'll open gifts on Christmas morning."

"What's Yule?" Rae asked me.

"I'm not sure," I admitted.

Dulcie tapped the tip of Rae's nose. "Yule is a celebration of the longest night of the year. We thank nature for the dark months that allow us to rest and rejuvenate."

"How do we celebrate?" Reeva asked.

"Will there be presents?" Gabe wanted to know.

"No presents," Dulcie answered, "but there will be lots and lots of special food. We'll decorate the table with pine boughs, pinecones, squashes, apples . . . anything harvested this season. And then, once we've eaten our fill, we will build a big fire outside and thank nature for the lighter, warmer months to come."

"Lots and lots of food," Keven mused as he brought his dishes to Rupert. "You know exactly what to say to motivate me to finish my task quickly. I'll do my best to be back by Friday night. That gives me two days."

He kissed his wife, laid a hand on Dillon's head, and went off to pack a bag.

"What are the rest of us going to do today?" Lucy asked. "It's a bright, sunny morning. We got a dusting of snow last night, but I don't think it will be very cold."

"Oksana and I are heading to the grocery store," Jurgen reported, "to buy all that food Dulcie is going to make for us."

"That *everyone* will make," Dulcie amended. "This is a group celebration, after all."

"We're leaving in about an hour." Oksana raised her voice so everyone heard her. "If you need something, write it down. And be specific." She leveled a look at Horace.

He held his hands up in a shrug. "How was I supposed to know what kind of shaving cream to get?"

"Ask your dads," Oksana suggested.

"Shaving cream?" Rupert asked, still washing dishes. "You're only eight."

Horace stroked his chin. "I felt stubble."

"It was probably dirt." Gregor ruffled his son's hair. "Try taking a shower before reaching for a razor."

"You and Rupert are going for gas, right?" Lucy asked Gregor.

"And a few other winter supplies. We've got ten five-gallon cans." He turned to Cybil and me. "I distributed what was in them into the other cars' tanks yesterday. If you were here two hours earlier, we would have had enough for you to get to a station."

"That's okay," I answered. "We got to stay the night and get to know you all a little better."

"I'm glad you did," Lucy said, ignoring Cybil's scowl. "The rest of us could go for a hike through the woods."

"Yay!" Dillon and the other kids cheered in unison, except Flavia who never seemed to smile. Our three shrugged to indicate a hike sounded like an okay idea.

"You mentioned that Dulcie and Fern are building cottages," I recalled. "I'd love to see them." ·

"I'm not building yet," Fern said. "It's still in the blueprint stage. Jurgen is helping me with that. I can show you where it will be, though. And I haven't been up to see Dulcie's plot in weeks."

"The garden is resting now," Dulcie admitted, "but you can see what we've got started on our cottage."

"Other than these overnight dustings," Lucy told me and Cybil, "we haven't had any snow yet. You'll still want to wear boots for warmth, though."

"We'll run up and get dressed." I motioned for Gabe, Rae, and Vanda to come with me.

"Don't rush," Fern called as she pulled a loaf of bread and jar of peanut butter from a cupboard and then grape jelly from the refrigerator. "I'm going to make lunch for us to bring and still need to get dressed myself."

"Does she ever stop cooking?" I asked Lucy.

Lucy smiled at the woman. "She loves taking care of people. I swear, this is what she was born to do."

We scurried up to our room, all three kids excited to go exploring. When we got there, Cybil took a seat in the reading chair.

"Our boots are in the station wagon," I said while pulling warm clothes out of my suitcase. "Cybil, since you're already dressed, would you—"

"I'm not going hiking," she announced like a surly teenager.

"But—"

"I'm grateful for their hospitality," she interrupted, "but just because this is where we ran out of gas, that doesn't mean I need to become pals with these people."

The kids stared open-mouthed, shocked by her angry tone.

I realized she wanted to get back on the road—to where, neither of us knew—but this crabby attitude of hers was pushing my patience to the breaking point. I waited until the kids had taken turns getting dressed in the bathroom, then shooed them out of the room and knelt next to my friend. "What's wrong?"

"I don't want to talk about it."

"If you changed your mind and want to go back—"

"No. I haven't changed my mind."

Thank heavens. Dare I tell her that I wasn't sorry to leave Kenosha?

She stood and stared out the window. "I knew I shouldn't do such a large event. But you and Bonnie pushed me."

When backed into a corner, even if she put herself there, Cybil would always strike like a cobra. Many times, I was her target. At least I had confirmation this was because of something that happened at her reading Friday night.

"This isn't my fault or Bonnie's, Cybil. Neither of us pushed you."

Cybil paced the room, no longer listening to reason.

Now what was I supposed to do? Stay here and keep pushing her for answers while risking my best friend continuing to use me as a punching bag? Or should I let Cybil wind down while I went with Lucy and explored the beauty of this area? The answer, while not a simple one, was obvious.

I pulled on my warm clothes and gathered my boots and jacket. "You know you can tell me anything, and I'm here if you decide you want to talk. For now, though, I think you need some alone time. Sit here and rage or go for a long walk or whatever you want to do. But if you still intend to take this out on me when I come back, you can find another corner in this big house to sleep in tonight."

"Rupert and Gregor are going to get gas. We're leaving once they put some in the station wagon."

"No, we're not," I said and nearly laughed at the shocked look on her face. "After hiking around the woods and getting all that fresh air, I will be tired. I want to stay one more night." Actually, I wanted to stay to find out what Yule was about but getting her to stay for two more days would take divine intervention of some kind. "Since I'm the only one who can drive . . ."

"You always have to throw that at me, don't you?" She glared at me and flung a hand at the door. "Go. Have fun with your new friends."

Chapter Five

"There's a spot off the road where we can park," Lucy explained as the thirteen of us divided between two vehicles. "We could hike the whole thing, but we never know what the weather will do this time of year. I'd rather we only have to trudge a mile to the cars than two or three back to the house."

The kids—Gabe, Rae, Dillon, Briar, Laurel, Flavia, Reeva, and Horace—all piled into Fern's VW bus with her and Vanda. Dulcie and I road with Lucy in her Bronco.

"You're sure you can't convince Cybil to come?" Dulcie urged. "This forest is like a balm for the soul. A day among the trees makes everything better."

"I don't doubt you," I promised, "but a day alone might be the balm Cybil needs. And I wouldn't want her mood to bring everyone else down. She's going through a tough time right now."

Dulcie didn't push it.

The truth was, I needed a little time away from Cybil too. She was my dearest friend in the world, but just because we'd spent nearly every day of the last twenty years together didn't mean that couldn't change. I was entitled to live my life according to my own desires. Wasn't I?

At the intersection of her driveway and the highway, Lucy took a right and headed east. A mile later, she turned onto a dirt road on our left, though calling it a road was an exaggeration. Really, it was two parallel tracks tires had worn into the ground.

Lucy turned off the Bronco. "We'll leave the car and van here. It's not quite a mile from Dulcie's plot to the spot where Fern wants to build her cottage."

I went to Vanda who was supervising the cluster of children all trying to exit the van at once. "How did the ride go?"

She shrugged. "How much trouble could they make in five minutes?"

I stared pointedly at her.

Vanda sighed. "They were fine, except Rae and Flavia. They do not like each other. No idea why."

"Did they do something," I asked, "or do you just have that feeling?"

She made a *V* with her index and middle fingers and tapped them beneath her eyes. "They stare and give each other the evil eye but do not speak."

"Good to know."

"And I think Reeva has a crush on Gabe."

How cute. "Thank you for supervising. Dulcie, Fern, and I will worry about the kids now. You have fun exploring this afternoon."

"Okay," she said without another word and wandered ahead of the group.

"Don't lose us," I called after her.

She waved a hand over her head, indicating she'd heard me.

We walked a couple hundred yards and came to a

makeshift bridge made of heavy wood beams and thick planks.

"Keven had his crew build the bridge," Dulcie explained, "so construction trucks could cross the creek."

"He owns a construction company," Lucy added.

"Take a right on the other side of the creek," Dulcie continued, "walk for three or four minutes, and you'll be at the five acres Lucy and Keven have so kindly gifted me."

"You're just giving them land?" I asked, amazed at her and Keven's generosity.

"Fern and I will own our houses," Dulcie corrected. "Lucy and Keven will let us live on their land. No paperwork or money involved."

"We've got two thousand acres," Lucy said with a shrug. "We can share a few."

"Take a right, munchkins," Dulcie announced on the other side of the surprisingly sturdy bridge.

She held her arms wide as though trying to corral them, but it was like a magnet was drawing them to the left. They all went through a natural opening in the brush. We followed and ended up in an almost perfectly circular opening thirty feet in diameter.

"Look at them," Lucy commented with an amused smile. "They're like a little pack of pups."

From the instant they darted through that opening, I got an uneasy feeling. My heart started to race, and my hands became clammy. Then my senses heightened. Instinctively, I tuned into the sounds around us as though listening for a predator nearby. My vision zeroed in on the spot where the kids were standing near the center of the clearing. There was something wrong here. Something bad. The next thing I knew, it was like an invisible force had shoved me. I stumbled and an instant later cried out and put my hand to my head as a jolt of pain shot through it.

"Effie?" Lucy took me by the arm. Dulcie bent to look me

in the face as I doubled over with the sensation. "Are you all right? What's wrong?"

Just that fast, everything was fine. "I'm okay. Really."

I paused, assessing my body for any other oddities—nothing—and assured them once more that I was fine. Then I looked at the kids. Flavia and Rae stood about fifteen feet apart, facing each other at the far end of the opening. Giving each other "the evil eye."

"We need to get out of here." I stepped toward them and copied Dulcie's outstretched arms. "Come on kids. Let's go. Rae, Gabe, out. Now, please."

They knew to not question me when I used that tone. Rae grabbed Gabe's hand and pulled him through the opening and back onto the path.

Dulcie and I waited until all the kids were out.

"What happened?" she asked.

"I had a vision." It had been a while, a long while, since one hit me like that. "Very helpful for doing readings and séances. Sometimes annoying when they come unbidden."

"A vision about this place?" She looked genuinely concerned. Understandable since her home would be just up the path.

"Sometimes I see things." I hesitated. "This time it was a feeling."

"Of what?"

"Death." Her eyes went wide, so I immediately amended, "All I know is something bad happened in this spot or will happen. It could be an animal. Maybe a person died there a hundred years ago or will a hundred years from now."

"I'll do a blessing," she said, accepting my words without hesitation. "The moon will be dark on the thirty-first. I'll cast a protection spell to banish the negative energy."

The moon will be dark? She'll cast a spell? What sort of community had we stumbled into? Should I be concerned? I wasn't. Mostly because there was nothing evil behind her statement. She said it as though announcing she was going to do laundry or make dinner. It was another item on her to-do list.

Tomorrow I will wash my clothes, make pork chops, and cast a protection spell.

And she just *knew* that the moon would be dark in eleven days? Lucy did tell me they followed the moon phases because of their religion. It probably had something to do with that.

"Coming?" Dulcie asked from the edge of the clearing.

"Yes, coming."

As I followed Dulcie, I heard Rae shout, "She is not" and then another child holler, "Ow!" On the other side of the opening, I found Flavia on the ground and Rae standing nearby with her hands clenched at her side. The others were gathered behind Rae in a semicircle.

"What happened?" I demanded.

"Rae pushed her," Fern explained. "Not hard. I think Flavia's feet got tangled, and she tripped."

"Are you okay?" Dulcie asked, pulling Flavia to her feet.

"Yeah." Flavia pointed a long finger at Rae. "She did it."

"Yes, we know." Dulcie's tone implied Flavia was a tattler. "Fern just told us."

I charged over to my daughter. "Why did you push her?"

Rae glared at Flavia. "She said I have a bossy mother."

"Because you told us to leave the clearing," Briar clarified.

"Well, I did say that, so I guess I am bossy."

Flavia didn't seem to know how to react to that. She probably suspected I'd deny it or scold her for disrespect.

"Rae," I began, "you need to apologize."

"No." She crossed her arms defiantly. "She's rude."

I pulled her closer to Flavia. "Say you're sorry for pushing her or you'll have to go back to the bus."

Through a clenched jaw and squinted, angry eyes locked on me, Rae hissed, "Sorry."

"Flavia?" Lucy prodded. "Your turn."

The girl looked at her as though Lucy had asked her to strip down to her underthings right there in front of everyone. "Why? I didn't lie."

"It's fine," I told Lucy. "Let's get away from this spot and keep the two separated until they cool off."

"This way," Fern called out and pointed east.

I took inventory, making sure we hadn't left anyone behind. Reeva and Laurel were already twenty yards ahead of us, apparently opting to stay clear of the drama. Gabe took Rae's hand this time and led her away from us. Then came Briar and Dillon. Flavia stayed near Fern. Who were we missing?

"Vanda?" I called out. Where was she? I told her not to lose us.

"Up here," came her reply from somewhere up the path.

All good.

Unused to this much nature, I told my racing heart to relax before I inadvertently brought on another vision. But the towering trees on our left, and the creek on the right at the bottom of a sudden, three-foot drop-off only made me more anxious. The kids were too close to the edge, weren't they? The creek was frozen, but who knew how thick the ice was. Soaking wet clothes out here were an invitation for hypothermia.

I turned my gaze away from the creek to find Lucy and Dulcie smirking at me. "What?"

"City girl," Dulcie teased lightly. "We can tell what you're thinking."

"It's okay," Lucy promised, "I was the same way when we first got here."

After only a couple minutes of walking, the thick trees gave way to another clearing.

"This is the start of my plot," Dulcie said like a proud mama. "We hiked out here last year, looking for the perfect Christmas tree, and came across this clearing. It was like I was meant to find it. With the creek right here, I'll have all the water I need for my garden. The natural opening in the forest lets a good amount of sunlight through, but Keven suggested we cut trees from this area for firewood and other building projects so even more sunlight can get through."

I stared in awe as a field of browned grasses merged into a huge garden with neat, tilled rows. "You did all that?"

"A lot of it. Keven's crew brought in a tractor and cleared it all for me first. I don't shy away from hard work, but this much land requires more than a hoe."

"And that will be your home?" I asked, pointing to three-foot-tall fieldstone walls forming a giant square.

"That's how far we got before the weather turned. When finished, it will be two stories tall with three bedrooms upstairs. The main floor will have a living room, bathroom, and a big kitchen with a fireplace. It won't be anywhere near as grand as Lucy's place, but I only plan for Briar and me to live here."

"I might have a bigger home," Lucy said, "but I'll never have a garden like she will."

While the kids, even Reeva and Laurel, ran in circles inside the walls of Dulcie's to-be home, I wandered a dozen yards out to the middle of her garden. There, I could see both the promise of the house that would stand there by this time next year and the lush garden that would surround it.

"What is she doing?" I heard Lucy ask Dulcie.

"I don't know," Dulcie responded.

With closed eyes, I *saw* Dulcie and Briar working in perfect unison, tending not only the food that would help feed the others who lived here but also making herbal medicines and crafted items for their homes.

The words *maiden*, *mother*, and *crone* whispered in my mind as someone else appeared in the vision. What did they mean? I called out to Dulcie, "Do you have another child?"

"No," she answered, "and no chance of one."

I kept my eyes closed and waited. "Any other child who might live here?"

"*Live* here? No." Dulcie seemed intrigued by my questions. "Why?"

"Because I see another girl. She has long black hair like yours, and I sense she will have a big impact on your little community."

Lucy laughed. "There are only fourteen of us. Not sure that could be considered a community."

"Fourteen for now," I replied. "More will come."

"I better plant more crops," Dulcie joked. "Although, I was thinking about fruit trees and berry crops on one of the acres."

"It wouldn't be a bad idea." I opened my eyes. "You will be very happy here, Dulcie. For a long time."

I blinked to clear the vision and then returned to them. My two new friends looked a little excited, a little bewildered. I was used to that. Anytime I gave a reading or séance and said something that affected my customer deeply, whether with emotions from loved ones passed or with hopes for the future, they all got the same expression.

"Where to next?" I asked, suddenly eager to see more of this place that made me feel more in tune with the spiritual realm than I had been since Jamaica.

Lucy smiled, her expression changing to one of excited expectation. "Dillon?"

"Yes?" his voice came from somewhere inside the square.

"Would you like to lead us to the lake?"

"Oh, yes!" He popped up from behind the wall closest to us. "Everybody, follow me."

Chapter Six

Dillon darted across the path straight toward the creek and leapt over the drop-off, the others following like lemmings. I was about to call after them when Lucy stopped me.

"Don't worry," she assured, "there's a foot bridge. He and Briar insist on taking the long way home when we come here. After ending up soaking wet from the knees down for the fifth time, despite there being a spot just upstream that is narrow enough for them to jump across, Keven's team lashed some trees together. The kids treat it like a balance beam."

At the edge, I found them crossing sideways, using a shuffle step, and holding their arms out to their sides. The kids loved it when we three did the same thing. The footbridge—thick tree trunks cut in half to make a flat surface—was as sturdy as the other one, which we could have driven over.

We followed Dillon along an obvious trail through the woods. When Dulcie explained that the kids walked this path nearly every day on their own after helping her in the garden, my concerns about us getting lost eased. But other ones arose.

"You let them walk alone?" I asked. "You're not worried about animals or injuries?"

Dulcie shook her head. "We haven't seen any animals that might hurt them. If they're around, they scatter when they hear us coming."

Not sure how I felt about that philosophy.

"As for injuries," Lucy added, "that could happen even if they were with us. We follow them sometimes but don't let them know. They like feeling independent. This path leads straight to the lake. From there, they follow the shoreline to the house. We know how long it should take them to get home, and there are consequences for abusing our trust. And I've warned them if they step one toe into the lake, I won't let them explore by themselves again until they're eighteen."

Guess that's the difference between growing up in the country versus the city. Or having parents who are more free and loose than me. I could be overly protective at times.

I took the caboose position in this train of adventurers. At one point, I looked back and saw nothing but trees, brush, and the path Dillon had led us down. I panicked, feeling almost claustrophobic in the middle of all this nature and couldn't get a deep enough breath. Looking ahead, I saw that the kids, even Flavia, were having fun playing some game only they seemed to understand the rules for.

There is no danger here.

The words were inside my head, but as I forced myself to relax, the sounds of the forest took over. I heard cracks and creaks and groans as the trees swayed with the breeze that didn't reach us on the ground. Looking up, the claustrophobic feeling grew stronger but only for an instant. Then, rather than feeling trapped, the canopy above made me feel protected.

I could no longer see the rest of the group, but I could still hear them. And even if I couldn't hear them, I reasoned, the path was obvious. Lucy said it led to the lake, which meant I would also be able to get to her house. I took a deep breath of pine-scented air and, within seconds, felt at ease.

Totally and completely at ease. When was the last time I'd felt this way? Certainly not while doing readings and séances for what was starting to feel like Bonnie's workhouse. I hadn't felt fully relaxed since before my husband had gone off to war.

No, further than that. Not since before that night in Jamaica.

As the memories tried to take over my feeling of peace, a strong gust of wind blew through the treetops, distracting me from the thoughts and dissolving the images trying to worm their way into my mind. I looked up and watched the trees' wild, swirling dance. As their branches and needles rubbed together, I was sure I heard them whisper *stay*.

And at that moment, I wanted nothing more than to do exactly that. I wanted to stay right here in this spot that filled me with such peace forever.

Stay, they whispered again but more softly. As though the offer was dying with each passing second.

When I looked ahead again, I saw Lucy watching me from a dozen yards away. Her head was tilted questioningly, and then a knowing smile lit her face. She beckoned me to catch up. As I took the first step toward her, it felt like a piece of my heart had pulled out of my chest to remain there in the forest with the trees that had invited me to stay. A moment I would remember forever.

I rounded the bend of the path to find the kids on their knees in a circle, Vanda standing close . . . waiting. But for what? "What are they doing?"

"Drinking from the spring," Dulcie said as though it was another normal item on her unusual to-do list.

Lucy placed a hand on my back, encouraging me to try. "It's the best, purest water I've ever tasted." At my reluctance, she laughed. "Goodness, Effie, it's perfectly safe."

"It is," Fern assured.

"This is the well that feeds our house," Lucy continued,

"and will feed Dulcie's and Fern's cottages. This bubbly little puddle is the source. The spot where it's perfect."

I watched the kids drink, exclaiming how cold and delicious the water was.

"You found this last year," I said as sure of this as I was that my name was Effie Crain.

"We did," Lucy confirmed. "During our expedition to find the perfect Christmas tree."

"Christyule," I murmured softly as another vision struck. In a flash that lasted no longer than a second, I saw, "A well."

Dulcie's head cocked in amusement. "What?"

"There will be a well here," I stated with absolute certainty.

Lucy and Dulcie exchanged a look, then chuckled. Fern looked as confused as I felt.

"What's so funny?" I propped my hands on my hips. Were they picking on my ability? On me?

"Sorry." Lucy blew out a hard breath. "Remind me to show you my sketch when we get back to the house."

I crossed my arms and waited for her to say more.

"Almost immediately after finding this spot," Lucy began, "we decided there should be a well here. Dulcie thinks it's some sort of holy spot."

"There is a high level of spiritual energy swirling here," I acknowledged, shivering at the feeling.

Dulcie gave Lucy's arm a gentle smack with the back of her hand. "See? Told you."

"It is a special place," Lucy agreed, "but if we're going to go through the exercise of building a well, I want it to be more welcoming than foreboding the way holy shrines can sometimes be. I envision a sort of park with places to sit and just . . . be."

"With a gleaming white well at the center," I stated when the vision in my head intensified.

"White?" Lucy asked.

"White marble." Dulcie seemed as sure of that as I was that there would be a well. "It represents purity, promotes peace, and is grounding and calming."

Lucy took a step back. "Guess I'll talk to Keven about white marble."

And he would make it happen.

Once the kids drank their fill, I knelt down and scooped up a bit in my cupped hand. They were right; it was the best tasting water I'd ever had. It was almost like I couldn't stop myself from drinking more and more.

"Come." Fern did the beckoning this time. "I want to show you the spot I chose for my cottage."

"Oh, good." Dulcie clapped her hands softly. "I've been so curious."

After only a few yards, the lake came into view. We were on the other side of the cove, Lucy's house directly across from us.

"Right here?" Dulcie asked, her eyes sparkling.

"Prime real estate," Lucy teased.

"Since that first day I visited here, I've been in absolute awe of Lucy's view," Fern said, breathless. "I immediately started dreaming of a little Medieval style cottage on the lake and was overjoyed when she said yes."

"Why wouldn't I?" Lucy replied. "Like I said, we've got more than enough to share."

"A big house," I corrected, surprised by my next vision.

"No." Fern shook her head. "It'll just be Laurel and me. Two bedrooms, a living room, nice size kitchen . . . Maybe three bedrooms, in case we ever have guests."

"I see guests," I told her, positive of this. "Lots of them."

Fern narrowed her eyes at me. "I'll start with three. I can always add on."

We went to the shoreline with the kids and watched them try to skip rocks. Only Vanda was successful, so the others swarmed her, begging her to show them how.

"Look." Lucy pointed out a stretch of shoreline in the shadows. "The lake is freezing. In a few weeks, it'll be all ice."

"That fast?" I asked.

She nodded with a certainty I didn't question. Who knew this place better than she did?

After eating the lunch Fern had prepared for us and had been carrying in the pack on her back this whole time, we decided it was time to head back to the house.

I didn't want to go. When we got there, we'd find that Gregor and Rupert had put a few gallons of gas in the station wagon's tank. Cybil would start demanding we hit the road despite my earlier insistence we stay one more night. I wasn't ready to leave these people or this place yet. Less than a day and it had already given me gifts I would cherish forever and worked some sort of magic on me. It restored a part of me that had gone missing long ago.

Maybe if I could get Cybil to tell me what had upset her so much, she would calm down enough to see what I saw: a place filled with people we were meant to find.

Chapter Seven

When we got back to the house, the kids, remarkably, still had energy to burn so played tag in the huge front yard. Inside, Oksana and Jurgen had put away all the groceries and were enjoying tea and cookies. I went in search of Cybil and found her in the bedroom in the same chair, same position she was in when I left nearly three hours ago. She appeared to be deep in thought over something. That was good. She had a lot to think about.

"Tell me you haven't been sitting there the whole time."

"Not the whole time."

She didn't volunteer more, and I wasn't going to encourage her silent tantrum by begging her to talk to me. Instead, I told her about the hike.

"Dulcie found an amazing spot by a creek, so she'll be able to water her garden. Lucy and Keven are letting her use five acres. Fern will be on an acre right by the lake. And there's a spring just a few yards from where her house will be." I sighed happily, remembering how I felt. "There's something mystical about that spot. The energy swirling around is so intense."

"Mm-hmm," she hummed.

"They're really nice people, Cybil. You're missing out."

"Rupert put an entire can of gas in the station wagon. Five gallons will easily take us to the next town."

"It should," I agreed, "but not tonight."

"Still being stubborn," she spat.

Now clearly wasn't the time to get her to talk. I hung my coat in the closet with Dulcie's clothes, tucked my boots in there, too, and opened the door to leave. "Oksana made tea, and there are cookies. I'm sure you're welcome to some."

Cybil finally came down when dinner was ready. Tonight Fern made a wonderfully hearty beef stew loaded with big chunks of vegetables that I peeled and cut up for her. There were also buttermilk biscuits and a white cake with chocolate frosting for dessert. Everyone greeted Cybil with either a "hello" or a warm smile when she came to the dining room and didn't say a word when she filled a bowl and took it back to our room.

After dinner, we gathered in the living room to watch *Lost in Space*, *The Beverly Hillbillies*, and *Green Acres*. Then we carried all the sleeping children up to bed and called it a night. It had been a busy day. And a magical one. For me at least.

Despite being bone tired from all the fresh air and exercise, I couldn't sleep. I thought constantly about those few minutes in the woods where the trees seemed to tell me to stay. But where? Lucy's house was full. Sure, Dulcie and Briar would move out when their cottage was finished, but that was still months from now. In the meantime, this was their room. We couldn't kick them out of it.

It was absurd for me to even be thinking about staying. Cybil would never agree.

A gust of wind blew outside and once again I was sure I heard *stay*. Or was that what I wanted to hear?

I agreed to leave Kenosha, but that didn't mean I had to go where Cybil decided. Could I let her go without me, though? Could I separate the kids? I chuckled darkly to myself. It sounded like I was contemplating a divorce. The thing was, Cybil and I had been best friends for more than twenty years. Not a single day had passed in that time when we hadn't been together for at least a few minutes. Every day for twenty years. Living apart from her would be like a divorce. Or a death.

At some point, I finally fell asleep. I must have tossed and turned all night because I woke feeling unrested just as the sky was starting to lighten. Poor Vanda was balanced on the edge of the mattress. She would let me know just how restless I had been when she awoke. Quietly, so as not to disturb any of the others, I once again crept out of the room. If we were leaving today, I wanted a little more time with Lucy.

I found her near the *Christyule* tree, staring out at the lake.

"Good morning, Effie," she said softly without even looking.

"How did you know it was me?"

"These folks have been living in my house for months. None of them are early risers. Yesterday was the first I'd heard that Fern gives me time alone in the mornings. Guessing you were the one coming up behind me was a safe bet. Let's grab some coffee."

She followed me to the kitchen, filled both of our cups and a small pot with coffee. After she pulled a cozy over the pot to keep the contents hot, she motioned for me to follow her. I thought we were going to the dining room. Instead, she took me to the sitting room across the hall from it. We each took a seat—me on the loveseat, her on a chair to my right—and it was like a bubble of silence enclosed the room.

"What's on your mind?" she asked me.

"Why do you think—"

"I've known you for about thirty-two hours. Not enough time to know you intimately, but you were very quiet after spending time in the woods yesterday. The trees spoke to you, didn't they?"

Did she mean literally or in an *I love being out in nature* way? Regardless, my answer would be the same. "They did. Did you take us along that route for that reason?"

She shook her head. "Like we said, Dillon and Briar almost always go home that way. It's not faster like they claim, but summers are short here, and being outside as much as possible is the best way to enjoy it. We have no reason to rush back home."

A sense of longing pulled at the center of my chest. I pressed my fingers to the spot. "Does everyone feel this way?"

She sipped her coffee. "What are you feeling?"

"That in less than forty-eight hours, I've connected with this place and you all, and I don't want—" The rest stuck in my throat. "It's a special place, isn't it?"

Lucy paused before agreeing, "It is. It called to Keven first. As I told you, he's a contractor. Someone heard that this plot in the Northwoods was for sale and thought he might want to develop it. I was miserable living where we were, and when he learned that there was two thousand acres of pristine forest on a lake, he snapped it up. For us, not his business."

"He could have made a lot of money putting in lake houses here." I glanced around the room, imagining other grand homes like this.

"He could have," Lucy agreed, "but before we'd let that happen, we came up to take a look. His company would have bought it from us if we decided it wasn't what we wanted. As soon as we got here, though, and I saw this little thumb of land, I knew it was the perfect place to put a house. There was no way anyone but us would ever own it." She took another sip of coffee. "When we were talking yesterday, you told me you left Kenosha with Cybil because you were repaying a debt. You didn't get to tell me why you had to leave Jamaica."

Yesterday I'd been enormously grateful Fern had come out

of her room when she did. Today I was praying she wouldn't, because if I was ever going to say this to anyone, it was here and now.

"It was the summer when we met the men who would become our husbands," I began, repeating some of what I'd already told her. "The four of us spent every day together for almost two full weeks. It was much more than a summer romance for me. Allen and I got *very* close, if you know what I mean."

Lucy waggled her eyebrows at me but said nothing.

I took a settling breath, but my voice shook as I spoke. "The night after Allen and Stan left, I went for a walk on the beach, and an island man came up to me and—" My words cut off.

Lucy reached over and laid her fingers on my knee. "You can tell me anything."

I nodded. "He started out asking me how my night was going. I said I felt a little sad because Allen left."

"Sounds like you knew this man," Lucy prompted when my words faded again.

"I did. Everyone did." I took a breath. "Then he put a comforting arm around my shoulders."

"He attacked you, didn't he?" Lucy guessed.

Bile burned my throat. "It's worse than that."

Gently, softly she encouraged, "Take your time, Effie."

I willed my racing heart to slow. When it finally did, I blurted, "I thought I killed him."

She sat straight. "All right, I didn't see that coming. You *thought* you killed him?"

"I wasn't sure. We were sitting on the beach, and the next thing I knew, he had pushed me down onto my back. I reached around for something to use as a weapon." With my cup and saucer balanced on my lap, I spread my arms and mimicked patting the sand. "My hand landed on something. It felt rough and hairy like a coconut. I have no idea why that would have been there. It was almost like I needed help and help arrived. Figuring I had only one shot, I hit him as hard as I could in the head with it, and he collapsed." My heart started racing again, like I was reliving the event. "It took all my strength to shove him off me. Once I did, he didn't move."

"Then what?" Lucy's rapt expression would have been comical if the topic wasn't so serious.

"I ran to find Cybil. She immediately knew something had happened. I was crying. My dress was filthy. There was sand all over me. I never told her who the man was because I didn't want to involve her that far. She wanted me to go to the police, but I couldn't do that."

Lucy waited a few seconds, then as though unsure she wanted to hear the answer, asked, "Why couldn't you go to the police?"

My voice dropped to a whisper. "Because he was one of them."

It took her a moment to understand. "You thought you killed a policeman?"

"I didn't know. For sure, I assaulted him. He was a powerful man, and I knew it would be my word against his."

"That's why you and Cybil left Jamaica?"

"Yes, because I was terrified about what he would do. He could spread lies. Threaten me to keep me quiet. Send thugs after me or my family or Cybil." I blinked away the memories of that night. "While I packed my bag, I begged her to come with me. She figured I just needed time to get my head together, so we'd leave for a while and then go back. Allen and Stan had given us their address in Florida, and she agreed to go there. We called them from the airport, and they were happy we were coming. They let us stay with them, and after a few weeks, I found out I was pregnant."

"Oh, Effie. Is Rae Allen's daughter?"

What was she saying? "Of course she is. How can you ask that?"

Lucy frowned, confused. "Well, the police officer. Could he be her father?"

After a few seconds, I understood. "Oh! No, I hit him with the coconut before he could do . . . *that.*"

She slumped back in her chair with relief. "Thank heavens. I assume the death of a police officer would have been big news. Did you ever find out if he lived or died?"

"He's alive," I admitted. "I was able to ask a family member about him during a phone call without giving away what had happened. In the end, he claimed he tripped in the dark and hit his head on that coconut."

"All right, at this point, you're in Florida and in the clear. Cybil has no idea what happened with the police officer, and you've told Allen you're pregnant."

"He asked me to marry him right away. As in that day." I touched the simple wedding band I had never taken off. Not once. "We really did love each other. Cybil, however, did not love Stan. She liked him well enough and eventually agreed to marry him, but she wasn't in love with him like I was Allen. She and I had a huge fight because she wanted to go home to Jamaica, and I refused. I was married, with child, and wanted to be with my husband. Finally, I told her if she stayed with me, I would owe her. Any time, no questions asked. We came up with the codeword *divinò*, and I promised if she ever used it, I would go with her. The stipulation being she could only use it once and she couldn't ask me to leave Allen."

"She used the word on Tuesday."

"Yes."

Lucy gave me an empathetic smile. "There were a lot more details than what you told me yesterday, but I understand why you wouldn't be fully comfortable telling a stranger that story."

"I promise, you now know the whole truth."

Lucy placed a hand over her heart. "Thank you for trusting me."

Like waves washing up on shore, I felt cleansed. But not completely. "Can I trust you with something else?"

"Of course you can."

I took a minute, debating how to tell her about the other big secret I'd been carrying around with me for far less time. "I've been living a lie in Kenosha."

Chapter Eight

" I think we'll need a refill for this." Lucy added more coffee to our cups from the small pot she'd brought into the sitting room. She added milk to hers and waited while I stirred sugar into mine. Then she nodded for me to continue.

"Cybil and I have been working with Bonnie for almost a year. For the last four months or so, I've been faking my readings."

Ashamed, I looked down at my cup and saucer on my lap.

"Do you honestly have this ability?" Lucy asked. "Your vision about the well yesterday was spot on, but it could have been a lucky guess."

That's what I told myself it was at first. Just lucky guesses. "Since I was a young girl, I have always felt different from other kids. I knew things were going to happen long before they did. For example, I knew when the boys in my village were wrestling and rough housing, one of them would get hurt. Yes, that could have been a lucky guess, as you say, but more often than not, I knew exactly which boy. Many times, I could predict what the injury would be, like a badly skinned knee, a cut that would need stitching, or a broken arm. It happened so often, the kids became scared of me and started calling me *Obeah*, which basically means Witch Girl. Some even accused me of causing the injuries. They teased me to the point that I couldn't play with them anymore. So I sat at home or wandered about by myself."

"And then Cybil came along?" Lucy guessed.

"Yes. She stood up for me, which meant the kids also picked on her. A friend of an obeah must be an obeah." I released a breath, feeling a little more relaxed. "Turned out, they weren't far off. We aren't witches, but as the saying goes, like attracts like."

"Cybil had the same ability you did."

"Similar. She doesn't do séances. Still, by the time we were teenagers, attitudes about us had changed. People in our village started coming to us for readings. It wasn't much, just a few a week, but then others on the island heard about us and eventually word spread to the tourists." I lifted my chin as though this was something to be proud of. "We set up a hut on the beach, and when we were 'open for business,' we had a line."

"And you were making money?"

"We were kids. We thought we were crazy rich. That was such a good time. Except for those who still believed we were unnatural."

"And what's different now? Why do you say you've been living a lie?"

I traced my finger around the rim of my cup. "Three months ago, Bonnie arranged for me to hold a group reading, much like the ones Cybil does. I was exhausted that night and couldn't form any connections to the spiritual world. I knew if I didn't give the audience something, they wouldn't come back. So I performed."

As I'd seen her do many times over the past two days, Lucy tilted her head in question. "What does that mean?"

I closed my eyes, pressed my index and middle fingers to

my temples, and in a trance-like voice intoned, "The messages are a little foggy today. I'm sensing a man . . . Do you know anyone whose first or last name starts with a *K* or maybe an *R*?"

When I peeked open an eye, Lucy was grinning. She played along. "Keven. Oh, and Rupert."

"Keven and Rupert," I echoed. "One of them is especially important to you."

Her grin turned into a chuckle. "Keven is my husband."

"Yes, I sense a romantic relationship. You will have some challenges ahead, but everything will work out."

"Let's try again," Lucy said, still playing. "I don't know anyone whose name starts with *K* or *R*."

I closed my eyes again and replaced my fingers. "I'm sensing that this person is someone you're very close with. Someone you either have or would like to have a deep relationship with." I opened my eyes. "And then inevitably, because they're so eager for a higher force to be playing a role in their life, they supply a name. 'There's someone at my church. He seems like a nice man.' And then I encourage her to talk to him and insist this will lead to a deeper relationship."

"But you never say a romantic one," Lucy guessed. "Simply talking with someone, even a stranger on the street, deepens your relationship with them."

"Exactly."

"And you kept *performing* after that first night?"

"Not every time, but more and more."

"Why? What do you think happened?"

My body felt heavy suddenly. As it had for the past weeks and months. "After that first time, I had my script. It was easier to perform on the days I was tired because that was far less emotionally and physically draining than forming a real connection."

"Is your gift like a muscle?" Lucy asked. "Did you overuse it and maybe needed to rest it for a while?"

"I abused it, is more accurate. I stopped respecting what had always come naturally to me and let Bonnie turn me into a show pony."

"And now it's gone?"

My voice grew thick with emotion. "I thought so. Until yesterday."

Lucy brightened. "What happened yesterday?"

"It was when we stopped at that clearing on the other side of the creek. I had a strong, undeniable vision and knew my gift was still with me."

She nodded, remembering. "You made us leave all of a sudden."

"I told Dulcie something bad had either happened there or will happen. Feelings of darkness hit me the moment we entered the space." My visions regarding specific people weren't always accurate, so I didn't tell either of them I had seen a fight break out among their kids. One that would result in consequences so dire they would resonate through the community for decades. Hopefully I was wrong. "Dulcie said she'd do some sort of protection spell?"

Lucy smiled. "One that is somehow connected to the moon. She does those kinds of things. After the incident at the clearing, when we were at Dulcie's acreage, you seemed to go into a trance. You said she'd be happy there for a long time."

My hand went to my chest. "I felt lots of love and positivity there. She said it was like she was meant to find it last year. I think she's right."

"And you told Fern to build a bigger house."

"I saw *lots* of people milling about." I paused, staring into the coffee in my cup. "And then something I've never experienced happened in your woods. When you all went ahead to the spring."

"My trees spoke to you," Lucy said. "What happened?"

"I stopped to listen to the sounds of the forest. I never realized how noisy nature can be." We both laughed at that, and then I became emotional again. "At first, the trees felt imposing, almost like giants that could pick up their trunks like they were long skirts and stomp on us mere humans with their massive roots. Then a feeling of absolute peace and security came over me, like the trees are here to protect us. I haven't felt so at ease since Jamaica. Since before the other kids started calling me obeah." I swallowed and blinked. "Since my mother would gather me onto her lap and tell me to ignore those mean kids."

Lucy had known exactly how I had felt out in the forest. I could tell by the way she looked at me before waving me over to the spring. And by the expectant look on her face right now.

"I felt like I belonged." My voice broke. "In that spot at that moment, I was exactly where I was meant to be."

Lucy placed her hands over her heart, one on top of the other, and seemed to almost glow from within. "I remember feeling the same way. I can't explain it, but there *is* something about this place." She seemed almost hopeful as she asked, "Do you still feel the same way? Like you belong here?"

Before I could answer, a herd of children burst into the room.

Chapter Nine

"Breakfast is ready," the kids announced in unison.

"Fern says to come while it's hot," Briar said, hands propped on her hips.

"If they ever have to choose one of them to be their leader," Lucy said quietly after they had scampered back the way they'd come, "it has to be Briar." The telephone rang as we left the room, and before going to answer it, she added, "You don't have to answer my question if you don't want to. Think about it, though."

Did I still feel like I belonged here?

The same questions that filled my head last night returned. If I did belong here, what did that mean for me, Cybil, and the kids?

In the kitchen, a big pot of oatmeal sat on a trivet at the center of the table. To prevent oatmeal plops landing from one end of the red, white, and green tablecloth to the other, Vanda filled the kids' bowls. There was also an array of add-ins—nuts, cut up fruit, granola, brown sugar, maple syrup. Our kids had never had oatmeal that way. We didn't get fancy with our food, mostly because we had to pinch pennies to ensure we had a savings. Because we made do with the basics, this was a real treat for them.

Maybe we should stay.

I did my best to dismiss the thought. It wasn't mine to make alone. And from the scowl on Cybil's face when she entered the room, I already knew what her answer would be if I asked.

She loaded her bowl, took a cup of coffee, and left the kitchen.

"Cybil," I called, trying to stop her.

"I'm going to the dining room," she snapped. "This table is full, and I'd prefer to eat in peace."

What was going on with her? It was more than me making us stay another night. Her crabby moods never lasted this long. Time to deal with this.

"Vanda?" I asked, and she looked up from her bowl-filling task. "I need to go talk to Cybil. Will you—"

"Keep them in line? Yes." She narrowed her eyes and pointed a finger at each of them in turn.

In the dining room, Cybil was sitting by herself at one table while Rupert, Gregor, Oksana, and Jurgen sat at the other. Why did she refuse to even try to be friendly with these lovely people?

"May I sit with you?" I asked.

She jutted her chin at the chair across from her in response.

I was stirring nuts and bananas into my oatmeal when Lucy entered the room. "Effie? Cybil? Sorry to interrupt. That was Keven on the phone. He says he's a little more than an hour away and would like you two to stay until he gets here."

"What's going on?" I asked.

She shook her head while saying, "I have no idea. All he would say was that it's something that you will want to hear in person."

"We'll stay, then," I promised, ignoring the fiery glare trying to set me ablaze from Cybil's side of the table.

"Why must you kowtow to these people?" Cybil demanded loud enough that everyone at the other table stopped talking, got up, and left the room.

My face burned with embarrassment as I looked apologetically at them. "I'm sorry."

"It's okay," Oksana promised from the doorway. "We finished eating a while ago and were just planning our day. Seems like you two could use some privacy."

My turn to glare at Cybil. "That was extremely rude. Even for you. And I am not kowtowing. We're guests in this home, they were gracious enough to involve *us* in their activities, and I was happy to go along. I thoroughly enjoyed my day yesterday. Can you say the same?"

She mumbled something I couldn't interpret.

"What's the matter, Cybil? I'm used to your moods, but this is a whole new level of crabby."

Without looking at me, she said, "I'm trying to figure out what's next. Okay?"

"Talk to me then. Let me help. Where do you want to go?"

Rather than answer, she filled her mouth with oatmeal, so I followed suit. If Cybil wasn't ready to talk, I could wait. Besides, I was curious to find out what Keven felt was so important.

She finished eating, and I was sure she'd scurry back to the room, so I said, "I've tried giving you space to work through your feelings, but you need to tell me something now. What happened at the reading Friday night?"

After a pause so long I figured she was still refusing to answer, she snapped defensively, "I didn't do anything wrong. The event went along like they always do. I walked through the crowd and got strong vibrations coming off one woman. I stood before her and sensed the name Nelson."

These things happened in different ways. Usually, we'd see images of people or places that only make sense to the person. Sometimes the visions wouldn't make sense until a later date, and we'd inevitably get a phone call or letter telling us we were right and a long explanation of what had occurred and why it was important. Now and then, we catch a name. For Cybil, there are sensations attached to her visions. Warmth was positive, and cold negative. For me, there'd be a color. A bright or cheery one meant this was a good thing. Dark and ominous, the opposite.

Cybil continued, "The woman said Nelson was her husband's business partner, and I advised it wasn't a good relationship to continue. She immediately became angry, saying I had accused her of having an affair." Cybil's nostrils flared in anger. "I never said the word *affair* and didn't accuse her of anything."

"Not a good relationship could mean any number of things," I replied. "Maybe her husband's friendship with the man was the relationship in question. Or Nelson could be doing something illegal or would in the future."

Cybil grunted while taking deep, calming breaths.

"Sounds like your words made this woman either angry or scared," I reasoned. "People react to both emotions in similar ways. I've seen that many times over the years. As have you."

Slightly calmer now, Cybil said, "I think if this woman had come to a personal reading or one with fewer people, it wouldn't have been so bad. She would have said I was wrong and left it at that. But she wouldn't let it go."

"What did she do?"

"Monday morning, Bonnie called me to her office. The woman was there. She accused me of being a fraud and said Bonnie was a charlatan. She showed us flyers she'd had printed. They warned people that Bonnie was running a scam, and she intended to post them all over town."

Cybil must have really poked at a sore spot for this woman. "Did you believe she'd do what she said?"

"I did. More importantly, Bonnie did. Bonnie told her she'd never gotten complaints about any of the other women working for her and put all the blame on me."

I gasped. "She didn't come to your defense?"

Fire blazed in Cybil's eyes. "On the spot, Bonnie canceled all of my events for the rest of the year."

"Did that satisfy this woman?" She had to be the one I overheard when I was out with Rae on Sunday. I couldn't believe all this happened and I was completely unaware. How wrapped up in my own world had I been lately?

"It seemed to. After she left, Bonnie told me we would reevaluate things at a later date."

"Why didn't you tell me?" I felt so hurt by this. And guilty at the same time. If anyone should have been accused of being a fraud, it was me for performing my readings rather than doing real ones.

"I was going to tell you," Cybil vowed. "Saturday I was still in shock. There never seemed to be a good time on Sunday. I planned to tell you on Monday, and then the woman showed up at Bonnie's farm. By Monday afternoon, Astra knew about it and word spread among the tellers faster than wildfire in a windstorm. The others started giving me grief, and on Tuesday, their kids joined in and started picking on ours. That was it. I was done."

I knew Astra had to be involved somehow.

"I've thought about little else since all of this happened on Friday," Cybil continued. "I've gone over and over what I said and the woman's reaction. You're right. She was either angry or scared, and I was not at fault. But that doesn't change the outcome. I reacted to the fallout rather than trying to fix the problem, and now neither of us have jobs. As for where I want us to go next, I have no idea. Where are two unemployed fortune tellers supposed to find work?"

Maybe we should stay. I wanted to say that so badly. At least until we had a plan. But it was nearly Christmas. We couldn't disrupt everyone's holiday that way.

"Okay," I relented, heartbroken. "Let's wait until Keven gets back and find out what's so important. Then we can go."

Cybil's whole body relaxed with relief. "I'm going to go pack our things."

"I'll let the others know we're leaving."

Rae and Gabe were not happy. They had already become "best friends" with the other kids. Fortunately, rather than hollering, they staged a silent protest by sitting in the corner, facing the wall, and insisting they weren't leaving this house.

"Are you sure?" Dulcie asked after I'd told them the plan. "If it's because of taking over our bedroom—"

"It's not that." I could barely look at Lucy. "Cybil is concerned about us not having jobs."

"None of us have jobs," Gregor stated. "Not in the winter at least. We find seasonal work from spring through fall and live off that money."

Oksana took a dish from Jurgen to dry. "We decided living here where we don't have to explain ourselves to those who won't accept us anyway is more important than possessions."

I didn't know exactly what she meant by not being accepted but guessed it had something to do with celebrating Yule and casting protection spells.

"Lucy doesn't charge rent or utilities," Rupert added. "We all pitch in for food and use what's left for personal expenses. Like Horace's clothes. I swear that boy needs new jeans and shoes every other week. Most of our money goes for that."

Lucy beamed as the others explained the situation. "I'm so happy to have you all here. It wasn't my original plan, but filling this house with friends makes my heart happy."

I didn't know what that meant either. Most of the time she and I spent talking, it was about me and Cybil. I barely knew anything about Lucy or the others.

"You mentioned you have a savings, Effie," Lucy continued. "If you decide you want to stay, whatever you can contribute will suffice until spring."

Dulcie wrapped me in a hug from behind. "As for the room situation, this house has a basement."

"We could put the kids down there or in the attic," Jurgen declared. "Even if Effie and the others don't stay, we can put the kids there." He gave Oksana a wink and slow nod. She grinned back at him.

"Didn't you say Cybil can't drive?" Fern quietly asked. "Far as I'm concerned, she who has the keys makes the rules."

I loved them all for offering reason after reason for why we didn't have to leave. "I'll tell her what you've said, but I don't know if it will work."

I went directly upstairs and stood at the door outside the bedroom we'd borrowed for the last two nights. Cybil was shuffling around inside, packing our bags. I grabbed the knob, prepared to go in and tell her we didn't *have* to go, but I just couldn't risk her dashing the bit of hope they'd sparked in me. No matter how wonderful these people were, no matter how welcoming, Cybil and I were a team. I had plenty of room for new friends in my life, but I would never do anything to risk what I had with the woman who had been by my side since the first day we met.

I let go of the knob and kept walking around the second floor until I discovered another door standing partially open. I peeked through the opening and saw a stairway. It must lead to the attic. I climbed the steps and found a large space with clusters of suitcases and boxes and other household things that must belong to Lucy's houseguests.

A row of windows on one of the walls caught my attention. The view of the lake from this high up made my breath catch. As if it wasn't beautiful enough from the first and second floors, I felt like I was queen of all I surveyed from here. Truly magnificent.

"We *could* put the kids up here," I thought out loud.

I'm not sure how long I stood there, staring out at the lake that was much larger than it seemed from ground level, but it must have been a good half hour. The next thing I knew, someone was calling my name.

"I'm up here," I called back, rushing to the stairs.

Lucy appeared in the doorway. "Great space, isn't it?"

"Shame to use it for only storage," I answered.

"Some day it will find its purpose." She pointed over her shoulder. "Keven is here."

"Okay, I'm coming."

I followed her first to the bedroom to pick up Cybil, then to the living room where Keven sat on one of the couches. On the other was a man neither of us knew . . . and Bonnie Bristol.

Chapter Ten

Cybil and I stood with our mouths gaping. What was she doing here?

"I assume you know Bonnie," Keven said, an aura of excitement swirling around him. A literal swirl. I saw red and yellow with flashes of orange surrounding him like a happy fog.

"Hi, ladies." Bonnie raised a hand in an earnest greeting.

Keven indicated the man with shaggy hair and round eyeglasses like John Lennon wore. "This is Richard Shapiro."

Richard stood. "Keven moved heaven and earth to find me, and I'm so glad he did."

Cybil fidgeted, uncomfortable with whatever this was. I felt the same. She asked, "Who are you?"

"We've never met," he began, his focus on Cybil, "but you know my wife. Soon to be ex-wife. She's the person who has made your life hell for the past week."

"The woman who's been telling everyone that Cybil is a fraud?" I mentally told myself to not take this out on him. Her actions were not his fault.

"Please, both of you, have a seat." Keven rose from the couch and moved to a corner to stand by Lucy.

Fern arrived silently with a big tray loaded with coffee and cookies. She set it on the table between the couches and then slipped out of the room again without a word. That's when I noticed none of the others were around. Lucy must have asked them to leave.

Richard filled and distributed cups to all six of us, then let out a sigh. "I've been rehearsing what to say the whole drive up here." When Cybil grunted softly, he added nervously, "Not to imply that what I'm about to say is disingenuous. I wanted to say it the right way. And it seems I'm already failing."

"What are you here to tell us, Mr. Shapiro?" I asked.

"Richard, please," he begged. "I'm not entirely sure why my wife attended your event on Friday, Cybil, but I suspect it was an attempt to glean a little insight into how much trouble she's in."

Cybil sparked a bit at that. "Trouble?"

Richard released a sigh, relaxing now that the topic had been opened, I guessed. Even his way of speaking turned less formal. "Look, she and I have been going through some messy stuff for almost a year. Three years ago, I opened an advertising firm in Milwaukee with a good friend."

"Nelson," Cybil guessed. She tapped her forehead. "The person I sensed."

"Yeah," Richard acknowledged. "He and I met in college, kept in touch during the first few years after graduating, and decided we hated working for other people. We opened our own firm, targeting people in our generation who are tired of things always staying the same. We've done well. Really well. Then I met Nancy."

His eyes widened briefly, silently indicating Nancy exhausted him.

"We hadn't known each other very long when I asked her to marry me. She had this way of motivating me to see how far I could push myself and convinced us to tap into the current culture. You know what I mean?"

We nodded. Big changes started happening in this country a few years ago, and many of us wanted to go on that ride. Being sensitive to spiritual activity wasn't something Cybil or I chose, but it was who we were and how we made a living. It also put us on the fringe of normal society with the other "weirdos and freaks" as people called us.

"We know exactly what you mean," Lucy supplied. "Why do you think we live where we do?"

"Your own little upscale commune." Richard's head bobbed up and down. "I love it."

Cybil squirmed again, probably not liking that we were all coming together over our beliefs. God forbid. I swear she liked being the odd one sometimes.

"You drove all the way up here from Milwaukee," Cybil noted. "Why?"

"Like I said, Keven found me." He looked across the room at him. "*How* did you find me?"

"I started with Bonnie," Keven answered. "Effie, I heard you and Lucy talking the other morning. You told her about working with a woman named Bonnie Bristol in Kenosha. Owning a contracting firm, I've got connections all over the state. It only took a few phone calls for me to find someone in the Kenosha area who had heard her name. They got her phone number and even made the initial contact with her for me. Then I drove down to talk to her in person."

"I was devastated when I saw that you'd left." Bonnie's clasped hands and knit brow pleaded with us to believe her. "You didn't even say goodbye."

At that, Cybil lowered her gaze to the floor. I bit my tongue so I wouldn't scream, *You fired her!*

"Keven and I spoke for a long time," she continued. "He told me this ragtag pair of tellers showed up on his doorstep, and he was trying to find out if I knew what had happened.

Oh, did I! This woman strode into my office, stuck her hand out at me and said, 'I'm Nancy Shapiro. If you don't know me, you've surely heard of my husband.' Then she proceeded to tell me she was the brains behind Richard's advertising firm and that she was furious about Friday's event." Bonnie turned to Cybil then. "That's when I called you into the office."

"Since Nancy gave Bonnie so much information," Keven said with a chuckle, "all we needed was directory assistance to locate Richard."

"She's a serial liar," Richard hissed. "I'm sorry you got caught in her net."

"Liar?" Cybil looked up again.

"You believe Cybil?" I asked, taking my friend's hand.

"Immediately," Richard answered. "When Keven asked if I'd come talk with you, I didn't hesitate. I wanted to thank you, Cybil."

It wasn't often that Cybil was left speechless. Unless she was pouting and looking for attention, of course.

"Thank her?" I asked for her.

Richard nodded, dark circles of exhaustion suddenly obvious beneath his eyes. "I knew something was going on between Nancy and Nelson. They were really sly about it. I guessed it was an affair. The attraction and chemistry between them . . . I have no idea why she agreed to marry me when he was also single and available. When you saw whatever you saw during that reading, and she started squealing like a stuck pig . . ." He shook his head then took a drink from his cup to steady himself. "Sorry. I'm a little bitter."

"Understandable." Bonnie put a comforting hand on his shoulder.

Her touch got him back on track. "Not only were they having an affair, Nancy was embezzling from the company."

"What?" I asked, devastated for this man.

"I was such a sucker." He blew out a breath. "Fell for everything she told me. About six months after we started dating, she said she didn't trust our bookkeeper. She was sure the man was stealing from us. Nancy *happened* to have experience with accounting, so Nelson and I agreed to let her take over and fired the man who'd been working with us from the start. After a few weeks of going through our books 'with a fine-tooth comb,' Nancy uncovered thousands of dollars in missing deposits."

"In other words, she stole the money from you," Lucy guessed.

"And Nelson knew it." Richard looked like he might be sick. "When Nancy started insisting you were a liar and a fraud, Cybil, it was because you had cracked open her scheme. Knowing that when caught in a lie people will often do crazy things to convince people they're innocent, I went to Nelson's house to talk to him about it. He was a mess. Literally made himself sick over the whole thing. In less than five minutes, he was sobbing and apologizing and telling me everything."

"Are you pressing charges?" Keven asked.

"Oh yeah. Making all of this worse, we had our bookkeeper, my friend, arrested for theft. He's been sitting in jail for months. As soon as they had Nelson's signed confession, they released him. Mark is a good guy and says he forgives me."

Cybil nodded. "Good. I'm sorry for what you went through but glad I was able to help uncover the truth.

"You came all this way to tell us this?" I asked.

"Absolutely," Richard insisted. "After what Nancy put her through, Cybil deserved a face-to-face apology."

Cybil's voice broke as she said, "Thank you for that."

"Will Mark come back to work for you?" I asked.

"Yes." Richard smiled big. "But not with this firm. I've made good money with advertising, which is great, but the work isn't satisfying. I've got an idea I'd like to pursue that's been floating around in my head for a while." He turned to Bonnie. "You might have some interest in it."

"Me?" She seemed intrigued, and more than a little *interested* in Richard.

"We'll talk about it on the drive home," he promised.

"Oh, come on," she purred. "You have to give me something."

"Okay. I have no idea if it will take off," he qualified, "but I've found that people are fascinated by knights and ladies-in-waiting, kings and queens, that kind of thing. I was in Malibu a couple of years ago, and they have something they call a Renaissance faire. It's meant to teach about the history of the period, but I thought why not create a Renaissance village where people appear to live and then invite the public to come for the experience?"

"Good thing it's a long drive back to Kenosha," Bonnie replied. "I want to hear every thought you have about this."

"And why are you here, Bonnie?" Cybil's anger at her over not defending her to Nancy had returned.

"I came to apologize. Simple as that." Bonnie both looked and sounded contrite.

I sensed there was more to her story, though. "Can't hide things from a mind reader, Bonnie. What else?"

She chewed her lip for a couple seconds, then blurted, "I want you to come back. The other tellers know the truth of what happened now and are horrified at how they treated you."

"*They* are horrified," I said pointedly.

Bonnie's hands covered her heart. "So am I, of course. I panicked."

We stared at her, waiting for more.

"Okay, here's the truth. You two are my biggest draw. Without you, the events won't be anywhere near as successful or well attended. Word of what happened with Nancy has spread and given people proof of your skills. Folks are begging to get readings with you." When we didn't reply, she continued, "I've even developed an advertising campaign to promote your events. They want readings with Cybil and séances with Effie."

I reached for a cookie on the tray. "In less than a week, the public started begging for us *and* you set up promotion? Busy week."

She slumped. "All right, there's no campaign yet, but I will make one. Everyone here is my witness. If you come back, I will promote you two as my headliners and give you ten percent of the profits for every show on top of your normal wages. And you don't have to live with the others in the community housing anymore."

Cybil turned to me. "Sounds like a good deal."

"We'll talk about it tonight," I responded immediately before Cybil promised something I didn't want. "Thank you for driving all this way to apologize. That means a lot."

Bonnie looked expectantly at me, as though I might change my mind and tell her here and now that we'd come back.

"We have your number," I reminded her. "We'll call you with our decision."

Chapter Eleven

L ucy refused to let Richard and Bonnie leave without giving them a good lunch and boxing up a meal for them to take in the car for the return trip. This gave Keven and Richard time to discuss Richard's Renaissance Faire idea while Bonnie continued trying to convince us to return to her fortune teller farm. I could tell by the look on Cybil's face that she wanted to go. I did not. Having to do those events made me feel like a product rather than a person with a gift. There was no way I could go back to doing that again.

It was nearly dusk by the time Richard and Bonnie left. Since we had no idea where or if we'd be able to find a hotel, we took Lucy and Keven up on their hospitality to stay one more night. Once we'd sent the kids to bed, I led Cybil up to the attic where we could talk without disturbing anyone.

"Cybil, I know you were able to help Richard, and that's great, but I have never felt that I helped anyone during one of Bonnie's shows. In Jamaica, yes. In Florida, sure. In Kenosha I feel like I'm an entertainer rather than a teller. And to be honest with you, I haven't done a genuine reading or held a real séance in months."

Her jaw dropped as I explained the script I'd come up with.

"Why didn't you tell me?"

"Because you seemed content and the kids were happy. It would have felt selfish to upend our lives because I'd lost my connection. And at least I was bringing in some money."

She switched between staring out the windows and at me. "I don't know what to say. I feel bad for you and understand how frustrating it must have been. But I also feel like you let me be the bad guy."

"What?"

"I'm the one who made us leave Kenosha. If you would have admitted the truth sooner—"

"You would have what? Quit your job and walked away from all the attention you were getting from Bonnie and your audience? Don't try to turn this one on me. I'm sorry you suffered all that fallout from Nancy, but I think everything has worked out for the best."

"Why? Because you found new friends?"

She was trying to bait me again. "If we hadn't come here, we likely never would have learned the truth about why Nancy attacked you that way."

"You're being dramatic."

"I'm not. Keven got the answers for all of us. The loop is closed."

Cybil grunted.

After a few silent moments of building my courage, I blurted, "I don't want to go back. It doesn't matter how good Bonnie's offer is, I can't be her headliner."

With her back to me, she whispered, "You want to stay here, don't you?"

My palms became clammy as I agreed. "I do. For a while at least."

She spun on me. "We're tellers, Effie. How are we

supposed to use our gifts here in the middle of the woods? How are we supposed to make a living?"

I considered her legitimate question. "Bonnie said people are begging to have readings with us. She can send them up here."

Cybil grunted harder at that.

"Either way, we have time to figure out the money part." I told her what Lucy said about contributing what we could for now.

Cybil crossed her arms and shook her head. "If it sounds too good to be true, it probably is."

I stood by her side and gazed up at the millions of stars. "We won't know if that's the case if we don't try. And it's not like we'd be held prisoner here. If we decide it's not working, we can leave."

"And return to Kenosha?"

Where my soul would continue to shrivel? I couldn't agree to that. Seemed we were at an impasse.

Chapter Twelve

I heard a lot of tossing and turning from the other side of the bedroom all night. Mostly because I was doing plenty of my own tossing and turning. Was this it? Was this the end of a lifelong friendship? Could I really let Cybil leave? Could I really stay without her?

The answer to that last question was yes. I'd only been with Lucy and the others for two days, but in that time, not only had I connected with them, this place had taken hold of me. Except for Jamaica, I'd never felt like I belonged anywhere like I did this two-thousand-acre plot in the Northwoods of Wisconsin. I might agree to go back to Jamaica, but I couldn't go back to Kenosha. No matter what it meant, I wouldn't.

At some point, I'd drifted off to sleep. I knew this because I was awakened by someone shaking my shoulder.

I squinted my eyes open. "Cybil?"

"Get up," she whispered. "Put on your warm clothes. And boots. Your suitcase is in the bathroom."

"What's—"

"Just do it. Please."

Please? I didn't hear that from her often.

I got dressed quietly and met her in the hallway. Without a word, she motioned for me to follow her. We went down the stairs and out the front door.

"Where are we going?" I whispered when we were out on the driveway.

"When you were out hiking with the others, I went for a walk too."

"Why didn't you come with us?"

"Because you were right. I needed time alone to think."

I was right? Something else I rarely heard from Cybil Grace.

"I found something. I want to show you."

At dawn? "We couldn't have waited until the sun was up?"

"Then the kids or someone else would have wanted to come with us. The sun will be up soon. We'll be fine."

She led me to where the creek passed under the driveway. On the other side of the creek, she took a right and headed down a short hill.

"Careful," she cautioned, "the leaves are a little slick. It's not far, though."

After a few yards, the hill's slope eased and then flattened. I gazed around at the pine trees that were thick but nowhere near as thick as they were along the path from Dulcie's cottage to the spring. We walked a little further and found a strip about fifty yards from the creek that had no trees. Maybe flooding washed away any pines that tried to grow here? Or maybe, like Dulcie's plot, they just didn't grow here.

Cybil pointed to our left. "Lucy's driveway is up there. The creek is behind us." She pointed to our right. "The highway is that way."

"A triangle."

In a tiny voice, like she was embarrassed to ask her next question, she whispered, "Do you feel it?"

I took a few steps away from her, looked up into the treetops, and closed my eyes. Every breath filled my lungs with pure, pine-scented air and restored my soul. And then a shiver that had nothing to do with the cold morning air made its way from my toes, up through my body, and out my fingertips and the top of my head.

"I do feel it." Afraid to admit exactly what that meant, I asked, "What do you feel?"

She stomped first her right foot and then her left. "That we are supposed to be right here."

Oh, please mean what I think, hope, and pray that means. "You want to stay?"

I held my breath, waiting for her answer.

"I want to talk to Bonnie about going down to Kenosha for special events during the year," she began. "If she can make it worth our while, we could make enough doing that to sustain us. We can also continue to sell our crafts at markets during the better weather months."

I had to exhale or I'd pass out. "Do you want to stay?"

"I'm sorry for being so crabby these last few days."

An apology? A third thing I rarely heard from her. I might pass out from sheer shock.

"You know it's hard for me to adjust to new situations. I'm not good at making new friends. This thing that Keven did for us, though, and the offer to stay and pay what we can . . . There is magic in this place."

"Cybil—"

"Yes, I want to stay. Right here."

I threw my arms around her. "Let's go talk to Lucy."

"Not yet. I want to stay in our triangle for a while longer. Just the two of us."

We watched as the sun turned the sky glorious shades of orange, pink, and yellow. We heard a loon call from somewhere out on the lake. Wind rustled the treetops, and I swear they said *welcome*.

I looked my dear friend in the eye as I said, "This is probably the best Christmas gift I've ever gotten."

She nodded. "Me too. When I found this spot, I believed we were brought here for a reason."

Bumping my shoulder against hers, I teased, "Took you long enough."

She turned us around so our backs were to the creek. "We could put a little cottage right here."

"Hmm. Maybe tucked back into the trees. We don't want to be too close to the creek if it floods in the spring."

"Fair point." She looked right and then left, taking in the open area that almost resembled a crescent moon. "What should we put here?"

"We've got plenty of time to figure that out. You, me, and the kids, we're going to live here for the rest of our lives, after all."

I didn't tell her I saw a row of vardos in this open space. And more than just our cottage back in the trees. This place had sparked my gift back to life, which meant I'd seen a lot as I wandered around Lucy's magical woods. So many good things would happen to us here. I would never tell any of them about the not so good times to come. In a place this glorious, we needed to live in the present and be grateful for every beautiful moment. We were strong. We'd make it through the not so good. One thing I knew for sure was that this community would grow, change, thrive, change some more, and keep on thriving. Lucy and Keven had no idea what their dreams would lead to.

Secret of the Hopeful Holiday

Chapter One

The GPS indicated I should take a left when I got to the road that ran along the Mississippi River. I was about to do that but took a minute to take in the view first. The wide expanse of slow-moving deep-blue water was breathtaking. The bluffs covered with naked trees on the far side, not so much.

"It must be beautiful here spring through fall," I said with a wistful sigh. "When all those trees have leaves . . . And just imagine the fall colors."

"You've become spoiled by the constant green from the pine trees surrounding our village," responded my friend, Morgan Barlow. "There's beauty in every season, Jayne. Appreciate what is."

Wise words from a woman who sometimes sounded like the human version of a fortune cookie.

Our lodging for the weekend was to be a two-bedroom suite at The Barge on Inn, which should be two blocks down after I turned.

"There it is." Morgan pointed at the three-story building right across from the river. "Oh, how charming."

Elaborate cream-colored cornices running along the

roofline and medium-blue louvered shutters on either side of each window had turned a plain rectangular red-brick building into a very inviting and, indeed, charming place. The abundance of Yuletide decorations amplified the charm factor. It looked like my goal for this four-day girlfriends' weekend just might happen. In no particular order, I wanted to rest, relax, get some Christmas shopping done, and spend uninterrupted time with my best friend.

My breath caught the moment we entered the inn's lobby. It was Christmas to excess in a good way. Wreaths with candlesticks and big red bows hung in every window. Trees set up all around were covered in twinkling lights and ornaments in the traditional colors of red, green, silver, and gold. Santa Claus watched from pictures hanging in random spots and from embroidered pillows perched on wingback chairs next to an inviting fireplace. Pine garland had been draped across the mantel and up the staircase banister.

It all made me think back to when I was a kid and would spring excitedly out of bed on Christmas mornings. I couldn't remember the last time I had felt that way about Christmas. When I was eight or ten? I loved giving gifts and had enjoyed learning about the Wiccan Yule traditions the people of Whispering Pines followed, but the holidays felt routine to me. Had for years. Like something I was supposed to do rather than a thing I eagerly awaited. Would I ever feel the magic of the season again, or was that just for little kids?

"You're a bit early," the innkeeper, Geoffrey, told us from the other side of the reservation desk. Check-in was at three, and it was almost two thirty. "Your room is ready, though, so I'm happy to check you in."

"And that is a two-room suite, right?" I verified. Bedrooms to ourselves, where we didn't have to worry about snoring and keeping each other awake, would go a long way toward me unwinding.

"Yes, Ms. O'Shea, we have you in the suite on the top

floor for three nights. And as requested, Ms. Barlow, we've put a mini freezer in one of the bedrooms."

"Bless you." Morgan placed her palms together in thanks.

"Our goal," Geoffrey assured, "is to provide perfect comfort, no matter what that means."

One thing Morgan was excited about for our weekend was getting a short break from her almost seven-month-old twins. She was breastfeeding them, though, and didn't want to pump and dump if she didn't have to. Bags of frozen milk would easily survive the three-hour return trip home in a cooler.

While completing the check-in process, Geoffrey explained that the inn was established in the mid-1800s and its quirky name was inspired by the barges that passed by on the river. "The massive flat-bottomed boats are pushed by little tugboats and transport goods like grain, coal, or building supplies. They float past almost daily from late spring through mid-November and always make me smile." He handed us our keys. "Welcome to The Barge on Inn and Blackwood Grove. I sincerely hope you enjoy your stay."

As we climbed the stairs to the third floor, I observed the inn's early American theme behind the holiday decorations. There was plenty of wood furniture, pieces upholstered in plaid or floral fabrics, braided rugs in various sizes, handmade baskets, wooden boxes, and wrought-iron hardware.

"Oh, wow," I breathed as we entered our suite, which was also decorated for the holidays with a small tree, garland and stockings hung on the fireplace mantel, and candlesticks on the windowsills. One bedroom was painted a muted olive green. The other a muted burgundy red. Both had four-poster beds with patchwork quilts. The sitting room was cream with olive and burgundy hand-stenciling that looked like wallpaper. "I feel like I stepped back in time two hundred years."

"Simpler times," Morgan agreed. Then she winced and pressed her arms over her chest. "Although they didn't have mini freezers and breast pumps back then. I'm going to take care of my milk, and then should we go for a walk?"

"Perfect. Neither of us sit this much at home. I'm starting to get hungry too."

"We can ask Geoffrey where we should have dinner."

Mine was the red room. I unpacked my one small bag and then flopped down on the bed. The extraordinarily comfortable bed. A sigh escaped me, and the exhaustion I'd been feeling for the past few months hit me hard.

The tourist season in Whispering Pines had officially ended with our annual Samhain celebration on October 31st. It had been an extremely stressful five months. On top of the standard amount of crime that occurred when thousands of people descended on a small village at the same time, there had been a tragic amount of death. I not only owned and operated Pine Time Bed-and-Breakfast, I was also a sheriff's deputy. It was my responsibility to keep the tourists and villagers safe. I'd failed miserably at that task and was having a hard time getting past it. When Morgan asked if I was interested in going on a road trip with her to Blackwood Grove, three hours south of us, I checked with my boyfriend, Tripp, to make sure he and my sister could handle our B&B without me for a few days.

"Four whole days of no B&B or deputy responsibilities?" he had asked while pulling me into his arms. "I think that's exactly what you need. I'm a little jealous you're going without me, but Rosalyn and I will be fine here."

After okaying the leave with the sheriff, I practically ran to Morgan's shop to let her know our girlfriends' weekend was on.

A light rapping on my doorframe woke me. I blinked, took a second to figure out where I was, and saw Morgan standing there smiling at me. "Did I fall asleep?"

"It appears you did," she said with a motherly tone. "It's only been fifteen minutes, so if you want to nap longer—"

"Nope." I groaned as I pushed myself into a sitting position. "I want to explore the town while it's still light outside. I checked over the mall's online map before we left; it's got a ton of unique stores. Figured we could walk past them, and I can formulate a plan of attack for tomorrow."

"Such a festive, relaxed approach to Yule shopping," she teased. "All right, let's go."

After pausing at the registration desk, we walked two blocks to the start of the mall. Blackwood Grove, according to its website, had become a shopping mecca in west-central Wisconsin. The developer turned what had been small homes into individual stores. What used to be the street that ran between the homes was now a lovely park with a meandering walking path, a large playground, and dozens of benches, where shoppers could rest or simply enjoy the area.

"This is lovely," Morgan declared of the park. "It speaks to my green witch self."

Dozens of trees grew throughout the half-mile-long park with small gardens growing randomly between them. Strings of lights spanned the park's width, draping from one old-fashioned lamppost to another. Wreaths with bows in red, green, or golden-brown hung from every lamppost as well. Small piles of snow added to the festive feel. And while every tree was decked out with lights, one huge pine tree at the center of the park was the focal point. It was covered in garland, large ornaments, and had a huge gold star on top.

"Golden-brown seems to be their prime color," I noted, "with green and red accents."

Morgan smiled. "This community isn't Wiccan like Whispering Pines, but at least half of the people who live here are Pagan. Green symbolizes renewal or ongoing life. Red is for blood that gives us life. The winter solstice is in a couple of weeks, so the ochre color is a nod to the slow return of more hours of sunlight."

"You like it here."

She slid an arm through mine, hooking our elbows together. "There's no place like Whispering Pines, but I feel very at home and welcome here."

As we walked, we passed by women's and men's clothing stores, children's clothing and toy stores, and others that sold plants, books, food, crafts, antiques . . . At the farthest end of the mall, next to an imposing-looking black hedge, we came to a rustic hut that would easily blend into a Louisiana bayou. It was painted emerald green and had gourds, tattered fabric garland, punched tin lanterns, and other voodoo-type adornments hanging from its porch. Then I saw the sign.

"That's Silver Moon Apothecary."

"Look at that." Morgan clapped her hands. "The girls did a great job."

Silver and Moon were the reason we were here this weekend. Or the reason Morgan was, at least. About two years ago, shortly after I moved to Whispering Pines, the two women came and spent a week with Morgan and her mother, Briar, learning how to run a New Age shop. They also got crash courses in blending herbs and oils, the best way to combine crystals and stones, and how to create an atmosphere that would keep customers coming back again and again. A few months ago, they sent Morgan and Briar an email inviting them to come and see what they'd created. Even though our tourist season was over, plenty of folks still came to shop for the holidays, so Briar opted to stay home and work in their store, Shoppe Mystique, and I took her place.

As I asked, "Do you want to go inside?" my stomach growled.

"I can wait. We'll be meeting Silver and Moon for breakfast in the morning. And you're clearly hungry."

It was only four thirty, but we hadn't stopped for lunch. "You don't have to convince me. Let's go get dinner."

Chapter Two

I consulted the map the innkeeper had given us to get to The Paddle Wheel Saloon, which he had recommended without hesitation for its great food and fun vibe. We had to walk all the way back to the other end of the mall closest to the inn, take a right to cross the street, and there it was. The saloon looked like something from the Wild West with a flat roof, second-floor balcony over the entrance, and a covered porch that wrapped around two sides of the sprawling building.

Whereas every store we'd passed by had adopted a more-is-more attitude toward holiday decorating, the saloon went simple. There were strands of lights around the porch posts, a few lighted snowflakes hanging in the windows, and a wreath with a red bow on the door. Inside, the first thing we noticed was a gleaming dark wood bar that was so big it took up an entire long wall and almost reached the ceiling of the tall dining room. The mirrored back bar, where the bottles of booze were stored, was outlined with white lights. The front bar, where customers sat, had white lights glowing from beneath the counter. There were at least twenty stools at the bar and plenty of dining tables covered with green tablecloths and flatware bundles in red-and-white plaid napkins. On the walls, tinsel garland adorned pictures, deer antlers, and an old clock. That was it—festive but on a low-key level.

Despite being a Thursday and barely five o'clock, the place was packed. There were a couple of empty tables, but every stool at the bar held a customer. One couple stood out sorely among the otherwise happy crowd. He was complaining loudly to the bartender regarding something he wasn't happy about. She had long, shaggy hair that was a cool shade of orangey pink. Not so cool was her body language: turned away with her head down, probably embarrassed by what was likely standard behavior for him.

"Hi, I'm Stella," greeted a large woman who looked like a weightlifter. "Two for dinner?"

"Yes, plea—"

Before I could finish, there was a commotion. One of the servers called out, "Stella, she's making a run for it again. Stop her!"

The next second, a petite woman bumped hard into Morgan and spun her out of the way. The woman darted for the door and was halfway out when it swung closed with enough force to capture her between it and the jamb. As in, despite her struggling to get free, she was good and truly held in place by that door.

"Dear Goddess," Morgan declared, "is she okay?"

"Is *she* okay?" I repeated. "What about you?"

"That's what I was going to ask," Stella agreed. "She hit you pretty hard."

Morgan flicked her hand in a dismissive gesture. "I'm fine. Promise."

"If you say so." Stella didn't look so sure. "Hang on for one more minute, and I'll take you to a table." She went to the door, grabbed the woman by the sleeve of her jacket, and the door released her. Stella pulled her back inside. "Get over there and pay your bill! This is the third time you've tried to skip out without paying. That's two times too many as far as I'm concerned. Don't bother trying to come back here again. You are officially banned from the premises." While escorting the woman to the bar, Stella looked past us at a third woman who was probably in her mid-fifties and had short blond hair. "Thanks for the help."

The woman gave a single nod as a satisfied look brightened her face. "Anytime." She crossed the dining room to a large round table in the corner where five other women were talking and eating. Oblivious, it seemed, to the event that had played out a few feet away.

Stella led us to a table across from the bar. "Ironically, that woman had a pocket full of cash. Did last time, too, if I remember right. I think she does the dine-and-dash thing just to see if she can get away with it." Once we were settled in our chairs, she handed us menus and told Morgan, "I'd like to offer you a free beverage. You're sure to have a bruise from that. Something warm? A hot toddy or Tom and Jerry?"

"That's very kind," Morgan replied, "but I'm breastfeeding so can't drink alcohol. Club soda with a lime will be fine."

"Free appetizer, then?"

"That she'll do," I answered for her. I'd already scanned that portion of the menu. "The jalapeno poppers. And make it two club sodas."

"Good choice on the poppers," Stella praised. "Ours don't come from the freezer; we make them fresh. I'll grab your drinks. Your server will be here in a bit with the appetizer and to take your dinner order."

By the time we had checked over the menu and made our decisions, a man in jeans and a Paddle Wheel Saloon T-shirt brought our poppers.

"What do you recommend?" I asked. "I always default to a burger and fries. But I love pulled pork."

"In my opinion," he began covertly, "our onion rings are

better than the fries. And you can't go wrong with the pulled pork sandwich."

"Sold," I said and handed him my menu.

Morgan opted for teriyaki salmon, wild rice, and a side salad. After he walked away, she asked, "What's the matter? You keep looking at the entrance."

"I'm trying to figure out what happened with that woman. That's not an automatic door, so it's not like there was a power surge or something that caused it to close and trap her. There's no wind that could have blown it shut. And it would have taken a gale force to hold it that way."

Morgan turned sideways on her chair to study it. "Perhaps there's a remote of some kind behind the bar. Push a button to hold the door in place, and the woman happened to get trapped. I've thought about having something similar installed at Shoppe Mystique to use during the busiest months. I'm only willing to let karma handle the shoplifters to an extent."

"There could be a button," I agreed, "but what are the chances of the thing trapping her that way? Closing on her at exactly the right time feels awfully coincidental, and you know how I feel about coincidences."

Morgan shrugged, clearly not seeing this as something to be concerned about. As a deputy, however, it was my job to notice unusual things. People acting strangely often ended up doing things I needed to get involved with. And something about the entire incident felt strange.

"And what about that blond woman?" I jerked my head toward the table in the corner.

"What about her?" Morgan leaned toward me and mimicked my conspiratorial tone.

"You didn't even notice her. Stella thanked her, but she wasn't anywhere near the bar to push a button when the incident occurred. How was she involved?"

Morgan took a popper from the plate between us, set it on the smaller one in front of her, and cut it in half. "I think you're tired from the drive, overstressed from the tourist season you haven't come down from yet, and are reading too much into the incident. Perhaps Stella was thanking her for something that happened earlier."

I frowned and was about to stuff an entire popper in my mouth.

"They're hot," Morgan cautioned in her mama voice. "You'll burn your tongue."

I set it on my little plate and cut it in half to cool. "You're right. The thanks could have been for something else. You really didn't see anything strange in that incident?"

"I told you what I think could have happened." She speared a popper half with her fork. "No one else reacted, so I'm not worried about it. You shouldn't be either. We're in Blackwood Grove, not Whispering Pines. You're not a deputy this weekend. Follow the locals' lead and let it go. We're here to relax."

I nodded. "Okay. You're right."

Follow the locals' lead. They weren't worked up about it. And even if they were, this wasn't my town so not my problem.

Our server arrived with our dinners a couple of minutes later. He was right about the pulled pork, and Morgan said her salmon was perfectly prepared.

"Those were the best onion rings I've ever had," I praised. "Do you suppose they've got a kitchen witch working back there? No, that's a Wiccan thing, isn't it?"

Morgan set her flatware and napkin on her empty plate and leaned back contentedly. "Actually, kitchen witchcraft has nothing to do with a religious affiliation. It's a magical practice of infusing food with positive energy. Or negative energy if you're cooking for a foe. That same principle applies to all forms of witchcraft. So they could have a kitchen witch back there, or they've simply got a really talented cook."

The blond woman from earlier and her companions

walked past then. One woman was about the same age as her, but the other four ladies were in their seventies or eighties. The first had short white hair and wore wide leg jeans with Converse sneakers. The second had long curly graying hair and was dressed in head-to-toe linen. Another in a leather motorcycle jacket had her white hair short on one side and a bit longer on the other. The last woman wore a multi-colored turban on her head and matching pants and tunic. What an interesting group.

Our server brought our bills, which we paid right away and then decided to leave because there were a lot of people waiting to come inside.

We had discussed a short after-dinner walk along the river, but the temperature had dropped dramatically since we entered the saloon. It wasn't quite as cold as it had been at home up north but was still chilly enough that we skipped the walk, not wanting to ruin our warm, happy tummy feeling. Instead, we headed up to our suite to snuggle under blankets by a cozy fire with mugs of hot chocolate. Geoffrey wasn't kidding about providing *perfect comfort*.

We talked and giggled until we were both ready for bed sometime after midnight. Maybe it was the cocoa and fire or maybe it was extended time with my bestie, something we *never* got at home, but I slept better than I had in months. The weird incident with the door was all but forgotten.

Chapter Three

The next morning, both Morgan and I were up early, as usual, so decided to take that walk along the river before meeting Silver and Moon for breakfast.

"What exactly will you be doing with them?" I asked.

Morgan tugged her heavy wool cloak tighter around her neck to block the chilly morning air. "Mostly they want to show me what they've done with their shop but are also looking for more instruction. Mama and I taught them the basics when they were with us, and they feel they're ready for more now. Silver is an herbalist and wants to know more about blending herbs and essential oils. She's also interested in my lotion recipe."

I stared at her in shock. "Are you going to give it to her?"

"Give her my recipe? Dear Goddess, no. I'll help her create her own. The main recipe I work with has been passed down through many generations of Barlow women and tweaked by each of us to make it our own. They'd let me hear about it if I gave it away."

Morgan was a very giving person, but I was happy to learn that certain things were kept top secret. "And what about Moon?"

"Her specialty is acupuncture. She wants to learn about using crystals to enhance treatments."

"What do you know about acupuncture?"

"Exactly nothing," she said with a laugh. "But I do know a thing or two about crystals. They're both curious about the little crystal cages I make for customers."

Morgan knew a ton about crystals. She filled small silver or gold filigree pendants with tiny crystal chips specially chosen to assist the customers with whatever was going on in their lives. The customer or whomever they gave the cage to would wear it as a necklace or tuck it into their bra or a pocket. They were among Shoppe Mystique's bestsellers.

"So this is a working weekend for you," I concluded.

"Only today and only until dinnertime," she insisted. "Then it will be our time. And tomorrow I have Yule presents to purchase."

Since there was no walkway directly next to the river, we had to walk on the road. When traffic started picking up as people went off to jobs or to drop their kids at school or whatever their days entailed, we decided it was time to head to The Comfort Diner.

We had spotted the back of Silver Moon Apothecary on our way past and decided to cut around the shop to enter the park on our way back. We turned and found ourselves facing an apple orchard that continued down the road to our left and around a curve. The thick hedge I'd noticed yesterday ran along it as well. We followed the hedge back toward the apothecary where, according to our map, it would take a sharp turn and continue north past a residential area. Just how big was this hedge?

Our route back took us past a beautiful, although oddly shaped, three-story white farmhouse. The only break in the hedge was the entrance to the farmhouse's driveway. Next to it, along the side of the road, was a large white sign with red lettering that beckoned people to come shop at The Apple Barn.

"How cute is that setup?" I noted. "Except for the massive, scary hedge."

Morgan explained that the hedge was formed from blackthorn bushes. "The story of the blackthorn is an interesting one. It would take a while for me to explain, however. Perhaps tonight while we drink more of that excellent cocoa, I'll tell you more."

"You can't leave me hanging like that. Give me something small."

"I'll give you two things. First, blackthorns are associated with the Crone phase of the Triple Goddess because they represent strength, protection, transformation, and death. Among other things."

"Don't mess with the crones?"

"I certainly wouldn't."

"Your mother is in her crone phase," I reminded her.

Morgan shivered. Jokingly. I think. "Have you ever seen Mama angry?"

"I don't think I have. She's usually pretty even-tempered."

"Well, let's just say everyone has a thorny side. Even Briar Barlow."

I laughed at that. "You promised two things about the shrub. What's the second thing?"

"Blackthorn is covered in extremely sharp thorns so serves as a natural barbed wire."

"In other words," I deciphered, "the people who own the orchard put up the hedge to keep people off their property yet welcome shoppers to their store. Interesting. Maybe it's a trap. Like the adult version of Hansel and Gretel. Think I need to check out The Apple Barn later."

About fifty yards past the apothecary, we came to what was quite possibly the most amazing playground I'd ever seen. There were towers of varying heights. Slides that were different in length and either straight or wavy or twisty. There were bridges to cross, hanging bars, swings, a rock-climbing wall . . . Everyplace I looked, I saw something new. How lucky the kids who lived here were.

Then I spotted the couple I'd seen at The Paddle Wheel last night sitting on a nearby bench. The pink-haired woman wore a puffy oversized jacket, and he had on a long wool coat and slouchy black beanie. It only took about two seconds for me to realize they were having a rather intense conversation, so I looked away.

After another hundred yards, we came to the diner. On the roof was a massive log covered with greenery and berries. One green, one ochre, and one red candle stuck out of it.

"It's a huge Yule log," I exclaimed. "How cool is that?"

"Very cool," Morgan said appreciatively. "It even looks like the candles are lit."

"You want to do that at Shoppe Mystique, don't you?"

She grinned and glanced at me out of the corner of her eye. "I do. Remind me of it when we get home."

A neon sign in a window next to the front door proclaimed *World's Best Pie*. That was a bold claim I was willing to test. A couple of times if necessary. Inside, it looked like a traditional 1950s diner.

"It's so retro," I said while a server brought us to a booth near the center of the building. The floor was red-and-white checkerboard. The seats of the booth benches and the stools along the breakfast counter were deep-green vinyl. Scattered throughout were also accents of the golden ochre color we'd seen around the town.

"You match the holiday color theme we've seen everywhere else," I told Nina, who was also the diner's manager according to her name tag. "And we really love the Yule log on the roof."

"There's a Yule log on the roof?" she asked.

"It's too big to miss," Morgan replied and then described it.

"Cool." Nina gave an approving nod. "I'll have to run outside and take a peek. That must have just happened. As for the floor and seat covering, those changed a couple of weeks ago. The floor was bubblegum pink and white before. The vinyl seats were turquoise." She made a face. "This is much more festive."

I laughed and jokingly asked, "You didn't change the building's interior specifically for Yule, did you?"

"*I* didn't, but something like that," she replied with a shrug and a wink. "What can I get you to drink?"

Morgan wanted herbal tea, and I asked for black coffee.

"For today's special," Nina informed, "the diner is serving sweet potato hash with a poached egg. It's apparently going with a theme, because its pie of the day is also sweet potato. Check over the menu, and I'll be right back for your order."

"We're meeting Silver and Moon here," Morgan told her.

"Oh, good. Haven't seen them in a while. I'll wait until they get here to take your order, then."

Once she walked away, I laughed. "She makes it sound like the diner itself chose the menu and decorations. What a fun place."

Morgan stood. "I'm going to use the ladies' room before Silver and Moon get here."

I glanced around at the very busy diner. It was packed full of all the traditional diner things: A breakfast counter and a window behind it where the chef placed orders ready for delivery. An old-fashioned three-head milkshake mixer on the counter. A pie case with four spinning shelves filled to capacity with the World's Best Pie. Tableside jukeboxes filled with classic rock-and-roll songs. And plenty of chrome.

Then I noticed the customers—young couples, older couples, friends, families, girlfriends, and guy friends. They were all smiling and chatting with their tablemates or nearby diners. A feeling of happiness . . . no, *jolliness* that could only be felt this time of year floated around like the heavenly aromas of coffee, toast, and bacon coming from the kitchen. The yearning feeling I'd experienced when we entered the inn yesterday hit me again, this time because now that I'd found some Christmas spirit, I didn't want it to end.

"One moment," a server told a middle-aged couple waiting to be seated. She raised her voice slightly and said, "We need to clear a few tables. And refill coffee cups, please."

Either the couple was hard of hearing, or she was sending a not-so-subtle directive to another employee. I couldn't spot a single clear table. Each was occupied or needed to be cleaned. The table closest to our booth was a complete mess. Whoever had been sitting there appeared to have tried everything on the menu if the stack of plates was any indication.

I took another swig of my coffee, looked back at the table . . . and it was clean. As in so spic-and-span I could eat off of it clean. But it had been covered in a pile of plates seconds earlier. Hadn't it?

"Okay," the server announced, "I can seat you now."

I lifted my cup to take another sip of coffee before someone came around to refill it . . . but found it full to the brim.

"What's the matter?" Morgan asked as she slid into the booth next to me. "You're white as snow."

"I . . ." I had to be seeing things, because like last night with the door at the saloon, no one reacted to what had supposedly happened. "Nothing. Guess I didn't sleep as well as I thought I did."

"You have been unusually stressed for months," she reminded me. "You may need all four days of this trip to fully relax."

She wasn't wrong. I stepped down as village sheriff not only because of the extreme guilt I felt for not preventing the awful deaths in Whispering Pines, but also because I'd made a

SECRET OF THE HOPEFUL HOLIDAY · 189

very bad decision about the person responsible for many of them. Which resulted in more people dying. What if I was never able to forgive myself?

Before I could travel too far down that pitiful path, Silver and Moon arrived at the booth. Morgan stood to embrace them both. Silver had dreadlocks that hung to her waist and had an almost childlike aura about her. She sat across from me and waved enthusiastically with both hands. Moon, with skin as pale as Silver's was dark, wore her hair in dozens of braids pulled into a high ponytail. After a quick round of how-have-you-been catchup and placing our breakfast orders with Nina, I asked what they recommended I do while Morgan was with them today.

"At this time of year," Moon began, "most people are here to shop. The best places to eat are here or The Paddle Wheel."

"*If* you're looking for a meal," Silver qualified. "If you just want a snack, there's So Mote It Tea teashop or The Sweet Spot bakery. They also serve non-alcoholic drinks and simple appetizers at the bookstore, Grimoires & Gimlets."

"All of those places are right here in the mall," Moon explained. "If you like hiking, there's a state park further down the road."

I loved to hike and suddenly wished I'd brought my Westie with me. Meeka loved nothing more than wandering through the woods.

"Oh, there's also the orchard," Silver said. "Everything has been harvested, so I'm pretty sure the Warrens have opened it for people to wander through." Something or someone near the breakfast bar caught her attention, and she tipped her head toward two women standing there. "There's Comfort and Dusty. We could ask if it's okay."

I recognized them, respectively, as the elderly woman wearing Converse sneakers and the blond woman we'd seen at the saloon last night.

Silver waved her arm and called out, "Dusty."

The woman turned and came over to our table. "Good morning, ladies."

Moon introduced her, Morgan, and me, and then Silver asked, "Is the orchard open for wandering?"

"It is. Who wants to wander?"

"I'm thinking about it," I said, studying her without being obvious. Something about her had my instincts tingling. "Morgan will be helping Silver and Moon at their shop today, so I'm on my own."

Dusty's eyes narrowed a bit, and she seemed to be studying me too. Then she smiled, and deep creases like quote marks formed around her mouth. "Feel free to wander if you'd like. Just stay on the roped-off path so you don't get lost. If you do go for a wander, stop by The Apple Barn afterward to warm up with some hot cider." The older woman called her back to the breakfast bar then. "Nice to meet you both."

"Who is she?" I asked, unable to hold back my curiosity.

"Dusty Hotte," Silver said, a hint of awe in her voice. "She's one of the Warren Witches."

"The Warren Witches?" I repeated.

"To understand the Warren family," Moon began, "you need to know the background of the town."

Nina arrived with our food then. Once she verified we had everything we needed and then left to check on another table, Moon began the history lesson while Morgan and I ate our savory sweet potato hash.

"Seeing as both Silver and I have been to Whispering Pines, we know that our towns are similar. Yours was founded fifty-some years ago by a woman who wanted a place to live where no one would criticize her for her lifestyle choices. Blackwood Grove came to be two hundred years ago because the Warrens practiced witchcraft, which was illegal and punishable by prison time or worse."

"Still is," Silver added. "Kind of."

I paused in my chewing. This sounded a lot like the Salem witch trials. But that was way back in the late 1600s. Things like that didn't happen in Wisconsin. Did they? Certainly not in this century.

"Back then," Moon continued, "there were many ordinary people, those who didn't use witchcraft, who strenuously objected to the persecutions. The witches, they claimed, did a lot to help them with cures and whatnot. To keep the Ordies happy and make amends to the persecuted, the witches were given plots of land where they could live freely. The Warren family was the first to receive land."

"The area inside that hedge is their parcel," Silver explained. "Well, it's part of it, they sold some . . . long story."

I reiterated, "They were free to live their lives however they wanted on their parcel."

"Were and are, correct," Moon agreed. "Hoping to be able to live the way the Warrens did, other people who practiced witchcraft moved here, and the town slowly grew around the parcel. Ordies who supported the witches and benefitted from their magic also came."

"That does sound a lot like how Whispering Pines came to be," I stated. "People found out about the freedom our founder, my grandmother, established and wanted to live the way she did."

Her mouth full of hash, Morgan simply nodded her agreement.

"And then"—Silver waved her hands in front of her own face—"chaos. The powers that be wanted to limit magic to the parcels only, but the witches objected to more or less being put on reservations and only being allowed to be their true selves in designated areas. After a great deal of debate and many protests, the lawmakers declared Blackwood Grove and the other communities surrounding the witch parcels to be *safe towns*, places where witches can perform all the magic they want without fear of persecution."

I was trying to keep an open mind about what they were saying, but they wanted me to believe the things I thought I'd seen: tables that cleared themselves and coffee cups that never emptied.

"So about the Warren Witches then . . ."

"Ah, yes." Silver continued, "The witches who live in Blackwood Grove each have an ability of some kind. The Warrens, however, take magic to another level. Dusty, her aunts Comfort and Gwynne, family friends Pepper and Jett, a couple of ghosts, and a passel of familiars all live in the farmhouse. Dusty's cousin, Carly, lives in a house at the north edge of the property with her kids and husband."

"Ghosts?" I asked. They were messing with me again.

Silver nodded. "Granny Sadie and Jett's husband, Freddie."

Fine. I'd play along, because they obviously weren't going to let this go. "Morgan and her mother, as you know, are green witches. What do the Warrens do?"

"Jett would be the closest to a green witch," Moon explained. "She oversees care of the gardens and the orchard. Comfort makes food, especially pies, that comfort people and allow them to work through their troubles. Pepper does amazing things with salt and pepper spells. Gwynne assembles spell kits with herbs, oils, and crystals that people line up at the gate to buy. Carly's skill is divination. And Dusty, along with having post-cognitive dreams, meaning she dreams about things that happened in the past—"

"Most of us do that," I interrupted.

"Yes," Moon agreed, "but Dusty dreams about things she couldn't possibly know. And they're *always* accurate."

"She's also a gray witch," Silver added.

"What's that?" I asked Morgan.

"I believe," she answered, "they perform spells that most would consider to be improper."

Silver nodded. "She does the wrong thing for the right reason. Not always. Only when someone asks for her help."

I laughed. "As a sheriff's deputy, I see people try to use that defense all the time. 'But I had really good intentions, officer.'"

Moon and Silver blinked at me.

"She uses her ability," Moon said evenly, "to restore justice. If someone has been wronged and can prove it, she will give them a spell to right the wrong."

Restoring justice. Righting wrongs. Moon was using words that I lived my life by. Still, in this case, it sounded like an excuse for committing crimes. "What kinds of spells?"

"Don't know," Silver said, "I've never used her services."

"Like Morgan and Gwynne can," Moon offered, "Dusty blends plants, oils, crystals . . . those kinds of things. She creates a spell, writes down the instructions for casting it, and gives the person all the necessary ingredients to make the spell happen."

I held back an unconvinced snort but said, "I only bought the gun and gave it to the killer, officer. I didn't pull the trigger."

This time, their stares turned to glares.

"You must understand why I'm skeptical," I insisted.

"If you were a regular Ordy, we would," Silver said. "But you live in a place where magical things happen all the time."

This stopped me cold. Magical things? In Whispering Pines?

Morgan patted the tabletop to get their attention. "Give her time to absorb this information."

I stared at my friend. "Are you saying you believe that *magic* really happens?"

"Living my life the way I do, where I do, how can I not?"

Was that it? Morgan had lived in Whispering Pines since the day she was born, surrounded by mysticism. I'd only been there for a little more than two years. She had grown up trusting in nature and believing that she could make things happen through the power of the Universe and manifestation. I was raised in an agnostic household and trained to only believe things I could see and qualify with facts.

"I apologize for the skepticism," I told Silver and Moon, "but as an officer of the law, it's ingrained in me to gather proof in order to believe something. How does one prove magic exists?"

Silver leaned toward me, her face glowing with childlike wonder. "How about this? Try believing in the magic of the holidays. That kind of easy magic is everywhere here."

If she had any idea how badly I wanted to.

I told her I'd try, but the thing was, I was far more likely to trust convoluted, smoke-and-mirrors explanations for the things I'd seen since arriving here than to accept what she and Moon were telling me. Because even though my personal life was practically perfect, so much had gone wrong on my professional watch recently that believing there were external forces at play was going to be very hard for me to do. I mean, if there was magic available, why did all those people die?

Maybe I needed to talk to Dusty about this restoring justice thing. Our methods may be at different ends of the spectrum, but we were at least fighting for the same thing. And maybe I'd pick up a few tricks from her. And possibly a new belief or two.

Suddenly, I was eager to explore the nooks and crannies of this town. Especially the area inside that hedge.

Chapter Four

Moon and Silver moved on from the Warren family to letting Morgan know what they wanted her help with at the apothecary. The list was long, so as soon as we'd finished our breakfasts, we headed over there. The three of them were so deep in discussion, they didn't even realize I had followed them. I'd been hearing so much about this shop, I wanted to see it in person. Plus, the outside was so amazing I couldn't imagine what the inside must look like.

As we walked, I paid attention to the stores we passed. There was a higher-end men's clothing store called Dapper, where I might find a gift for the owner of our village, River Carr, who was also Morgan's husband. Maybe they has something for my boss, Martin Reed, too. And possibly for Tripp, but he was more of a jeans and flannel kind of guy. So was Martin, come to think of it.

A yarn shop stood next door to Dapper. I'd learned how to weave and had been thinking about learning to knit, but it felt disloyal to shop at a craft store here when we had such an amazing place in the village. Although, there was no harm in taking a peek. I put an asterisk next to that one on the map. Across the park was a place called Earthly Delights. I had no clue what they sold but was intrigued enough by the name that I had to check them out.

I'd been so focused on the shops and abundance of traditional trimmings—most folks in Whispering Pines preferred nature-based Northwoods decorations—I didn't realize I'd fallen behind. Morgan, Silver, and Moon were almost to the apothecary, so I jogged to catch up.

"You came," Morgan noted when she saw me behind them.

"I wanted to see what it looks like inside."

"Excellent," Silver declared. "We're always happy to show off our shop."

Unbelievably, the outside was just a teaser for the inside, which was amazing in a different way. One wall was covered with shelves containing crystals and stones. Another was lined with bookcases, each painted a deep muted shade of teal-blue and filled with mismatched bottles of dried herbs.

"Are the walls . . ." I didn't even know what to ask. The paint shimmered and swirled in shades of purple, teal, and magenta.

"Would you believe me," Moon began, "if I told you they were enchanted?"

Probably not. Fortunately, she didn't seem to be expecting an answer, so I didn't give her one. The walls had to be covered with some kind of screen, and the swirling kaleidoscope of colors was being projected onto them. That had to be expensive, but it was a really cool effect.

Like in Morgan's shop, tables of different shapes and sizes were scattered across the sales floor and topped with merchandise—jewelry on one, lotions and potions on another, essential oils on a third . . .

On the wall across from the entrance, a loft stuck out about a quarter of the way over the sales floor. The space looked like a miniature bookstore with packed-full cases running the width of the store and cozy-looking wingback chairs at each end. The ceiling was also *enchanted*, as Moon claimed, with a night sky filled with stars and a moon that slowly moved through its phases. Very cool.

Their Yule decorations blended in seamlessly. In the center of the shop stood a black tree that bent over at the top. I smiled at its resemblance to a witch's hat. It was covered in tiny white lights and larger bohemian-style ornaments in shades of primarily deep purple and rich teal with pops of acid green and magenta.

"You don't match the rest of the town," I noted with a smile and nod at the tree.

"In any way, shape, or form," Silver acknowledged. "We've marched to our own tune our whole lives. That's kind of why they stuck us way down at this end of the mall."

"That's not why," came a voice from beneath the loft. "I brought this shop here from New Orleans twenty years ago, and it's been in this spot ever since. Long before the mall was here." One of the women I saw at The Paddle Wheel last night, the one wearing a turban with a matching tunic and pants, emerged from the shadows. Today, her outfit was the same except in shades of purple and teal, which meant she also blended with the shop.

"You're early," Moon noted. "We don't open for another hour."

The woman glanced at Morgan and me. "I felt called to be here." She extended a hand to Morgan and, with a slight Cajun accent, said, "I'm Pepper Boudreaux."

"The salt and pepper witch," I recalled.

"Indeed." Her hand moved from Morgan's to mine, and when she paused momentarily, I thought of Lily Grace back home, one of our fortune tellers. Whenever Lily Grace touched me or did a reading for me, it always came true in some form or another. As an officer and her friend, I'd come to rely on her visions to help me work through problems.

Had Pepper sensed something the way Lily Grace did

when our hands touched? How could I believe that was possible but not the other things Silver and Moon had told me?

"Among other things, Pepper reads tarot for us," Moon explained. "She's very good."

"Can I interest you in a reading?" Pepper asked me.

"Not today but thank you."

"I won't be here tomorrow," she cautioned.

The tone in her voice made me think this was something I shouldn't miss. Besides, it's not like I had to be anywhere. I was free to do whatever I wanted today.

"Okay, let's draw a card."

"Actually, we'll draw three," she said, leading me to her reading corner beneath the loft on the left. A small room filled the space on the right. A sign on a door there read *Acupuncture*, so that had to be where Moon treated her customers.

In Pepper's corner, a beautiful round dark wood table and two chairs waited. The heavy table had thick, spiral-carved legs, and the chairs resembled miniature thrones. The edge of the table and the backs of the chairs were intricately engraved with suns and moons. Down the center of the table ran a dark-teal velvet cloth. On it, were a pair of wrought-iron candlesticks, a crystal ball, and a small black ceramic bowl containing different colored stones. There were also three different tarot card decks: one with a celestial theme, the second with forest images, and the third with wolves.

"Choose a deck," Pepper instructed, "shuffle them and then choose three cards."

I reached for the forest deck but then diverted to the wolves.

"Are wolves important to you?" Pepper asked.

"There was a wolf I saw around our village last winter. He hung out by my house for a few days too. So, yes, I have a soft spot for them." I smiled, remembering Farkas, then held up the cards. "Should I be thinking anything while doing this?"

A grin turned Pepper's mouth. "You're not new to this."

"New to tarot. Not new to mystical beliefs."

"Your reading will address a question," she explained. "A three-card spread will, obviously, address three aspects of your question. For example, your past, present, and future. You, your path, and your potential." She paused slightly before suggesting, "A situation, the challenge surrounding it, and advice for moving through it. You can tell me what you're thinking or not. It won't change what I see either way."

The last one. I wanted answers for moving through a challenging situation but kept that to myself. As I shuffled the deck, I thought about my village and the mess it had become. I was supposed to make it a safe place, but it seemed to only be getting messier.

A safe place . . . Like this safe town? Was Blackwood Grove *really* safe if the founding family had to live behind a spiked hedge? Maybe our towns were even more alike than they seemed.

"Draw three?" I asked when I felt I'd shuffled enough.

She took the deck from me and fanned out the cards on the table. "Place them in a row, face down."

As I did, she tipped the stones from the little bowl into her left hand and cupped her right one on top of it.

Before turning over the cards, she said, "Listen to me, child."

I nodded and looked her in the eye.

"I am not a fortune teller. I don't claim that what I read is any kind of vision or guarantee." She fisted her hand holding the stones, touched her fist to her forehead and then held it to her chest. "Tarot delivers a message for you to hold in your head and your heart. It's meant to help you focus, not provide a roadmap. Does that make sense?"

"A message to focus on. I understand." I'd take anything I could get at this point. I was desperate to help my villagers.

She turned the cards face up and took in their overall

message. "You feel stuck in whatever your current situation is and can't find the right path forward."

Skeptic that I was, my immediate thought was that this could be true for just about anyone at any time. Still, she was one for one.

She tapped the first card. "The Three of Wands reversed or upside down. You're frustrated about your present situation. There are obstacles blocking your path." Her head tilted to the side. "Or is fear preventing you from moving forward?"

My mouth went dry.

She placed a finger on the second card. "The Six of Swords upright indicates the path you want to take is the right one. It may not feel like it, but even though this direction seems fraught with obstacles and fear, it will lead to a place of healing or a fresh start."

Tears prickled my eyes. Dear Goddess, I hoped that was true.

She slid the last card across the table closer to me. "The Chariot indicates pushing through conflict in a positive direction. If you keep pushing, keep striving to succeed, you will. Reversed, as this one is, it indicates your energy isn't focused. You're scattered and are suffering self-doubt."

I worked part time as a deputy, managed the village all the time, *and* ran a B&B with Tripp. Every day brought some sort of chaos from both tourists and villagers. I felt constant pressure, both real and self-imposed, to honor my grandmother's wish that I heal the community she created. Yes, I was definitely scattered, and my stage of self-doubt was closing in on paralysis. A tear broke free. Embarrassed, I swiped it away and whispered, "What do I do about it?"

Pepper placed a hand on my arm. "Remember, this is not a foretelling of the future. It's a message—"

"It's a message that's one hundred percent accurate." A sense of desperation made my chest constrict. I looked imploringly at this woman who'd offered me a direction and asked with more intensity, "What do I do?"

She tapped the Chariot card then held her palm to my cheek. "The card suggests surrender."

"I can't give up—"

"That's not what it means, child. It means stop trying to do it all yourself. Surrender and allow others to help."

More tears fell, and I laughed weakly. "This isn't the first time I've heard that advice."

"When messages repeat in your life, it's best to pay attention." She placed the card back in its spot on the table in its reversed position. "Do you have any other questions for me?"

My mind was absolutely spinning and wouldn't land on anything solid. So I asked, "What do I owe you?"

She shook her head. "Consider this your first Yule gift of the season. Take a minute to collect yourself." After returning the stones to the bowl, she left me alone with the cards. Which I took a picture of so I wouldn't forget which ones they were.

To recap the reading, I was frustrated because the path I was following kept getting blocked by one obstacle after another, including my own fear. But it was the right one and would lead me to the right place. That was hopeful. Finally, I needed to stop thinking I was the only one who could get us to that place. I needed to let my villagers help. That, too, was hopeful but also a huge step out of my comfort zone.

I closed my eyes, breathed deep, and let the energy of the apothecary flow into me. One of the things I'd learned from Whispering Pines was that there were forces at play in our lives we couldn't explain. Some were good, others bad. This reading might only be a message for me to focus on, but as Pepper said, when the same message kept repeating, the Universe was speaking, and it was best to pay attention.

I blew out a hard breath, wiped the tears from my face, and squared my shoulders.

Morgan looked at me with concern as I approached her. "Are you okay?"

"I'm fine. The reading hit a little close. Incredibly close, in fact."

"Do you need to talk?"

"Not right now. I'll tell you about it at dinner tonight. What time are we meeting?"

"Six o'clock at the saloon again?" she offered.

"It's either there or the diner, right?"

"Unless we leave town."

I shook my head. In an awkward way I couldn't explain, I felt . . . *safe* here and didn't want to leave Blackwood Grove until it was time to go home. "The saloon is fine. I'll let you get on with your consultation."

Morgan rubbed a comforting hand up and down my arm. "You're sure you're okay?"

"Seriously, absolutely fine. It's always a little disconcerting when people who know nothing about you zero in on a big aspect of your life." I smiled at the turban-wearing witch a few feet away. "Pepper is very intuitive."

Pepper placed her palms together and bowed in thanks.

"Off to explore?" Silver asked excitedly. "I'm always envious when people get to experience the town for the first time."

What a nice way to look at it. "Think I'll do some shopping and maybe go wander through the apple orchard."

Silver clapped her hands. "If you do, remember to check out The Apple Barn. Along with being super cute inside, they've got a great selection of kitchen and home things."

"Sounds like the perfect place to shop for my boyfriend," I replied. "He's the cook in our house."

On my way out of the shop, I passed a table of essential oil blends. One was called *Ease*. Smaller text below the name claimed *instant relaxation with just a sniff*. So I sniffed. It was like the immediate, soothing comfort of vapor rub applied to a congested chest, only rubbed onto my brain. My swirling thoughts settled, and I really did feel significantly calmer. More Blackwood Grove magic?

I waved goodbye to the group and headed off in search of good things.

Chapter Five

At the intersection of the apothecary's front walk and the path that wound through the mall park, I debated which way to turn. Left to the apple orchard or right to the shops? Figuring the crowds would only get heavier as the day went on, I decided to tackle the mall first.

I studied the map the innkeeper gave me and made notes regarding which stores I wanted to shop at and for whom. My gift-buying list wasn't long, but I tried to be thoughtful about what I gave people. As I walked, inhaling the crisp river-scented air, I thought again about the message from the tarot reading. Specifically, to trust that even though it didn't feel like it most of the time, I was on the right path. Too often, I felt like I was laying the path and trying to follow it at the same time.

"You need to follow the path that appears," I murmured to myself.

"Excuse me?" a woman nearby asked. "Were you talking to me?"

"No, sorry. Talking to myself. Bad habit."

She swatted a *don't-worry-about-it* hand at me. "Honey, I do the same thing." She held up a sheet of paper and shook it. "I've got twenty-seven names on my Christmas list this year and limited time to shop, so I need to purchase as many gifts as possible this weekend. There will be a lot of self-muttering, trust me."

I wished her a good day and smiled as she walked away humming *Jingle Bells*. How wonderfully different it was to simply be a part of the crowd instead of the deputy everyone came up to with complaints.

The first gift I bought was for my sister. Rosalyn complained that the B&B was cold in the winter even though Tripp and I were fine. In fairness, we were usually running all around the house while she was on her computer most of the day and didn't move much. If we turned up the heat, Tripp and I would be sweating, and our gas bill would soar. At Swank, a women's clothing store, I chose an amazingly soft alpaca and mohair turtleneck sweater, a thick pair of cozy wool socks, and fingerless gloves. Add in the occasional mug of tea and Rozzie should be toasty warm.

In the antique store next door to Swank, I found a fountain pen set in a gleaming red wooden case. I wanted to talk to Tripp about it and was going to ask the shop owner to hold it for me until I could. Then I remembered my cellphone actually worked in Blackwood Grove. We had zero cell coverage in Whispering Pines. I took a picture, emailed it to Tripp, and then called him to look at it.

"I can see it sitting on River's desk," I said.

"Oh yeah," Tripp agreed. "The case looks handmade. You know how he feels about things like that."

River had impressive woodworking skills so greatly respected other artisans. And red was his favorite color. "It's gorgeous and a great price."

"I vote yes. How's everything going there?"

I told him about the unusual things I'd seen around the village. "Then a witch named Pepper did a tarot card reading for me, and it was scarily accurate. Honestly, it freaked me out a little." I gave him a rundown of the three-card spread.

He didn't have a response for the weird stuff I was seeing. Probably because he was used to seeing weird things happen around our village almost every day. Or he assumed I needed more relaxation time. Regarding the reading, however, he said, "Blackwood Grove sounds like a sister town to Whispering Pines."

"It does kind of feel that way." My words faded away as I caught a glimpse of the woman with pink hair and the man in the wool coat through the store's front windows. They didn't look right together, and not just because they appeared to be from opposite ends of the social spectrum. She looked like she came from the rough side of a big city while he would easily blend into any financial district. They might be brother and sister or longtime friends. They could be coworkers. Maybe he was trying to help her somehow, but she was fighting him. I could come up with a dozen possible scenarios. What stood out to me, though, was the way she walked with her hands shoved deep into her jacket pockets and her shoulders hunched so far forward she looked like she was folding in on herself.

My instincts told me something wasn't right, and since I almost always trusted my instincts, I thought about going after them. But by the time I crossed the store to the windows, they'd disappeared into the crowd.

"Babe?"

"Sorry." I blinked and returned to my call with Tripp. "Something out the window caught my eye."

"You're not a cop this weekend."

He knew me so well. "I know. What are you doing?"

"Baking bread. And it's just about ready to come out of the oven."

My mouth watered at the thought of how the house must smell. "I'll let you go, then. Miss you. Love you."

"I love you too. Have fun with Morgan."

The slight emphasis on those last words meant *remember you're there to decompress.*

"I will," I promised and put my phone back into the belt bag I wore across my chest and zipped inside my jacket.

I made one last lap around the store, paid for the pen set, and asked where to get a good mocha. The lady behind the counter assured me that both So Mote It Tea and The Sweet Spot served excellent mocha lattes. That bar was very high, however, because the best mocha in the world came from Ye Olde Bean Grinder in Whispering Pines.

"If you have to choose," she concluded, "go to the teashop. Unless you also want a pastry, then save yourself a stop and go to the bakery."

I thanked her, crossed the park toward the teashop, and as I opened the door, I found the same couple blocking the entrance. If I trusted the Universe, which I did, I kept crossing paths with these two for a reason. Currently, they appeared to be in the middle of a heated argument. That would explain her closed-off posture earlier. A shelving unit filled with books, magazines, and board games on one side of the door, and a wall on the other prevented me from skirting around them. I had no choice but to wait for them to notice me and move out of my way. It only took two seconds to realize they weren't arguing; he was reprimanding her.

"You made me look like an idiot," he growled.

"How did I do that?" she objected, her voice soft and soothing.

"You changed your drink order."

"Craig, all I did was switch from oat milk to soy milk. The lady behind us in line said oat milk froths better, and I thought I'd give it a try."

"The order was already placed."

"But the barista hadn't started making it yet. She said it was no big deal."

This was one of the dumbest arguments I'd ever heard. And I spent most of the summer dealing with drunk people.

"It is a big deal." The volume of Craig's voice rose along with the angry red flush on his face. "I order for you, and then you change it? No. From now on, you take what I give you."

There were multiple ways to interpret that directive. I didn't like any of them.

"But—"

"No." He closed the small gap between them until they were so close his nose was almost touching hers. "If you're so indecisive you can't make up your mind before we get to the counter, you deserve nothing."

The woman hunched her shoulders and ducked her head as though bracing for a slap or punch. My sheriff deputy persona screamed at me to step in and help her.

"In fact . . ." Craig took the cup from her hand and tossed it in the nearest garbage can. "We're leaving. Let's go. What a complete waste."

I wasn't sure if he meant she was the waste or the discarded coffee. My blood boiled, but before I could say anything, he charged toward the door so suddenly I had to press myself against the wall, or he would have smashed right into me. A blink later, he was face down in a slush pile outside. The coffee he'd been holding spilled all over the ground. Inside the store, a few of the customers who'd witnessed the interaction cheered or laughed.

Furious, he sprang to his feet and stared between me and the pink-haired woman standing behind me. "Which one of you did that?"

"Did what?" I was beyond annoyed with his attitude.

"Pushed me or tripped me . . . whatever."

Ignoring him, I faced the woman, looking at her up close

for the first time. Her eye makeup made her look half asleep or high on something. I hoped it was her makeup. "What's your name?"

"Amy," she answered meekly.

I turned to the man. "You were three feet away from Amy before she even took a step. I was pressed up against the wall so you wouldn't plow me over. You fell all on your own, buddy."

I looked back at Amy again and found Dusty standing near the counter ten feet away, watching our interaction. She met my eye and tipped her head in acknowledgement.

Amy was now standing close enough to me that our shoulders were practically pressed together. She looked scared of her boyfriend, or whatever Craig was to her.

"Are you okay?" I asked softly. "Do you need help?"

"I, um—"

"Amy, come on," Craig barked. "Let's go."

She flinched at his voice but didn't say another word before walking off with him. If he would have grabbed her or if she had given me any indication she needed help, I would have intervened. She left voluntarily, though. Should I have done more?

"I'm so sorry you were involved with that," a man wearing a So Mote It Tea apron said to me. "I'm Russell. My wife, Maggie, and I own the shop. What can I get you? On the house."

The whole time he spoke, my attention was on Dusty who now had her back to me and was talking to the woman behind the counter. Maggie, I presumed. First at The Paddle Wheel last night, and now this. There was nothing in the doorway that Craig could have tripped over. There was no floor mat in the way, no threshold strip he could have caught the toe of his shoe on. Nothing. He probably tripped over his own feet. I'd done that plenty of times. But Silver and Moon said Dusty was a gray witch. That she did the wrong thing for the right reason in order to restore justice. Like causing a man to fall on his face after publicly humiliating the woman he was with? Had Dusty somehow caused his fall?

From ten feet away? That was impossible. Wasn't it?

"Miss? Are you okay?"

I blinked to find . . . Russell looking at me with concern. "Yeah, I'm fine. Trying to figure out what just happened. Do you know that couple?"

He placed a hand on my upper back, seemed to freeze for a moment, and then led me to the counter. "They stop in here sometimes, so I know their names but don't really know them. I think they live in the area but not in Blackwood Grove. Please, what can we get you?"

His wife smiled and nodded. "We want to make sure you leave our shop happy."

"Okay," I finally relented. "I'd love a mocha with a double-pump of vanilla and extra whipped cream."

"Extra-large double-vanilla extra-whip mocha coming up," Maggie stated.

Had I said extra-large? Or did she just know that's what I always ordered at home? No, I needed to quit jumping straight to the unexplainable or paranormal or whatever for these situations. Most likely she was simply ensuring I left happy by giving me the largest drink possible.

As I waited, I thought rationally about the things I'd witnessed. Craig falling on his face could simply mean he was a klutz or that his karma was coming back at him. There also had to be a logical reason for the table clearing and coffee refills at the diner, like I'd been looking around for longer than I realized and hadn't noticed a super-speedy employee reset the table and fill my cup. Maybe I hadn't drunk as much as I thought. As for The Paddle Wheel's door, there *could* have been a button behind the bar that closed and held it in place.

And perhaps Stella *had* thanked Dusty for something completely unrelated.

"Question for you," I began after Maggie slid my drink across the counter to me. I was going to ask if Dusty did something to Craig, but that would make me sound like a crazy person. Besides, I wasn't a cop this weekend. But I was a caring citizen. "Russell said that couple, Amy and Craig, comes in here sometimes."

She nodded. "I've seen them. He's a class A jerk, isn't he?"

"Is he always like that?"

"Always? No. Why are you asking?"

I explained that I was an off-duty deputy and even showed her my badge as proof.

"You carry your badge even when not on duty?" she asked curiously.

"I never know when I'll end up involved in incidents. Having my badge makes things go more smoothly."

"Makes sense." Maggie reiterated her earlier question. "Any reason you're asking about that couple?"

I blinked at her. She saw the interaction. That's why they were offering me a free drink. Didn't it upset her? "Is it normal around here for people to publicly berate each other? Do people not notice things like that?"

She smiled, acknowledging my concern. "That's not it at all. People tend to stay out of others' business, though."

"It's my job, at home, to directly insert myself into people's business." I laughed to break the tension forming between us. "I'm worried that was more than an argument. Amy could be in some kind of danger." And now I was regretting not stepping in asking more firmly if she needed help. "Since you see them around here on occasion—"

"Be aware."

"Right."

Her on-guard attitude softened. "As a regular citizen, it's

hard to know when to intervene and when to let people be who they are."

"That can be hard for officers too." I tapped my abdomen. "My gut is telling me something might be wrong here, so I wanted to make you aware too."

The slow bow of her head said she heard and understood.

"Thanks for the mocha." I held it up to both Maggie and Russell. "Happy holidays, you two."

Chapter Six

T he mocha was very good. Not the best I'd ever had but a solid contender for second place. The hit of caffeine restored me and left me motivated to do more Yule shopping. I'd had good luck at my first two stops, so my next was the bookstore next to the teashop.

Grimoires & Gimlets would fit in perfectly in Whispering Pines if we didn't already have our own amazing shop. This place was half book store, half pub, and had a magical, witchy vibe that hit me in all the right spots the instant I walked in. The forest-green walls and cozy seating on the book side was very inviting. Hundreds of little orbs that looked like moons or planets along with larger crescent-moon-shaped lights hung over the bar on the family-friendly pub side.

I was tempted to stay right there until it was time to meet Morgan for dinner. In case I decided I'd had enough shopping before six o'clock and figuring an escape from reality sounded like a good plan, I bought myself a fantasy novel to curl up with. I hadn't gotten lost in a story since last winter.

Tucked in among the books on the shelves were candles, figurines, antique bottles, and other mystically themed items. I spotted what I thought was a locket on one shelf. The silver case engraved with a pentacle made me immediately think of Morgan. I imagined her tucking pictures of loved ones, snips of her twins' hair, or crystal chips inside it. When I opened it, though, I found what appeared to be a smooth jet-black stone.

"What is this?" I asked Tabitha, the bookstore/pub owner, who looked like a witchy librarian. She wore a long black dress with fluttery sleeves, lace-up booties, and a slouchy beanie hat that resembled a deflated stereotypical witch's hat. Cute.

Tabitha explained, "It's a scrying mirror. We have larger ones too." She pointed out a hand mirror on a nearby shelf and a big oval-shaped one hanging on the wall.

I gazed into the black surface of the pendant. "I can't see my reflection."

"You're not meant to. Scrying mirrors are for divination, to help open your mind, or for connecting with beings in other realms."

I studied the pendant closer. It looked like it used to be a pocket watch. "Tell me more about opening my mind."

Tabitha perked with excitement. "The concept is that gazing into the surface allows you to connect with your psyche." She swirled her hands around her head. "Our minds hold a vast amount of knowledge, and without help, we can only access a tiny portion of it. The mirrors help you tap into those treasures."

"The answers are there," I summarized, "we just need to get at them."

"Exactly."

I got the pendant for Morgan and added a pocket-size scrying mirror for myself. She would probably wear it because it was cool looking, and I figured tapping into the vast knowledge of my mind sounded like a good idea. A book and a mirror for myself when I was supposed to be buying Yule gifts. It felt a little indulgent, but I rarely bought myself anything other than necessities, so why not?

Next was a store that sold plants and plant-related items. I found an adorable floppy sun hat and matching gardening gloves for Briar. She had complained a couple of times this past summer about the sun beating down on her neck. This hat would take care of that problem; the brim was huge. Both the hat and gloves were covered in cartoon flowers, snails, lady bugs, and gardening tools. The best part was the big patch on the front embroidered with *Show us your bloomers, you dirty hoes!* She'd love it.

By that time, the park was getting very crowded, and I was starting to feel a bit claustrophobic around all the people. Odd since I spent most of my mornings surrounded by tourists while patrolling the village. Apparently I was yearning for space as well as relaxation. Time to leave the mall and head over to the orchard.

It was lunch time, so I grabbed a cup of hot cocoa and a meat pie from a food truck parked on the street between the mall and its parking lot. Then I sat on a bench beneath one of the heaters and enjoyed every bite of the savory pie while watching kids running around the playground. From my seat, I could also see The Apple Barn. I'd planned to go to the inn, drop off my purchases, and then go for a walk, but the big red barn with white trim was suddenly calling me.

"One more stop," I murmured like a pep talk, "and then I'm done shopping for the day."

With a warm belly and a curious attitude, I headed for the Warren Witches' property. I thought about wandering through the orchard for a few minutes, but not with all these bags. Maybe tomorrow. Instead, I followed the path through the mall park straight to the hedge. From a distance, the blackthorn bushes simply looked like a creative way to delineate their land from the rest of the town. Up close, I immediately understood the natural barbed-wire concept. The line of bushes was a good fifteen feet tall and ten feet wide. The needle-sharp thorns Morgan had mentioned covered every branch and ranged from an inch to more than two inches long. I looked for an opening to pass through, but there wasn't one, and there was no way to squeeze through without getting skewered like a voodoo doll. I had no choice but to head left toward the river, take a right at the road, and then another sharp right onto the Applewood Farm driveway.

I paused on my way past the huge white farmhouse to take a closer look at it. Traditional pine garland draped along the railing of the covered porch, and pine wreaths with red bows hung in each of its dozens of windows. As my gaze traveled upward, I looked a little more closely at the structure. The main and second floors appeared to have rooms tacked on in random places. Like maybe they decided a room needed to be bigger so expanded it or added on a new one.

"And I thought we had interesting buildings in Whispering Pines."

As I studied the house, I could have sworn someone was standing in a top-floor window. Embarrassed to be caught staring, I looked away and resumed walking, but couldn't stop myself from glancing back at the window once more. No one was there. Maybe one of the ghosts Silver had mentioned at breakfast hung out up there and watched people. I chuckled at the thought.

The driveway continued straight into a small parking lot next to the barn but also curved to the left to a locked gate. The farmhouse was on the other side of the gate. I continued straight and just inside the parking lot was an antique apple-red truck, decorated from bumper to bumper with holiday lights. From the bed, employees sold caramel apples, candy apples, and cups of hot apple cider. On the far side of The Apple Barn's entrance, kids of all ages gathered around a pen to pet the little goats hopping around inside. A few feet from the pen, other kids waited in line by a giant cartoon apple dressed like a Christmas elf. There was a cutout where the elf's face should be. The kids peered through the oval and grinned while their adults took their picture.

The atmosphere was festive and fun for everyone and made me feel that, even as an adult, the season could be magical.

Inside the shop, I was immediately charmed by the stone floors and fairy lights encircling rustic beams that might have once held up a second floor. Now, the beams gave the illusion of a ceiling. Pine garland loaded with red and white berry sprigs and yards and yards of ochre ribbon hung from the beams in great swooping scallops. Trees decorated with traditional or apple ornaments were set up all around the barn.

"Welcome," a cheery voice greeted me.

I smiled at the woman, about my age, with short light-brown hair poking out from beneath a Santa hat. "Cute place you've got here."

"Oh, thanks. We do love the holidays." She pointed around the barn. "Real quick, we have clothing and household items up in the loft at the back. Frozen and refrigerated foods are in the cases on that wall. On this side, we've got packaged food, various ingredients, and great seasonings. The tables scattered around hold various health-and-beauty supplies, jewelry, and tons of other awesome gifts." She paused to think, then shrugged. "You're sure to find something I'm forgetting. I'm Nicola, by the way." She handed me a black wire handbasket. "Feel free to ask if you need help with anything and come back for another basket if you fill that one. We'll hold the full one behind the counter for you. Carly is also circulating around the main floor, and I think I saw Aunt Gwynne helping us in the loft today."

I started at the shelves of packaged foods, and my attention immediately zeroed in on pasta shaped like tiny apples. A recipe on the back called for Granny Smith apples, caramelized onions, bacon, and cheddar cheese. All things I liked, especially the bacon and cheese. The pasta went into the basket for Tripp. I also added apple butter, interesting herb blends I thought he might like to experiment with, and applewood chips to throw on the grill. Then I spotted a set of applewood serving boards that loosely resembled two people nestled against each other. They made me think of Tripp and me, so I added them to the basket too. If I was in any other store, the sheer volume of apple things would be over the top. Here, it was just enough.

The health-and-beauty table held some of the same products they sold at Silver Moon Apothecary, including the *Ease* essential oil blend I'd sniffed earlier. They must use the same distributor.

After scouring every display on the lower level, I headed up into the loft. The first thing I saw there was an applewood keepsake box shaped like a triple moon goddess symbol. The crescent moons slid to the sides to allow the full moon at the center to flip up. It would be the perfect place for Morgan to store her scrying mirror pendant and other treasures, so in the basket it went.

Next I came to a table piled high with super cozy-looking blankets in a variety of colors and sizes. I didn't see an apple on any of them, but a little sign on the table indicated they were hand-knit by a local woman. The charcoal-gray lap blanket looked like a great gift for Martin, and I grabbed a second in navy blue for our other deputy.

My basket was overflowing at that point and getting quite heavy, so I set it on the floor to search through a display of sweatshirts, T-shirts, tote bags, and mugs with either *WW* or *AF* in a font that resembled apple tree branches. Or perhaps blackthorn branches. Below the WW in a smaller font was *Warren Witches, Applewood Farm, Blackwood Grove, WI*. Beneath the AF was simply *Applewood Farm, Blackwood Grove, WI*. I chose black waffle weave WW hoodies for myself and Morgan as a memento of our weekend.

Then I noticed I'd made a real mess of both the blanket

and shirt tables. I bent to set the hoodies on top of the basket and when I stood again, both tables were neat and tidy.

My jaw dropped, and I glanced at a woman with wild gray hair dressed all in linen standing nearby. She'd been at the saloon with Dusty last night too. "Those tables were just messed up, weren't they?"

"It took us a while to get that spell right," she replied. "At first, items just got ripped out of customers' hands when they picked them up to look at them. Or they'd set things in their baskets, and the items would fly back to the shelves." She tapped her forehead. "Both the mind and the magic go a little wonky as you get older."

I stared at her. "The . . . um . . . what?"

She slapped her hand over her mouth. Through splayed fingers, she whispered, "Oops. I'm not supposed to say things like that."

"You're not supposed to say things like that," I repeated. A sigh escaped me, and I muttered mostly to myself, "I think *my* mind has gone wonky."

"That's possible," she answered, "but you're quite young so probably not. For me, it's like my brain gets tired and goes to sleep at inconvenient moments. Although, my brain is seventy-eight years old and entitled to nap whenever it wants to as far as I'm concerned. How old is your brain?"

"Twenty-eight next month," I murmured, wondering how I kept stumbling into these odd situations.

The woman swatted a hand at me. "*Pfft.* Like I said, you're probably fine. I'm Gwynne, by the way."

Feeling infinitesimally better after her comment, I asked, "Aunt Gwynne?"

"Right." Her smile faded slightly. "Do I know you?"

"No. Nicola told me you were working in the shop today." I gazed a little longer at the woman. There was a shadow of confusion behind her eyes that made me sad. "Are you one of the Warren Witches?"

She held the edges of her long linen vest out to the side and curtsied. "Gwynne Warren. Pleased to meet you."

I bowed my head in return. "Jayne O'Shea. I'm here for the weekend with my friend Morgan—"

The shadow cleared away. "From Whispering Pines! Oh, Silver and Moon have been talking for weeks about the famous Morgan. I haven't met her yet, but it's lovely to make your acquaintance, Miss Jayne."

"And yours." I pointed at my basket and adopted the tone of a rabid fan purchasing merchandise from a favorite celebrity. "I'm buying two of your shirts for Morgan and me."

She raised her chin and waggled her shoulders side to side. "Well, we are kind of a big deal around here."

I liked this woman. And I felt like I could trust her. "Can I ask you a strange question?"

"You'd be surprised how many people ask me that exact thing." She held out her hand as though to say *please, ask away*.

I told her about how since arriving last night I was certain I'd witnessed a woman get trapped by the door at the saloon, a table clear itself, and my coffee cup never emptying no matter how much I drank. "And now the merchandise on these tables appear to have straightened all on their own. I'm *sure* I saw those things . . ."

"But?"

"Did I really?"

"Or are you hallucinating? Have you slipped a cog? Do you need to be fitted for a jacket with long arms?" Gwynne teased with a grin. After a long pause, she said, "Silver and Moon reported that remarkable and unexplainable things happened in your village when they were there."

I opened my mouth to object that the things I had witnessed here were nothing like what happened in Whispering Pines, but the words wouldn't come.

Instead, I thought of all the people who felt summoned to

a village in the middle of Wisconsin's Northwoods they'd never even heard of. Then once they got there, it turned out to be the exact place they needed to be at that exact moment in their lives. I thought of our natural spring that somehow washed away troubles. Then I thought of how the trees whispered to . . . well, me. I hadn't heard anyone else make that claim.

"Magic," Gwynne began gently, "in whatever form it takes, is a hard thing to accept, isn't it? Many people believe there is magic in the holiday season. Children especially are sure of it, and the rest of us tend to nod and agree with them. Then, at some point, we stop believing and agreeing. As adults, if the magic happens here"—she tapped her head and then her chest—"we call it divine intervention or accept it as trusting in a higher power. Here or here"—she set one shaky finger next to one of her eyes and another next to an ear—"we dismiss it as, 'My eyes are playing tricks on me' or 'I'm hearing things' or 'I must be losing my mind' or 'I've been really stressed lately and not getting enough sleep.'"

My cheeks flushed warmly, and I stared at her for a long moment, processing her words. "I'm not sure you answered my question, but I like what you said."

She sandwiched my hand between hers and patted it. "Trust what you believe, Jayne. And it's okay to question what you see."

An elderly woman in our village, Mallory, *believed* there were fairies roaming our woods even though none of the rest of us ever saw them. Another villager, Reeva, spoke lightheartedly sometimes about the *frolic of fairies* in the trees in her backyard. We chuckled and dismissed it as her goofing around. But what if she wasn't? What if she saw them too? Why did we accept without question that Mallory saw the creatures but barely acknowledge that Reeva might as well? Why was it okay for children or childlike adults to believe in magical things but not "normal" adults?

"Thank you for your thoughts, Gwynne. I think I need to sit with them for a while."

"As you should."

She helped me carry everything down to the checkout counter.

"Looks like you needed that second basket," Nicola noted.

"Nah," I answered with a wink. "I found Gwynne instead. A much better solution."

Chapter Seven

I'd no sooner left Applewood Farm's driveway when I realized I didn't get a bottle of the *Ease* oil. If I'd experienced anything truly magical today, it was the way that scent instantly eased my tension. It had become a chore to carry all my purchases, however, and I doubted my arms would hold out for too much longer. I could grab a bottle at the apothecary tomorrow. That turned out to be the right call, because by the time I was back at the inn, my arms were aching from the weight. Maybe I should have taken Nicola up on her offer to deliver my bags to our suite.

"Looks like you had a successful day," the woman behind the counter said when I walked in the front door. "Let me help you. I'm Irene, by the way."

"Jayne." I considered being a martyr and finishing the job myself, then gladly relinquished half my load to her. As we climbed the stairs, she commented that the inn was booked solid until after New Year's, and I told her we had a similar situation at our B&B.

"Oh, you're in the biz." She stood in the open doorway of the suite, and we shared stories about memorable guests.

I considered telling her I was also a deputy, but that would have changed the whole tone of our conversation. It was nice to just be Jayne the B&B owner for a few days. "We've only been open a little more than a year, but so far, we're really happy we made the decision to go for it. My boyfriend is a natural at innkeeping."

Irene glanced at her watch and frowned. "Wish I could stand here and chat more with you, but I should get back downstairs. New guests will be arriving shortly."

"Before you go, can I ask a question?"

"Sure. Wait, let me guess. You *saw* something today?"

Gwynne told me to trust what I believed and not be afraid to question what I saw. I told Silver and Moon I needed proof in order to really believe things. So I had to gather more evidence to figure out what to believe about this town.

"Something I heard actually. Someone said Blackwood Grove is a safe town?"

Silver and Moon gave me a full explanation, but I'd play dumb to see if Irene agreed with them.

She gave no indication that my question was odd or that I was being gullible. Instead, as factually as stating snow was white and the sky blue, she said, "Witches live here. I won't name names. There are too many non-witch folks who will attack or abuse those who have abilities. Not saying that you would . . ."

"No offense taken," I assured her. "Can you tell me about them? The witches, I mean."

"Yes." She drew out the word as though trying to decide how to proceed. "Some of our witches have nature skills, like those who work at the apple orchard or on the farms. Others have the ability to see into the past or future. Some can locate lost objects or missing people. A few can communicate with those who are no longer with us. Then there are those who can sense things about people or places with a simple touch."

The simple touch comment made me immediately think of Russell. He had put his hand on my back to guide me to the counter and seemed to freeze for a moment. Had he sensed something about me?

"That's just a sampling of their abilities," Irene continued. "They really are a talented bunch, and to tell the truth, I'm a little envious." Her face glowed in a fangirl way. "Being around them is partly why I decided to move here."

Lily Grace channeled my grandmother during a séance once. She also got readings about me or a case I was working on if she touched me. Like Russell seemed to. Morgan, Briar, and the other green witches worked with nature. The kitchen witches could do amazing things with food. The fortune tellers could see into the past or future. They all could cast blessings that cleansed an area of bad energy, and those blessings were even more powerful if they performed them together. Many of the people who visited us felt that the village itself held a sort of magic.

"What about Blackwood Grove?" I asked.

"You mean does the town have abilities?" She shook her head. "Only the witches. The Warren property seems to have an aura of magic if you want to call it that. They say that's because so many family members and friends died there over the years and their spirits have remained. The rumor is that they joined into a single entity and give a sort of personality to the place. I can't say if that's true or not, because I've never been inside the farmhouse, but I understand it's an experience."

Whispering Pines had only been around for fifty years, but many people, villagers and tourists alike, had died there. Not long after moving there, I came to believe with all my heart that the village itself was as much a living thing as the trees surrounding it. It was a place like no other, and like Silver and Moon had, I noticed and accepted the "remarkable and unexplainable things" that happened there. Why was I fighting that the same could be true here?

"People think the Warrens' diner has a similar sort of aura," Irene added and chuckled. "Guess it was getting crowded at the farmhouse, so a few spirits moved down the street."

"The Warrens own the diner. I hadn't realized that." If what *they say* was true, that explained some of what I experienced there. "I heard there are other safe towns. Are they all like Blackwood Grove?"

Irene tilted her head side to side, weighing her response. "On the surface, I guess. Their witches have the same sorts of abilities ours do. But every town, safe or ordinary, is different in its own way, isn't it?" When I nodded but remained silent, she asked, "Have I answered your questions adequately?"

"You have. Thank you, Irene."

"I'll be down at the desk. If you'd like to chat some more, about witches, safe towns, B&Bs, or whatever, feel free to grab a coffee and come on down."

I considered her offer, and while I was more at ease, I still felt unsettled. Other than spending time with Tripp, there were three ways I decompressed—walking among my pine trees, staring up at the stars and moon, or being near water. It was still daytime, so no stars to gaze at yet. I could go for a hike or go wander around the apple orchard, but I really wanted quiet and stillness. That left water, which meant sitting by the river.

With my new book and travel mug full of hot cocoa in hand, I headed downstairs.

"Heading out again?" Irene asked a little sadly. Guess she wanted to chat more.

"Thought I'd sit by the river for a bit."

"Nice idea." She pointed across the street. "We have a small landing over there with a couple chairs and a portable heater. Hang on." She stepped into a small room or storage closet behind her and returned with a wool blanket. "It's a little chilly. You can borrow this."

I thanked her, crossed the street, and descended a short staircase. The dock was snug with just enough room for the chairs and heater. I'd seen a larger boat dock across the street from the diner, but it had a lot of traffic with people going down to get closer to the water. This little one was hidden from view and currently vacant. After turning on the heater and tucking the blanket around my legs, I stared at the water flowing slowly by and exhaled. I tried to read my book, but the river kept drawing my attention, so I closed it and let the setting relax me. A lone leaf floated by. The empty tree branches gave me peeks at the slowly darkening western sky. Tiny bits of snow remained around on the shadowy sides of trees and rocks. The sun had melted it everywhere else as though reminding us that its time in the sky would soon start growing longer each day. Morgan was right, there was beauty in every season.

After what felt like only a few minutes of sitting there watching the sun set through the tree branches, the lamp post on the street above turned on. Another few minutes and the sky turned full dark. Snow started to fall softly, the flakes staying on my mittens just long enough for me to admire before melting into the wool. The next thing I knew, the alarm on my cell phone was alerting me that it was time to meet Morgan for dinner. If I didn't have Lucy Lake in my backyard at home, it would have been painful to leave the little dock.

I returned the blanket to Geoffrey, who was now working at the registration desk.

"Your cheeks and nose are bright red," he noted. "How long were you out there?"

"I'm not sure," I answered. "Two or three hours, I think. Isn't it great how nature can totally absorb us at times?"

He tipped his head in agreement. "Regardless of whether

you're on it or near it, the river will wash your worries downstream."

I paused, thinking of The Well in Whispering Pines, and smiled. After bringing my book and mug to the suite, I headed through the still falling snow to The Paddle Wheel, purposely getting there a few minutes early so I could gather more evidence. This time about that door.

Chapter Eight

S tella was working behind the bar tonight instead of as the bouncer. I chose a barstool and treated myself to a hot buttered rum, made with apple cider instead of hot water. Yum! When Stella had a break between orders, I asked her about the door.

"What about it?" she seemed confused.

"We were here last night—"

"Oh yeah, I remember. I gave you free poppers."

"Right. I'm just a little confused about what happened with the woman who got squeezed between it and the doorjamb. Was it meant to do that?"

She smiled slyly and, like any good bartender, didn't give away any secrets. "Kinda cool, wasn't it? That woman had dashed on us twice before, so she was on our radar."

And that was all she said.

I debated pushing her for more of an answer, but at this point, she could tell me it was a button behind the bar, and I'd believe her. She could say Dusty had somehow zapped it with a bolt of energy at just the right time, and I'd probably believe that too. She could tell me the frolic of fairies flew down here from Reeva's backyard, and I'd accept it. Maybe. Ultimately, it didn't matter. Something happened . . . and justice was restored. I'd leave it at that.

Morgan arrived just as I was finishing my drink, and we decided to sit at the bar to eat tonight. She never stopped smiling as she told me about her day with Silver and Moon. In fact, she went on for so long, our food arrived and she was still gushing about it. "They were just so excited and grateful to learn anything I could offer."

"I'm glad you were helpful to them."

She gave a contented sigh. "You seem a little more relaxed."

"I sat by the river for three hours. Maybe less."

"Ah. A water infusion for my nature girl."

That wasn't me at all two years ago. Whispering Pines, both the people who lived there and the village itself, changed my entire life.

"Something's still bothering you," she stated while digging into her bowl of quinoa and roasted autumn veggies. "Did you have success shopping?"

"I had great luck," I admitted and stirred the beef stew I'd chosen to help it cool a little.

She set down her fork and turned toward me. "What happened?"

"Nothing *happened*. Not to me, at least. There were all these unusual things going on around me, though."

"What do you mean by unusual?"

She retrieved her fork and ate silently while waiting for me to explain. I decided it would be easiest to just give her the chronological sequence of events, but as I organized my thoughts, the *things* didn't seem so odd anymore. Probably because no matter who I talked to about them—Gwynne, Irene, Stella—no one saw anything strange about them. It typically took three days for people to become completely enchanted and accepting of Whispering Pines. When they left, they'd insist it was the most magical, wonderful, restful place they'd ever been and vowed to come back again and again. After a little more than twenty-four hours here, especially after the last six or so, the line between unusual and normal had blurred.

Instead of telling her about the events, I asked, "Do you believe in magic?"

She actually covered her mouth and laughed out loud. "You know how I feel about nature and universal magic."

"Yeah, but I'm talking about the kind I always assumed to be fictitious."

"Fictitious," she repeated. "Funny, I recall when you first came to the village, one of your favorite words was *woo-woo*. You spoke disbelievingly about the woo-woo going on and how crazy it was that everyone thought they could make things happen by putting their trust in karma. I couldn't tell you when you stopped using that word or when your feelings changed, but as far as I can tell, you're now completely on board with the magic of Whispering Pines. In fact, there are many times when I've heard you say, give it three days."

I dunked a big chunk of biscuit into my stew's gravy and shoved it in my mouth.

"Tell me about the tarot reading Pepper gave you."

"It was a lot more intense than I expected," I began. "First, she gave me ideas for things to think about while I shuffled the cards. Like past, present, future type things. Working through a challenging situation seemed most appropriate for my world, so I shuffled and then laid down three cards. Pepper said the cards indicated I was frustrated because I kept running into obstacles, that I was heading in the right direction, but I needed to let go and stop trying to do it all myself."

Morgan's eyebrows shot up, and she choked on her food. She grabbed her water to wash it down, then said, "I'm not sure the fortune tellers at home could have done better."

"Right? Gotta say, it freaked me out." I speared a carrot

chunk from my stew bowl. "The thing is, I don't know how to let go."

"Why?"

That's not what I expected her to say. I figured she'd insist *of course you do* and give me ideas for proceeding. As I thought about my answer, it occurred to me that this was the crucial point in our conversation where if we were home, someone would come up to say hi or sit down at our table and we'd never circle back around to finishing the topic. How nice to know we could probably sit on our barstools until closing time and work through our crises without being interrupted. Well, my crises. Morgan seemed to have everything under control. Except motherhood, but I couldn't help with that.

"I think," I began, "I'm afraid that someone else will get hurt. I'd rather do it all myself than risk that."

Morgan signaled Stella for a refill on her club soda, then said, "How about we practice? Let's work through a potential problem you might encounter at home."

"There's a potential problem going on here." I told her about Amy and how I was worried she was in danger with Craig.

"What did you do about it?"

"I spoke with Russell and Maggie at the teashop, because they witnessed an incident there this morning. They promised to pay close attention if the two come in again."

"Very good. You got someone else involved. Now let them handle it."

I shook my head. "That goes completely against my training. My job is to serve and protect, and even though I'm not a cop here, I can't just let it go."

She sipped her club soda, then asked, "Do you suppose they have police officers here? If you truly feel this woman is in danger, would it help to speak with them?"

I gaped at her. "Why didn't I think of that?"

"Because you have a hard time asking for help. We just

talked about that." She grinned at me. "You have a solution, so I say use the tarot's advice, talk to someone here who can take over, and then step away."

I sopped up the last of my gravy with my last bite of biscuit. "Why am I always the one who needs therapy?"

She laughed again. "You don't need therapy. You question and analyze things instead of just accepting what doesn't fit with your beliefs. That's a good thing. And you're willing to alter your beliefs when new information is presented."

That was quite possibly the best answer she could have given me. I bumped my shoulder against hers. "I love you, you know."

She pressed her shoulder against mine. "Now, we only have a day and a half before we need to go home. Let's enjoy ourselves."

We kicked that off by asking Stella which dessert we should get.

"You're in an apple-themed town," she stated as though the answer was obvious.

"Apple pie?" I asked.

Stella looked both ways then leaned across the counter. "Don't get the pie here. If that's what you want, go to the diner. There's none better. *Anywhere.*"

"Well, we're here and comfortable on our barstools," Morgan declared, "so I will have an apple dumpling."

"Apple crumble with vanilla ice cream for me," I requested.

While we waited for our desserts to arrive, two women came up to the bar to order drinks. As Stella got them, one of the women said, "This will be the fourth Christmas."

"I know," the other said. "Try not to lose hope."

Stella came back with two bottles of beer, and the first woman handed her a twenty. "Keep the change."

"You're sure? That's double what you owe," Stella advised.

"I'm sure," she answered. "Merry Christmas."

"And to you." Stella touched her hand over her heart.

As they turned to walk away, the woman told her friend, "That's about as jolly as I can get. I'm trying, but I swear it's going to take a freaking Christmas miracle for me to ever get in the holiday spirit again. I just can't. Not without my Jamie."

Or did she say Amy?

Chapter Nine

M organ heard the name too. "You know what the chances are."

I turned to look at the women as they headed for the pool tables near the front door. I estimated them to both be in their late forties or early fifties. One of them—Her mother? An aunt?—had the same narrow eyes and puffy lips as Amy. Maybe that meant Amy hadn't been strung out on anything. Knowing she might have all her faculties in place eased my mind somewhat. It meant that, if necessary, she might be able to fight back against Craig.

My heart raced as I replied to Morgan, "I think we can both agree the chance of that being a coincidence is slim."

"Jayne," Morgan replied, her voice full of caution.

"Oh, come on. This feels like the Universe begging me to get involved."

Something behind me caught her attention. She sighed and jutted her chin at whatever it was. "There's a police officer in the other room. Talk to him. It would be cruel to go to that woman and get her hopes up."

She was right about that.

I crossed the saloon to Officer Balinski, according to his

name badge, and asked if I could speak with him privately. He led me to a quiet corner, and I introduced myself as a deputy and showed him my badge. I pointed out the woman with long auburn hair and told him about Amy and Craig.

"Might be nothing," I concluded.

"But Christmas miracles do happen," he said.

I froze at his echoing of the words the woman just used. "Sounds like this would be a good one."

He asked for descriptions of Amy and Craig and wrote them in his notebook. "I'm off duty for the night, but I'll go back to the station and see if we've got anything in the system on them."

"Any chance you'll let me know if something comes of this?" I pleaded. "You know we rarely get to know the outcome of these things. I'd really like to know about this one if possible."

"I'll tell you what I can when I can," he promised. "How long will you be here?"

"One more day. Heading back Sunday morning. We're staying at the inn, and after that, you can reach me at the Whispering Pines sheriff's station."

"Whispering Pines," he repeated, adding that to his notes. "Up north. What brings you here?"

I pointed out Morgan waiting at the bar. "My friend came to help Silver and Moon at their apothecary. I tagged along to decompress."

He smiled. "Is it working?"

"Sort of." I glanced over at the woman who resembled Amy. "A Christmas miracle would seal the deal for me."

"I'll see what I can do about that." He shook my hand. "Pleasure to meet you, Deputy O'Shea. Hopefully, I'll be in touch soon."

As we walked back to The Barge on Inn, through just enough fluffy snow to make the town look like a winter wonderland, I told Morgan what Officer Balinski had said. I inhaled a long breath of chilly air and blew it out in a big cloud. "I feel lighter."

"I promise I'm not trying to be a little black rain cloud, but—"

"I know. Really. This might not be anything, but just think if it is."

She squeezed my elbow, locked with hers, tighter to her side. "That would be wonderful."

In our suite, we changed into our jammies, turned on the fireplace, and settled into the same spots as last night. She told me more about her day with Moon and Silver. I told her about the stores I'd gone to today, and she noted the ones she for sure wanted to visit tomorrow on a fresh mall map.

"I'd like to make a quick stop at the apothecary," I said. "They have an essential oil called Ease that really calmed me. Unless you have something similar at Shoppe Mystique."

"My specialty is tea and crystals, so if you found an oil blend from someone else that works for you, feel free to purchase it." She winked and added, "Feel free to purchase others' tea, too, just don't tell me about it."

The next morning, neither of us were especially hungry, so coffee, fruit, and pastries in the morning room off the inn's lobby was enough for breakfast.

"First stop is the apothecary?" Morgan confirmed while adding milk to her tea.

"Right. Shouldn't take more than a minute or two."

"Jayne?"

I turned to find Officer Balinski coming over to our little table by a window overlooking the river. My hopeful heart skipped a beat as I stood. "Do you have good news?"

"Not yet, but I wanted to verify everything you told me yesterday." He read what he'd written and added a couple of details. "Okay. That's all I needed."

"Did you find anything helpful last night?" My sparkly outlook after talking with him at the saloon led to a really good night's sleep. His stern demeanor this morning, however, was tarnishing my sparkle.

"Nothing I want to report yet."

"To report *yet*," I repeated. "Does that mean you found something regarding Amy?"

The look in his eyes gave away nothing. "Like I said last night, I'll let you know what I can when I can. I'm sure you understand."

I didn't like being on this side of an investigation. "I do."

* * *

"I don't remember selling *that* much yesterday," Silver said, checking their essential oil stock. "We must have, though, because I can't find anymore bottles of Ease. Sorry, Jayne."

"Check at The Apple Barn," Moon suggested. "Dusty makes it for us, so they'll probably have some."

"That explains why they carry some of the same health-and-beauty items you do." I asked Morgan, "Do you want to go with me?"

"Absolutely," she said with a decisive nod. "I've heard so much about this place, I'd feel like I missed out on something if I don't experience it."

We took a left out of the shop and walked toward the scary hedge.

Morgan stepped closer to investigate it, reaching toward but not touching one of the thorns. "A prick from one of these can result in a rather serious bacterial infection. It's said that these bushes are where the curse in the *Sleeping Beauty* fairy tale came from."

"The pricking of her finger," I said with a smile. "Truth in fiction. Love it."

I led her to the road and up the driveway on the other side. Today, a woman wearing jeans and an *Applewood Farms* tunic met us at the door.

"That's a really popular blend this time of year with all the craziness of the holidays," Carly said searching their display. "Hmm. Looks like we're out too."

Disappointed, I replied, "Well, that's good for you. Can I order some for you to send to me?"

"I have a better idea. My cousin, Dusty, is in her Sanctuary. Since we need more anyway, let's go see if she'll whip some up. Let me grab my jacket from the back and track down Nicola to watch the register."

"I'll wait for you here," Morgan said. "I want to look around."

Carly led me toward the locked gate I noticed yesterday. It opened as we approached. "It knows me," she explained.

Right. Or she had a sensor in her pocket that signaled it to open.

As we continued past the big farmhouse and toward an adorable white carriage house with a small, covered porch, I asked, "What's the Sanctuary?"

"It's Dusty's workshop. She makes all her potions and spells up there."

On the other side of the apple-green front door was a wooden staircase leading up to the second floor.

"Dusty?" Carly called. "Are you up there?"

"I am," came Dusty's reply.

"Is it okay for me to bring Jayne up?" Once she got the approval, she told me, "It's rare for an Ordy to be allowed up there."

This felt weird. Were other customers brought to the Sanctuary when the shop ran out of products? And when did I tell Carly my name?

At the top of the stairs was a single large room with mismatched shelving and cabinets lining the walls that looked worn from hundreds of years of use. Each one was a different color—red, jade, purple, or sapphire—so they had a collected over time feel. Each was stuffed to capacity with small apothecary-style bottles, baskets, books, and wooden boxes. Dried plants hung from beams in the ceiling. At the center of the room was a massive wood table covered with mixing bowls, a mortar and pestle, candles, loose papers, and a grimoire on a stand.

"What a great vibe," I murmured.

"You should have seen it before it changed." Carly's tone was the same as Nina's when she implied the diner had decorated itself.

Dusty was sitting in the far corner in a wingback chair next to a huge fireplace with a happily crackling fire. Her head tilted quizzically when she saw me, then she recalled, "We met at the diner."

"I've seen you at other places around town as well," I noted. "Jayne O'Shea."

"We're out of Ease oil," Carly told Dusty, "and Jayne would like some."

Dusty stood and set the old leather book she'd been reading on the chair. "That won't take long." She took a handled basket from beneath the big table, went to the far side of the room, and started plucking bottles off the shelves and placing them in the basket. Then she set the bottles from the basket in a row on her table, and like an old-timey scientist, started carefully drizzling oils into an old glass beaker. "You must be who my dream was about."

"Your dream?." Then I recalled Silver telling me about Dusty's post-cognitive dreams.

"They're more rare, but I do have pre-cognitive ones as well," she said as though adjusting my thoughts. "I saw a little white dog running after something pink. That one was more obscure than normal. Usually, they're simple and visually clear, so I can tell exactly who or what the dream is about. This one needs interpretation. Does it mean anything to you?"

If I hadn't been used to Lily Grace's bizarre visions, this would have freaked me out. "I have a West Highland White

Terrier named Meeka. Since I got here, I've been crossing paths with a woman named Amy—"

"Of course." Dusty's hands dropped to her table as though I'd turned on a lightbulb for her. "The woman with pink hair. What do you know about her?"

"Not much, but I'm almost positive something is very wrong between her and her boyfriend. Or whoever this Craig guy is." I told her what I'd observed. To be honest, Dusty intimidated me a little, so I was happy to know something about this situation she didn't.

"This is my favorite part," Carly said, nodding at her cousin.

We watched silently as Dusty added small crystal chips to the beaker and swirled the contents. After a few seconds, the liquid inside flashed a serene shade of blue-green and then returned to its previous colorless state.

"All ready," Dusty proclaimed.

She poured the beaker's contents into small bottles and started adding labels when a music rang out from somewhere. She pulled a cellphone from a pocket on her cross-back apron.

From the way she answered, she was familiar with the caller. As she listened, a furrow between her eyebrows deepened and she nodded along with whatever was being said. After a minute, she replied, "Understood. The Sweet Spot and bring Jayne."

I stiffened at the mention of my name. When she hung up, I asked, "What's going on?"

"We need to meet Beau at the bakery in forty-five minutes," Dusty explained.

"Who's Beau?"

"Officer Balinski."

My heart rate picked up in a hopeful way. I noted the time on my watch. "Why am I supposed to come? Does this have something to do with Amy?"

"It does. You'll find out more when you get there."

I didn't like being involved with something and not knowing the details.

She finished applying labels to the bottles and returned the oils to the shelves, saying something about them ending up in the wrong place if she didn't do it herself. Then she divided the new bottles of Ease between two brown paper bags. She gave one bag to Carly.

"The other bag is for Silver and Moon. I'll drop it off when we walk past. And this is my gift to you." She handed me one of the bottles.

"Thank you. Before we go to the bakery, I need to stop by The Apple Barn and get my friend, Morgan. She's doing some Yule shopping there."

"No rush," Dusty replied. "We've got time."

Inside the barn, Morgan had just stepped up to the checkout. While I waited, I noticed ten bottles of Ease on the table with the other blends.

"It was the strangest thing," Nicola said when I asked about them. "I found those right after you and Carly left. They were just right there."

I suspected the same would be true at the apothecary. Why did I feel like this had been some kind of setup? To bring Dusty and me together? Why? Whatever was going on, I definitely wanted Morgan with me at The Sweet Spot.

"We'll deliver this to The Barge on Inn for you this afternoon," Nicola told Morgan and added a tag with our suite number to the stuffed-full shopping bag.

Morgan thanked her then told me, "This place is a treasure. Are we ready to move along?"

After thanking Nicola for her help and waving at Gwynne, who looked down at us from the balcony, we followed Dusty around to the back side of the barn.

"Don't we have to go down to the street?" I asked as we headed straight for the hedge. Then I noticed a path worn into the grass that appeared to run straight through the prickly branches.

When she was inches away, Dusty held out her hand, and like an electric door on a building, a section of the hedge shivered and slid in on itself.

"It knows those of us who live here," Dusty explained at our shocked expressions. Or mine, at least. Nothing seemed to surprise Morgan.

We stopped for two minutes at the apothecary. Yes, they had found more oil, too, but were happy to take the fresh bottles as well. Then we started down the path toward The Sweet Spot.

"We've still got half an hour," Dusty said, checking her watch. "I've got a couple of things to take care of first, so I'll meet you back here."

"Hang on." Anxiety was building inside me. "Whatever this is, it feels big. Can you tell me something? Anything?"

She looked me in the eye and placed a hand on my arm. "Jayne, please, trust me. We've got everything under control. I'll be back in thirty minutes."

Who was *we*? Her and Officer Balinski? Before I could ask, she turned and sped off.

I glanced at Morgan, who only shrugged.

Guess I didn't have any other choice than to . . . relinquish control and let Dusty take the lead. My tarot reading was coming into play, and I hadn't even left Blackwood Grove yet.

Chapter Ten

T hirty minutes felt more like thirty hours. Time ticked by like a clock with wearing-down batteries. I followed Morgan around Dapper, where she found something "perfect" for River. I didn't even pay attention to what it was. All I could think about was what would happen at The Sweet Spot. By the time she was done at that shop, we still had ten minutes before we had to meet Dusty.

"I'm working off a ton of nervous energy," I told her. "Let's get over to the bakery so I can get something to eat before whatever this is goes down."

"Good idea." She patted her tote bag. "I need to pump as well, so I hope they have a place where I can sit."

The wife and husband owners were more than happy to let Morgan use their office in back.

"It's very comfy," Kelsey assured. "My quiet place when things get crazy on the sales floor. Come with me."

I got a mocha and a chocolate peppermint brownie and chose a table toward the back of the dining area to devour my chocolate fix.

A few minutes later, Craig and Amy walked in and got in

line. He seemed very smug about something. More importantly, Amy looked even worse than she had yesterday.

Unwilling to sit by any longer, I went up to the counter to get another napkin and overheard Craig say, "I won two free drinks and doughnuts."

"Congratulations," Kelsey praised, taking the coupon he set on the counter.

As I turned to go back to my table, I met Amy's eyes. I was about to ask if she was okay, but she shook her head in short, crisp bursts. Her eyebrows pinched together as though she was scared or in pain. Either way, her message was clear: please don't say anything.

I put my hand to my heart, hoping she realized that meant I was here to help. I returned to my table and sat where I could see her, and she could clearly see me. As Kelsey reviewed the options with them, Amy looked back at me. Craig jabbed her with his elbow and directed her attention back to Kelsey. Then, while he pointed out exactly which pastries he wanted, Amy gave me the sign I'd been waiting for.

She held her hand behind her back, palm facing me, fingers spread wide. She folded her thumb to her palm then methodically opened and closed her fingers over it three times. The hand signal for *I need help*. Or *I'm in danger*. Or *please help me*.

Less than a minute later, they walked right past me. I met her eyes again and nodded. Message received. Craig led her to the only available table. It was in the farthest corner and had a reserved sign on it, but he pushed it aside and sat anyway.

I had to wait for the right moment. If I acted too quickly, it could all go badly. If I waited too long, she could be gone again. I sat and sipped my mocha, barely tasting it. Craig wasn't big, but he was bigger than me and looked quite muscular, so I'd likely lose a physical altercation. That meant somehow I had to lure Amy away from him. Just as a plan was coming together, backup arrived. Dusty walked in and directly to my table.

"That's her." I casually pointed out Amy who was sitting with her side to us. "She just flashed me the hand signal for help. I've got a plan. If you stand near the door—"

"Amy Beeler?" Dusty called out as though seeing an old acquaintance.

Beeler?

As I sat there wondering how she knew Amy's last name, Amy sat straight and said, "I'm Amy." She half stood and Craig hissed at her to sit down, then told Dusty to, "Get lost, lady."

I started to repeat my plan to Dusty, but she crossed halfway to their table and spread her arms wide. "I haven't seen you in forever. Come give me a hug, girl."

Amy looked over her shoulder at Dusty, then shot a glance at me. When I nodded it was okay, she rose half way out of her chair.

Craig said something I couldn't hear that made Amy sink back down.

Her desperate expression suggested this was the best chance she'd had to get away from this man. What control did he have over her? Was she afraid he'd harm her physically? Did he have some sort of psychological hold over her? Had he threatened someone she loved? Whatever it was, I wasn't going to let her leave this building with him. When she dared a looked at me again, I nodded more urgently and mouthed, "Go!"

She was out of her chair and halfway to Dusty before Craig realized she had moved. He stood, ready to charge after her, and froze. As in, it was like his feet had become stuck to the ground. At the same time, Dusty stood like some sort of witchy superhero with her hand held out to him in a stop gesture. It was impossible, but it somehow seemed she was preventing him from moving despite his clear struggle to free his feet from the floor.

As one curse word after another streamed from his mouth, Amy started to panic. She went to his side, and soothed, "No, it's okay, baby, everything's fine."

"It's not fine," I said, standing next to Dusty. "I saw your signal."

"Your what?" Craig demanded. "What did you do?"

Amy stared at him and then Dusty, a debate clearly playing out in her mind. She was obviously scared of what would happen if she left with him but equally terrified of what would happen if she didn't.

"I didn't do anything," Amy insisted. "I have no idea who this woman is, but she doesn't know what she's talking about." She knelt and tried to free Craig's feet, but they were well and truly stuck to the floor. Then she tried to undo his boot laces, but they wouldn't untie. "Let him go," she hollered, glaring at Dusty.

Behind us, customers were gathering, ready to act if necessary. But would they help us or Craig?

Before anyone could do anything more, the front door opened, and Officer Balinski entered. He strode straight over to Craig and put handcuffs on him. "Craig Kerr, I'm arresting you for the unlawful restraint of Amy Beeler."

"What?" Amy objected and tried to shove the officer away. "No, leave him alone. It's not like that."

Unable to stand there and do nothing for another second, I pulled her away from the men. "It's okay, Amy. You're safe."

"Of course I'm safe." In a low tone, she insisted, "Please, let it go. Ignore what I did."

I held her gaze but said nothing. After a few seconds, she stopped trying to get around me and all the fight left her body. She would have dropped to the ground if I hadn't held her up. I guided her to a chair and stayed at her side until Dusty lowered her hand, and the officer led a still cursing Craig out of the shop.

Had she really held him in place with . . . the power of her mind? Could she perform hypnosis of some kind? Were there magnets in the floor? I could come up with a dozen crazy options but, instead, let it go. What happened happened, and sometimes it was easier to just accept things that couldn't be explained.

Morgan stepped out of the back room, paused at the scene playing out in the dining room, and then came over to Dusty and me. "I was gone for ten minutes. What happened?"

"I'm not entirely sure," I admitted.

Just then, another officer entered the shop, a young Black woman with a massive curly ponytail.

"Come with me," the officer gently told Amy. Her name tag read *L. Chapman*.

"Where?" Tears streamed down Amy's face as she stared, shaking and scared, at the officer. "What's going to happen to me?"

"Nothing bad," Dusty assured her. "I promise, everything will be fine."

As the officer escorted Amy out of the shop, Dusty said, "Come to the station. It's on River Road about a mile past the inn. You can't miss it."

She left before I could respond.

"Do you want to go with me," I asked Morgan, "or stay and do your shopping?"

"I'm going with you. I already missed out on something big. I'm not missing the rest of this."

She ordered a hot tea and pastry to go, and after a quick stop at the inn to drop off her shopping bags and breast pump, we hopped in the car and drove to the station. Dusty was right, it was easy to find. Inside, she met us in the lobby with Officer Chapman. They had Morgan and I sign in and then took us back to a conference style room. There, Amy was sitting with the woman from The Paddle Wheel who resembled her and two men.

"Amy's family," Dusty explained. "Mom, dad, and brother. They've been trying to get her away from Craig for almost four years. It apparently started with him not wanting to attend a significant family function, and her bowing out to stay with him. That led to him dictating when she could see them, speak with them, or even text them. He moved her every six months, give or take, so they never knew where she was. They made complaints to the police early on, but because Amy insisted she was fine, there was nothing the police could do."

"How did today happen?" I asked, unable to take my eyes off the family, who sat in such a tight circle their knees were all touching.

"You," Dusty answered.

Morgan placed her hand on my arm and gave it a squeeze.

"Me?"

"You noticed something was off," Dusty explained. "You trusted your instincts and took time to pay attention when you saw them around town."

Which was often. Almost as though we were purposely put on each other's paths.

"Amy also said you asked her if she was okay," Dusty continued, "which apparently no one else has ever done."

"It only takes one voice," Morgan added, "to start something."

Dusty nodded. "And in this case, the thing you started was giving Amy the spark of courage she needed to flash that hand signal at you. You cared once, she told us, so maybe you'd care again."

My heart swelled, and tears stung my eyes.

"As for everything else that played out," Dusty continued, "Beau told me his plan when he called me. We enlisted the shop owners' help. Beau printed out coupons for those free bakery items Craig said he'd won. Then Beau, Officer Chapman, and I dropped them off at the shops with descriptions of Amy and Craig. Amy's hair made them easy to identify. We enlisted the help of the customers at the bakery too. Beau wanted the couple to sit at that table in the corner so Craig couldn't make a run for it. Kelsey told every customer that table was reserved. I came in and did my thing, and Beau arrested Craig."

I blinked at her, stunned. "You three pulled all of that together that fast?"

Dusty shrugged. "It's amazing what can happen when you ask for help."

The biggest message from Pepper's tarot reading. Was this whole weekend one big Universal set up? "Can I talk with Amy?"

"Let me check with her," Officer Chapman said.

I watched through the big window on the conference room wall as she went inside and said something to Amy.

Amy spun to face us and then ran to the door. She threw herself into my arms and sobbed. "Thank you, thank you, thank you. I didn't think I'd ever see my family again." She pulled away but held my hands in both of hers. "I don't even know your name."

"I'm Jayne O'Shea. I live up north in Whispering Pines and am here for the weekend with my friend Morgan."

Morgan pressed her palms together. "We're so glad things worked out this way for you."

The next thing I knew, Amy's mom was pulling me into a hug. "A true Christmas miracle and you are our Christmas angel. We can never thank you enough."

Amy's father and brother hugged me next, each one filling my heart even more. They asked if there was any way they could thank me. As in a gift of some kind.

"I just wanted to get her away from him," I told them. "Your reunion and gratitude is the best gift I could get."

We chatted for a few more minutes, and then Officer Chapman walked Dusty, Morgan, and me to the lobby.

"How much longer are you here?" Dusty asked, following us to my car in the parking lot.

"We'll be leaving sometime tomorrow," Morgan told her. "We're not in a rush, but I promised to be home by dinnertime."

"Come to the farmhouse for breakfast in the morning," Dusty said. "I'd love a little more time to chat. You can meet my aunts." She narrowed her eyes then, creases crinkling the corners. "Or maybe you don't want to meet the aunts. They're a handful."

"Gwynne and Pepper are two of them, right?" I asked.

"Gwynne is my blood aunt. Pepper and Jett are close family friends, so it's easier to just include them under the auntie umbrella."

"Well, Gwynne and I had a nice little talk in The Apple Barn yesterday," I said, "and Pepper gave me an amazing tarot reading. I'd love to see them once more and meet the others."

Dusty gave a crisp nod. "All right, then. Is seven o'clock too early?"

"We're both up with the birds," Morgan assured. "Seven is fine."

"See you then. The gate will know to let you in."

"The gate will know," I repeated to Morgan when we got in the car. "Why do I feel like we could stay for another week and not understand this place?"

Morgan said nothing, which made me wonder if she knew things she wasn't sharing. Then again, I had thought that many times since meeting her.

Chapter Eleven

F or the rest of Saturday afternoon, Morgan and I wandered around the town and made great progress on our shopping lists.

"We should come back here next year," Morgan mused. "I got almost all my shopping done in one day."

I almost said it was like magic but let it go.

Bone-tired from the day, we decided to have dinner delivered to our suite that night, but when we got back there, we found we didn't need to order anything. Amy's family had found out, probably from Dusty or Officer Balinski, that we were staying at The Barge on Inn and had two huge baskets of food and another with both alcoholic and alcohol-free beverages delivered as a thank you for freeing Amy from her captor. There was even a holiday-themed bouquet that my green witch friend proclaimed was gorgeous.

"I think I'll try to replicate this when we get home," she said after investigating it thoroughly. "It would look perfect on the checkout counter at Shoppe Mystique."

Like we'd done the last two nights, we got into our pajamas, lit a fire, then munched our way through the baskets. As bedtime approached, we both grew a little sad knowing this was our last girlfriend night together. This must be how guests felt when it was time to leave our B&B.

"We'll do this again," Morgan promised. "I wasn't joking about coming again next year."

I woke to the sun slowly lighting my bedroom and lay there hugging my pillow. Thoughts of all that I'd seen and experienced over the past three days in Blackwood Grove filled my mind. Some of those things *could* be explained as tricks of some sort. But what other than Universal intervention could explain Amy and I being together on this small patch of earth and repeatedly crossing each other's paths at just the right time? Coincidence? Maybe, but couldn't coincidence be considered a sort of magic? Whatever the label, I helped an abused, controlled woman get away from her tormentor and back into the arms of her loving family. If that wasn't a Christmas miracle, I didn't know what would be.

"Time to go home?" Geoffrey asked us as we checked out of our suite.

"We've been invited to breakfast with the Warrens first," I said.

"The diner is a great place for breakfast," he replied, nodding his approval.

"It is," Morgan agreed, "but we're going to the farm."

His jaw dropped. "To the farm? As in, inside their house?" When we said yes, he shook his head in disbelief. "Did you win some kind of lottery? No one but family and visiting witches get inside the farmhouse."

A few minutes later, I pulled to a stop at the Applewood Farm gate and rolled down my window, expecting a voice to ask who I was and why I was there. But there was no speaker that I could see. Instead, the gate opened, so I drove through, following the driveway around the house until I saw Dusty step out the back door.

"Glad you made it," she greeted. "Come on in. Breakfast is almost ready."

We entered a mudroom with a dozen cubbies for hanging coats and storing shoes, then into the most amazing kitchen I'd ever seen. The ceilings soared a good twenty feet in the air. Immediately to our left, next to a large fireplace, was a dining table that could easily seat twenty people. At the back of the room was a twelve-foot-square island with what looked like professional-grade appliances.

"My boyfriend, Tripp, would absolutely love this kitchen," I told Dusty. Then I noticed four other women waiting to greet us.

Dusty made the introductions. "I believe Jayne, Gwynne, and Pepper have all met."

We smiled and waved at each other.

"Morgan and I met at the apothecary," Pepper said.

"We did," Morgan agreed. "And I met Gwynne at The Apple Barn yesterday."

The woman with short gray hair and Converse sneakers said, "I'm Comfort. I hear you saved a young woman's life."

My first reaction was to humbly deny the praise, but then I smiled proudly. "I guess I did. But Dusty gets half the credit."

I remembered the fourth woman from the saloon. She had gray hair cut very short on one side and longer on the other.

She held up a hand. "I'm Jett."

"The green witch," Morgan noted with respect.

Jett smiled and, in a gentle Scottish accent, replied, "Not many refer to me that way. If anything, they call me an earth witch. Either way, the gardens and orchard are my happy place."

Morgan and Jett wandered off to take seats at the table and chat.

"It will be just the seven of us for breakfast," Dusty informed. "There are many more family members, but that would be overwhelming for you. They overwhelm me."

The room lights flickered then.

"Breakfast is ready," Pepper announced from near the range.

When I turned to choose a place to sit, I found the table that had been bare a minute ago was now not only set for seven, there was a small mountain of food waiting for us to dig in.

I glanced at Dusty. "I shouldn't ask how that happened, should I?"

"It's easier to go with the flow," she advised. "If it helps, the house still amazes me sometimes too. And I grew up in it."

Breakfast, which Dusty and the aunts credited the house with making, was very good. Like my coffee cup had at the diner, my plate seemed to never empty no matter how much I ate. At some point, it became like that three-day break-in period at Whispering Pines when people stopped questioning the odd things they saw and fell in love with our village. Whatever was going on in this house and town, I wasn't going to question it anymore. If it was all a trick of some kind, it was a very good one. If it really was magic, I loved it.

The seven of us sat at the table laughing and chatting for two hours. A variety of animals—cats, a basset hound, a cockatoo, and even a black squirrel—wandered around, crawled into laps, and snatched scraps off plates. I swear, at one point, I saw a tiny old woman in a mustard-yellow cardigan sweater out of the corner of my eye. When I looked straight at her, however, no one was there.

"Granny Sadie," Gwynne whispered. "She's a ghost."

I paused, then replied, "So is *my* grandmother."

When everyone appeared to have eaten their fill, I asked if I could help clean up and heard a *huff* sound coming from . . . everywhere at once.

"That's the house's job," Dusty said.

Okie dokie. "Can you and I chat for a bit, then?"

"As in away from the chaos?" She tilted her head toward the mud room. "Follow me."

We took mugs of coffee outside to the patio. It should have been cold out there, but it was like a bubble of warmth surrounded the pretty little spot. We didn't even need jackets.

"What's on your mind?" Dusty asked once we'd settled into seats.

"The events of yesterday. How did all of that come together?"

"Beau said when he searched for a missing woman named Amy in Wisconsin, he found a formal complaint the Beelers had filed regarding Craig. He called them and asked them to come."

"They were already here. I saw the mother at The Paddle Wheel last night."

"They live in the area," Dusty explained. "Mrs. Beeler and her friend were here to shop. When Beau described Amy's pink hair, she figured it wasn't her daughter, because Amy's natural hair color is the same as Mrs. Beeler's. But they have followed every lead that has come up, so they came back, and this time they hit the bullseye."

"Amy's hair must be why they didn't notice her while they were shopping," I mused. "If Mrs. Beeler was on the lookout for her auburn-haired daughter, she would have looked right past a young woman with pink hair. And Amy walked with her head down and her hair covering her face."

"For Amy to be right here, so close to her family . . ." Dusty shook her head. "Craig kept her hidden in plain sight."

Shifting topics slightly, I asked, "Why did you get involved? I mean, you charged right up to Craig. He could have hurt you."

She shrugged off the concern. "I wasn't worried about myself, but Amy was so beaten down it was obvious she couldn't take much more. As we both know, you can't force someone to leave their abuser."

"No, you can't. If they're not *really* ready, they'll either stay or go back. Amy still could."

"Fortunately, Craig will be locked up for a while."

"And she has a loving family who will support her." I studied Dusty for a moment.

"Go ahead," she prompted, "ask what's really on your mind."

"I heard you're a gray witch," I answered immediately. "Which means you do the wrong thing for the right reason in order to restore justice?"

"More or less. I provide the means for people to restore their own justice. The quick explanation for that is I create spells, kind of like your Ease oil, that people use to get the result they want. I don't judge, only give them what they ask for."

"Even if it means someone gets hurt or dies?"

"That's where the gray part comes in." She gave a tight smile and appeared to be remembering something. "I can also prevent things from happening. Like stopping Craig from grabbing Amy and disappearing with her into the mall crowd."

"You detained him until Amy stepped away and the police officer moved in." My mind still wanted a logical explanation, but I couldn't come up with one for what the other bakery customers and I witnessed. "Would you have pushed it further than holding him there if necessary?"

Dusty grew quiet for a moment. "If a person is in danger —physical, mental, whatever—I'm willing to step in and do what needs to be done. I'm in my fifties, the age where women find themselves becoming invisible. Not literally." She winked. "For me, that offers a layer of protection. You also charged right in and pulled Amy away from him. *You* also could have gotten hurt but didn't hesitate."

I nodded. "Our methods are different, but our desires are the same. Stop the bad guy."

She held her mug up in a toast. "Exactly."

"Except, I have a badge."

"True, but in this town, no one will try to stop me."

There was a slightly sinister edge to her reply that raised a bit of gooseflesh on my arms.

"Jayne?" The door opened, and Morgan stepped out. "I hate to say it, but we should probably start heading back."

I sighed. As much as I missed Tripp and loved my village, I wasn't ready to leave Blackwood Grove yet. Being basically incognito for four days was really nice. Fortunately, it was only a three-hour drive from Whispering Pines, so a return trip during the offseason wasn't out of the question.

We said our goodbyes to Dusty and the aunts and headed out of town. When we passed a sign that said *Thanks for visiting, come again soon!* I looked at Morgan and asked, "What did we just experience? I mean, it was real, wasn't it?"

Morgan smiled. "When we got here four days ago, you would have phrased that differently. You would have said, 'What did we just experience because that couldn't have been real.'"

I laughed. "You're right. I would have. I like believing that there's magic in the world. And not just at this time of year." After another mile, I said, "Far as I can tell, you didn't question anything. Is that because you grew up around witches and nature magic?"

She pondered that before answering. "Perhaps miracles and magic aren't as miraculous and magical as we'd like to think. Maybe the miracle is that magic is always around us. It's just a matter of whether we're willing to see it."

As usual, my friend left me hopeful but with much to think about.

It would be easiest to start small with this *magic all around us* thing, so I would focus on the magic of Christmas. Or ChristYule as the first residents of Whispering Pines called it. They each had slightly different beliefs and traditions, so they merged them. That's something I noticed in Blackwood Grove. Some called it Christmas. Others Yule. Some just called it the holidays or the season. It all meant basically the same thing.

"We'll need to make a quick stop on the way home," I announced.

"For what?"

"Red, green, gold, and silver ornaments." A little thrill rushed through me. "I think our nature-themed tree needs a bit more sparkle."

Also by Shawn McGuire

WHISPERING PINES Mystery Series

THE WITCHES OF BLACKWOOD GROVE Mystery Series

GEMI KITTREDGE Mystery Series

THE WISH MAKERS Fantasy Series

About the Author

Mystery and fantasy author Shawn McGuire loves creating characters and places her fans want to return to again and again. She started writing after seeing the first Star Wars movie (that's episode IV) as a kid. She couldn't wait for the next installment to come out so wrote her own. Sadly, those notebooks are long lost, but her desire to tell a tale is as strong now as it was then. She lives in Wisconsin near the beautiful Mississippi River and when not writing or reading, she might be baking, crafting, going for a long walk, or nibbling really dark chocolate.